It may be easier to patch up an old home than a broken heart. But along the Louisiana bayou, where beauty and danger mingle all too seamlessly, thoughts of romance may have to simmer on the back burner . . .

Twin sisters and fellow divorcees Sunny Taylor and Eve Vaughn have established their home repair and remodeling business with an eye toward quality and personal attention. So when they're approached by hunky Dave Price to fix up his bayou fishing camp, they're more than happy to take the job—especially since they both secretly think he may prove to be more than just another satisfied customer . . .

The ramshackle campsite could certainly use a woman's touch. What it does not need is a dead body—but that's what the trio stumble across. Clearly, the poor soul was murdered—and once the town tongue-waggers get going, Sunny, Eve, and Dave come under suspicion of the police, not to mention potential clients . . .

Now, with their futures on the line, their brewing love triangle will have to wait. Helped—and harried—by the twins' mother and her retirement home's cadre of amateur sleuths, the trio starts snooping on their own. But when another dead body turns up, they'll have to get their hands dirtier than a swamp-bottom snake if they hope to clear their names . . .

Books by June Shaw

Twin Sisters Mysteries
A Fatal Romance
Dead on the Bayou

Published by Kensington Publishing Corporation

Dead On the Bayou

A Twin Sisters Mystery

June Shaw

LYRICAL PRESS
Kensington Publishing Corp.
www.kensingtonbooks.com

Lyrical Press books are published by
Kensington Publishing Corp. 119 West 40th Street New York, NY 10018

All Kensington titles, imprints, and distributed lines are available at special
quantity discounts for bulk purchases for sales promotion, premiums, fund-
raising, and educational or institutional use.

To the extent that the image or images on the cover of this book depict a
person or persons, such person or persons are merely models, and are not
intended to portray any character or characters featured in the book.

Special book excerpts or customized printings can also be created to fit
specific needs. For details, write or phone the office of the Kensington
Special Sales Manager:
Kensington Publishing Corp.
119 West 40th Street
New York, NY 10018
Attn. Special Sales Department. Phone: 1-800-221-2647.

First Electronic Edition: August 2017
eISBN-13: 978-1-5161-0093-4
eISBN-10: 1-5161-0093-X

First Print Edition: August 2017
ISBN-13: 978-1-5161-0096-5
ISBN-10: 1-5161-0096-4

Printed in the United States of America

For Bob and all my family—You are my reason for being

Acknowledgements

My family and friends, I don't know what I would do without you. Thank you for all of your encouragement and love.

For years I saw through SOLA, my RWA writers group in New Orleans, that becoming an author of books people wanted to read was possible and increasingly probable. What a tremendous group of friends.

I learned so much about writing mysteries from countless people in Mystery Writers of America, Sisters in Crime, and the Guppies. It's amazing how much other writers want to share with you and want you to succeed. Thank you.

Thank you, God, for all of the blessings in my life, especially the people. Thanks to all the folks from South Louisiana. Y'all rock like no others, bless your hearts.

Working with Lyrical Press has been truly amazing. Marci Clark does an excellent job editing my work. Managing Director Renee Rocco is wonderful and has people continue to work on books until they shine, so I guarantee you any errors that might still occur are all mine.

To you, my readers, my words on the page would sit alone without you. I can't thank you enough for allowing me to share my imagination with you. I really love to have you contact me and write reviews. Reviews truly help authors survive.

Chapter 1

I had never seen my identical twin Eve so content and so miserable. While cicadas screamed and the sun began its slow descent, a small group of family and friends stood in her windy front yard, one emotion of hers twisting into the other when the corners of her clear blue eyes lifted and an instant later drooped. Their sparkle dulled and her face saddened as she looked at the baby in her arms that she would soon need to give away.

The wind blew her flame-red waves across her face while she snuggled her weeks-old grandchild Noah, pressing the pink-faced bundle against her tall slender body as though she needed him there for her to continue to breathe.

Her daughter Nicole stepped closer to them and pulled the white medical mask off her own face and stretched out her arms. With a soft sigh, Eve pressed a lingering kiss on the baby's forehead and handed him over.

"Oh, my God, how wonderful it feels to get to take him home." The young woman who looked like a small replica of her mother planted kisses all around the boy's tiny face. "Mom, thank you so much for keeping him." She squeezed my sister's hand.

"The pleasure was mine." Eve's shoulders remained stiff, as though she were forcing herself to stay back, although she probably wanted to keep both of them inside her arms.

I knew the feeling, but surely not with as much intensity as she experienced. I reached the index finger of my right hand out, slid it beneath Noah's fingers, and for the last time felt the snug grip of his small hand. Yes, I also wanted to keep the only child in our family around. I also longed to rock him again on Eve's comfy rocker bought only for him, and smell his new baby-powdery smells, and snuggle with him. I lived on the next street, so I had been around him often. Now they were taking him to another state.

"Aunt Sunny, thank you for helping Miss Eve take care of him." Nicole's husband Randy, a nice fellow of average height and build, gave Eve and me quick hugs. "Y'all need to come out and see us in Houston sometime."

Both of us nodded, neither saying a word while they buckled the babe into his sturdy infant seat in the backseat of the car, but others who'd had dessert with us didn't remain quiet.

"Y'all stay safe," our mother called to them. "And keep him warm." It wasn't winter here in south Louisiana, and even if it were, the temperature might be eighty-five. We'd learned our mom had wrapped Eve and me in blankets so much after we were born that summer about forty years ago, we kept a rash coating our bodies so that strangers feared coming near. They thought we had measles, but we actually sported heat rashes. "You don't want that precious boy to catch a cold or the flu," Mom said.

Her words made Nicole and Randy jerk their faces toward her, their previous happiness replaced by fearful expressions with eyes tight and brows furrowed. The flu was what made them need to avoid their newborn. Nicole had come down with the virus soon after he was born, and shortly afterward Randy developed a worse case. They couldn't be near Noah unless they were outside, and even then they needed to wear medical masks. No other family lived around them. That's why those of us in bayou country got the pleasure of his company for a while. But now he was leaving us.

Dave Price, the handsome businessman Eve and I were attracted to—although my feelings remained secret thus far—stepped closer to us on the circular drive while the young family pulled away. "Flu germs wouldn't stay in their car or their house, would they?"

I waited for Eve to reply, but she only sighed and watched the car. She had invited Dave to join our family for the bread pudding I'd made and she'd served and to see the baby before he departed.

"They've been decontaminating everything," I said. "They used sanitary wipes on every surface a number of times and sprayed so much disinfectant that a germ would feel terrorized about taking up residence on any fiber in their home or cars."

"Great. I know they'll be thrilled to be together."

I knew they would, too. I only wished they could stay closer to us.

"That sure is a cute baby." The slender, frightfully pale woman who had remained across the yard from us kept her eyes toward the family's car until it moved out of view. "I'll be going home now."

"It was nice of you to come out here to see him," I told her, although I could have been speaking to the wind for all of the response I received. The woman, Mrs. Wilburn, took long steps toward her house, the one to the right of my sister's. I realized that even though I lived close and came to Eve's place often, this was only one of the handful of times I had seen her neighbor outside. It was definitely the first time I had seen the woman's small, dark eyes not look mean. Usually seeing them spear me from her window next door almost brought a Christmas carol out of my mouth, a horrible trait of mine that fear sometimes triggered. This day she had come here because she'd seen the baby. I normally referred to her only as "your snoopy neighbor" when I mentioned her at all to Eve since I had seen Mrs. Wilburn's eyes peering toward Eve's place many times through the front window facing Eve's as though someone placed her there to stand guard.

Now her young adult son Royce took her place between those curtains. He often stood right behind her at that window. At the moment, his expression appeared grim. His lips seemed extra tight pressed together and his normally stern eyes looked sad. Why? Sudden thoughts came that maybe he wished to become a father. Or was he already one, but for some reason couldn't be with his child? All we'd heard about him since he returned to stay with his mother was that he had many debts from trying to gamble for a living in Las Vegas.

"I need to get back to the manor. Sunny, you're going to bring me? I can't wait to tell my friends all about that little boy." Mom's snowy hair bounced in the sunshine while she moved, shoving the strap of her white purse up on her shoulder with the hand most twisted from the rheumatoid arthritis that made her insist on residing in Sugar Ledge Manor, the assisted living home in town, instead of with Eve or me. Mom was one of its youngest residents. She gave Eve a hug and scurried to my truck.

I squelched my instinct to ask Eve if she'd be okay. Of course she wouldn't. Not now, and probably not for a few days at least. She had kept that baby almost a month and dreaded having him taken away. I gave her a one-armed hug and stopped myself from again suggesting she go and stay with the young family awhile.

"They need their time together with their newborn," she had said after both parents received their doctor's approval to take their baby home, and I agreed.

I suggested that Dave stay behind with Eve, which I believed would give her some comfort. He was her soulmate, she'd told me, even if she had never shared that idea with him. He knew she cared about him because she was more outgoing and pushy with men than I was. But he also knew she had previously loved many others, having married and divorced three men, who still showered her with signs of affection like jewelry and cars. The only thing my ex left me with was such a dread of sex that imagining myself doing that quick, miserable deed normally pulled a carol out of my throat. Except when I was around Dave.

A relationship with him was something I wanted to explore. Eve and I had gotten to know him a few months ago when she had his company install an alarm system in her house. During the few times I'd been around him, I felt he might care for me, too, although this wasn't the time to admit it to my sister. She had urged me to find a man to get into a romantic relationship with because I'd avoided romance since the unpleasant experiences with the man I'd married. I had been ready to tell her about the person I wanted when excitement interrupted my admission. Since then we'd been busy with the baby.

With unusual wordiness, Mom didn't let me speak. She chattered all the way across town, admiring one thing and another about the baby—his tiny eyes, little lips, curly fine hair, his looking like his mother, which meant like Eve and me—and the minute she stepped down from my truck, repeated those descriptions and many others about her first great-grandchild to the people she saw outside the manor. She didn't need me to go in with her, which was fine since I wanted to get back to Eve.

When I arrived, her front yard and drive were empty. Disappointment sat inside me since Dave already left. I questioned my reasoning and knew that no, I didn't want him there for me this time.

I rang the doorbell and then used my key to let myself in. "Hey, I'm back," I called while I entered. When she didn't respond, I rushed through her picture-perfect spacious den that normally had nothing out of place. Now a small pink and blue striped blanket lay on the coach beside a blue plastic baby bottle holding a trace of milk. Instead of the room's usual vanilla scent from candles, it carried the enticing smell of baby.

Stepping into her art room beyond the den, I found Eve flinging black paint from a brush onto a canvas on a stand. "Your art is matching your mood."

She didn't reply or glance at me. She dipped her brush in a can and stroked big black marks on her painting. Nothing else was in this room where she used to create colorful, bright paintings until someone broke into her house and destroyed all her work. Those paintings had represented men she'd dated, their brightness and size representing her feelings toward them. The one she had created for Dave had been brightest of all. It was their relationship she expected to experience.

With all of her first artwork gone, she would have started on more that represented men. Instead, a grandchild popped into her life, and she treasured each moment with him. Obviously, her happy moments had vanished.

I watched her long minutes while she seemed not to know I was there. I ached inside for her and wanted to do something. "Call if you need me," I said.

Getting no response, I made my way out the front door, shoulders as heavy as my spirits because I could do nothing to help her feel better now. Probably Dave left so early because she had ignored him, too, and gone straight to her dark paints.

Outside, I heard a welcome sound. Somebody nearby was using a hammer. A glance to the left of Eve's house let me see her fairly new neighbor, Jake Angelette, knocking a short stake into the grass beside her yard.

"I sure wish I could do that." I felt a mournful look gripping my face and stepped closer.

Jake was a financial advisor in his mid-forties. Dimples formed when he smiled and made him especially not bad to look at, although my sister looked at men much more than I did. He was divorced and sometimes dated, she had told me. I wished she would date Jake and leave Dave for me.

Jake stopped working. "You can't?" He nudged his chin toward scattered items in his open toolbox. "Don't you and Eve own a remodeling and repair business?"

"We do."

"Then I'm sure you both know how to handle tools really well. Eve looked right at home using that power nailer when I helped her board up that sliding glass door someone smashed at her house."

His mention of that horrible incident when she almost died sent shivers down my back and arms. "Of course we can use tools. Our daddy was a good teacher. But I have problems with my shoulder that have developed more difficulties and my doctor won't give me clearance yet to work on people's houses. We have customers waiting." My insurance wouldn't cover medical attention if I did physical work for others now. And if he didn't know that being shot had caused my problem, I didn't need to discuss it with him or anyone else who hadn't heard about my encounter with a gunman. "I'm developing sketches for someone's remodeling that we have subcontractors working on." And I hoped Eve's sadness cleared so she could come up with more creative ideas.

"I hope your shoulder gets better fast."

"Thanks." I noticed the wood he had knocked in the ground. "You're making a fence?"

Dimples deepened in his cheeks. "Almost everybody around here has one." He pointed to the white vinyl one that ran behind his lawn and the similar one on the opposite side of his house.

I took a couple of steps away and turned. "You have your permit, don't you?"

"I need one?"

"If you're going to build a fence over six feet tall to match both of theirs, you do. Most people don't realize that." It was one of the many recent rules for permits that made people avoid some remodeling in the first place.

I needed to drive around only one block to the rear to reach my place. With houses less fine than on Eve's street and plants selected and planted by people who were paying on those homes instead of landscapers, lawns here didn't look as lush. Cars were less fancy. Most of us had carports instead of closed garages. Sometimes the differences in our places bothered me, but not anytime lately. We had experienced happy times since Eve became a grandmother. I still couldn't believe my sister's child gave birth. We were still so young. But Nicole had done like Eve and married at an early age. Baby Noah thrilled us. But now Eve was wretched. I wished I could make her feel better.

Parked on my carport, I recalled one of the tools I had noticed in Jake's open box. Our dad had a ball peen hammer just like it, a tool that, as a child, I had thought was adorable and liked to hold. With its small rounded head and no claws, it was one of the hammers our carpenter father hadn't used too often. Remembrance of him and Eve's unhappiness made tears swell inside my throat.

I entered the storeroom at the back end of my carport, fingered my father's worn tool belt, and tied it around my waist. I'd gotten to keep most of his tools after he passed on, but had found only claw hammers. I picked one out now. Grabbing the closest nails and a couple of short two-by-fours, I angled one piece across the other, leaned them against a plastic sawhorse, and slammed the hammer with my right hand. The hit felt good.

What should have made Eve content was having Dave around. He was the man she had been searching for all along, she believed, yet he had told me he didn't have the same interest in her. *Slam.* The nail went deeper. No, I didn't want him to fall in love with her. I only wanted her out of her current dark mood. *Slam. Wham.*

If she and *Jake* got together, a new romantic relationship sprouting in her life would pull her out of any doldrums. I made sharp taps with my hammer on smaller Brad nails while I tried to conceive a plan and almost missed hearing the ring of the phone in the pocket of my slacks.

"How is she?" I believed a man asked, although I was finishing a strike against a nail. "Sunny, this is Dave," he said, and I pulled back my hammer before letting it hit again. "She was in such a sad state that I hated to leave her that way, but she insisted I go." Concern gripped his tone.

She always wanted Dave around, the closer the better.

"She doesn't want me there, either." I set the hammer down. Instead of being exciting about Dave, I remained concerned about my sister. "I think it won't be long before she can work off the misery she's feeling from baby withdrawal and be ready for real life again."

"I certainly hope so." When I didn't respond, he said, "What are you doing?"

I glanced at my silly woodwork. "Just playing around with a hammer to get some frustration out."

He hesitated a long minute. "You could come and play around and get more frustration out at a place I need to repair."

His words intensified my hearing and interests. Dave said *repair*, one of my favorite activities. He also invited me to his place. Did live chickens have heads? "I'd love to do that."

"Wait," he said, making my chest deflate and my five-foot-eight height shorten. Was he going to tell me not to come? "I know you aren't supposed to work for clients yet so I won't be a client, but I will want to pay for your assistance."

"Oh no, I wouldn't take your money." I surely needed more income, but not from him.

"Here's what we'll do. You come and look over the old fishing camp I bought and let me know how you think I can fix it up, okay?"

"Just tell me when and where."

Chapter 2

The next morning I drove around the block to Eve's house to check on her. The air was still as I rang the doorbell and waited. She didn't come to the door, so I let myself in. "Eve, it's me." Shivers raced around my back while I entered, a carol trying to start in my throat. I knew I feared finding someone again trying to kill her. Singing Christmas carols when I was afraid began when I was a child alone with our older sister and someone shot her, and I didn't know what else to do while I waited for help. That affliction competed with my dyslexia for which of them often made me feel more like a rabbit that ought to burrow in a hole, although my self-worth was gradually improving.

I didn't see her immediately but checked the alarm box inside her foyer, my own body's alarm relaxing a pinch when I found *Home* glowing in green and then saw her across the way. Dave's company had installed this system.

Instead of being dressed in a stylish pantsuit or dress, Eve still wore a lavender silk robe over her matching nightgown that was partly visible beneath the robe's hem. Through the open doorway beyond her den, she didn't look toward me, not even when I stepped up beside her. She stuck her brush into a can and thrust wide black strokes across those already ruining her canvas and didn't pay attention to the black splatters on her sleeve and tie of her robe.

"That isn't a recent lover, I hope."

"My disposition." She slashed at her canvas with more furious strokes.

I watched her create no pattern, but getting her annoyance out. "Anything I can do?"

For the first time since I entered her house, she turned to me. "Leave."

My sister shooting me such an irate word and stare stopped my breath. I released it, knowing her heartbreak came elsewhere. *Let me know how I can help* almost came from my mouth, but she would probably just shout, so I kept the offer inside and let myself out.

Driving away, I opened my windows and sucked in fresh air, feeling a need for some. Eve would feel better soon, I told myself, my own disposition lifting once I aimed my truck at Bayou Boogie Woogie.

South Louisiana was home to a great number of these slim waterways with irregular borders. Many bayous forked off the Mississippi and split again and dumped their waters that were normally brown but sometimes green into the Gulf of Mexico. The numerous manmade canals were much straighter. All of them made fishermen happy with countless fish of all kinds. I knew where Bayou Boogie Woogie was, although I had never driven so far down the road beside it.

My breaths quickened while I motored, regular houses becoming less apparent, and I knew I was approaching his camp. Dave was the first man I believed I might truly love, although I had married once. Poor self-esteem probably made me agree to that marriage. Now I felt a mutual attraction with Dave, although he never actually said so or acted on romantic feelings during the few times I'd been around him. With Eve experiencing such unhappiness now, I would wait until she perked up before I made her aware of my interest in him. It would be cruel to do otherwise.

My heartbeats thrummed faster during the drive. Rustic unpainted cypress buildings sat up on piling or squatted all along the waterway. A couple of ancient small camps leaned toward the bayou like they were trying to decide whether to or not to slide in and swim. With my truck windows open for the unique swampy smell, I enjoyed the gumbo of scents from algae-tinted water to that of fresh crabs, which made me hungry for some. Occasional shrimp boats moored with their trawl nets raised like butterfly wings emitted the odor of shrimp peelings left out in the sun, not all that pleasant, but combining with the others to create something I could smell nowhere else, and I wanted as much of that scent as I could get.

Fewer buildings sat along this road and fewer still the number of vehicles, mostly trucks, parked around them. These were fishing camps, unlike some of the finer ones in other areas down here, although their owners enjoyed these getaway places just as much. Tall wild lavender irises, white lilies, and purple hyacinths decorated the water's edges. In the bayou, three small turtles sunbathed on a slim branch. A snake slid through low dry grass into the brown water. Not far past it, a snowy egret searched for food. Farther along, I was thrilled to spot a roseate spoonbill that resembled a flamingo soaring over the water. A large blue heron sat on a wharf and an adolescent boy stood on a different wharf with a fishing pole bending over. I eyed the pole, wanting to know what he would bring in, but then spotted Dave's truck. Any interest I had in that fish vanished. I pulled behind Dave's truck on his gravel driveway, swallowed, and got out.

An electric saw whined from about seventy yards beyond, where a man on his wharf sliced through wood. Out in the water behind these camps, an alligator slid along the bayou's surface, its heavy tail propelling it in a steady rhythm.

"It isn't a thing of beauty, but I don't plan to live here." Dave stood three feet beside me, his surprising nearness making me gasp. "Oh, it's that bad?" His hot chocolate eyes were bright beneath his slightly longish black hair.

"No, not at all." I'd hardly glanced at this structure he'd bought and was speaking about him, not any walls, windows, or roof.

"Look through the place before you decide that."

Right. Check it out instead of you. "I just saw an alligator." I pointed, and he took steps closer to the bank. We watched it slide farther away from shore.

"I heard there are a lot of others around. We'll try to stay out of their way and hope they stay out of ours, okay?" he said.

He smiled, and I laughed. I had lived down here long enough to have seen a few gators, although not nearly as many as folks from other places seemed to believe we encountered. Many people lived down here all their lives, and the only gators they saw resided in Audubon Zoo in New Orleans. Most of us southerners still felt a small thrill of excitement and a tingle of fear when we witnessed one. Most of us, except for gator hunters, respected them and would be afraid to encounter one up close.

"You like to fish enough to want a camp?" Lots of people owned camps, but the men's love for fishing or hunting was normally passed down from fathers, uncles, and grandfathers. Since Dave had only lived in south Louisiana a year or so, his interest in outdoor sports surprised me.

He cupped his hand below my elbow to lead me back up the drive. I tried to ignore the distracting feelings that came from his touch. Dave guided me past the stacks of two-by-fours and plywood in the carport to a door.

"I've only been fishing a few times with a friend who had a boat. Since I wasn't very good at it, I made the fish happy. I thought they wouldn't mind if I went out around them again." He stepped closer to me as we walked to the doorway and made me happy, too.

I stopped moving and stared at him. "You've only fished a couple of times, and now you want a camp? Do you own a boat?"

With a laugh, he shook his head. "Not even a fishing line yet, but I'm hoping to get both of those soon. First I want a place where I can spend the night and wake up before the sun does since I was told that's when the fish bite best."

"Usually, but not always." I moved away from him so I could pay attention to the structure. After all, that's why he wanted me here. We had entered a kitchen, an old-fashioned one with a sheet vinyl floor, white freestanding stove, small white refrigerator, and scratched stainless steel sink.

"It sounds like you know a bit about catching fish. Maybe you'll go fishing with me and give me some tips." He stood near, his smile reeling me in.

"I'm not the best, but I have caught my share." Pulling my interest away from romance, I touched the laminate countertop. Its sparkles of gold brought out the antique finish that lent a suggestion of real marble. "This is nice. I don't see any cracks or chips, but I don't know what you plan to change."

"Probably not a whole lot right now. This was someone's camp, and that's all I'll use it for. I'll just fix up a few things gradually." He took steps away from me and waved his hand toward the floor and the walls.

"Maybe a fishing line will come first," I said with a grin, looking forward to going out in a boat with him and teaching him how to cast. My mind then conjured images of him and me working together to make improvements in here. We could change that vinyl floor, add a wharf in back over the water, and see what else we could do with the rest of this place. The more I imagined us as a real couple, the more I felt drawn to him—a place I should not be yet with my sister so fragile. Our other sister had been murdered. Keeping this sister on solid footing remained most important right now.

I hoped more than ever that Eve would come out of that gloomy state soon. I didn't have much experience with romance, but the vibes I received from Dave's smiles, nearness, and suggestion made me more assured that he might also be interested in me.

We walked together down a small hall. Feeling his closeness even more, I barely glanced into the two bedrooms, bath, and utility room. In the wider living area, I stopped. "I know most camps aren't fancy, and I don't find any real problems here. But how about if I bring Eve over to check it out with us? She might come out of her doldrums or see something I'd miss."

He agreed, and we walked out the door to the carport.

"So you think this place has potential?" he asked.

"Definitely."

"Sometimes I'll want to just come out here to relax and feel the breeze and enjoy the wildlife."

"That's an excellent idea."

"I could do some of the fixing up myself, but I work a lot of hours and could use a few suggestions and help with implementation."

Ideas flowed through my head for things that might improve this place. But what he wanted to use it for and all-out sprucing clashed in my mind. "A lot of decisions will depend on how much you want to spend on this project."

"That's something I haven't decided on yet."

"I'll bring Eve over to get her suggestions."

He smiled the intense smile that made me decide I had better get away from him. Dave pulled keys from his pocket, unclasped a link on his key ring, and pulled one key off. "Take this. That way you can bring her in even if I need to be at work."

"I won't come inside if you aren't around unless we agree to do some work here. We haven't agreed to that yet." As tempting as it was to have a key to a place he owned, I kept my arms against my sides and my hands closed.

He worked up a slow smile. "All right. I'll be here tomorrow after four. Maybe you can both get here then."

"I'll bring her."

"Good. Now if you give me a minute to lock up, I'll drive back to town with you." He hustled back inside.

I didn't need his truck on the road with mine, but somehow the image of his large midnight blue truck following mine brought comfort. He came out a couple of minutes later and walked to the driveway. Apprehension made me stand in place, feeling like a schoolgirl who wondered if we should kiss each other good-bye.

We shouldn't, I figured, at least not now.

The whine of an electric saw made me grateful for its distraction. Dave and I glanced toward the source of its sound on the neighboring wharf and then looked at each other. I swallowed when his gaze found my lips.

"I should go." I made myself turn away, threw myself into my truck, and started the motor.

A mirror let me see he watched, a tight smile on his face with what I felt was a knowing expression. He knew I cared about him. I didn't want it so obvious.

* * * *

Eve wasn't excited about checking out the building, even if it meant the man who normally thrilled her would be there. She kept making dark marks on canvas when I got back to town and told her about him wanting us there.

"I'll pick you up tomorrow," I said and hoped she would let me.

There was no use trying to get her to work with me now on the remodeling job we already had going for a customer. The job was large, would pay well, and while my shoulder took whatever time it needed to heal, we were having the subcontractors and helpers we often used complete parts of it. The young couple had bought the house because they loved the location and its basic floorplan and didn't want to start with a new one. They wanted the brick house refinished in stucco to give it a modern feel. That was possible, we'd told them. They'd asked to have the nondescript front door replaced with a wide, attractive entrance. I looked over paperwork and plans we'd agreed on so far and drove off to see how things were coming along.

The number of trucks at their place pleased me. We hadn't had our summer rains yet, so working conditions had been good. Georgia Andrews walked out of the house with her alligator purse when I drove up.

"Hey, Sunny, I need to go, but come in for a minute and see the front door we chose."

I exchanged greetings with workers and followed her to what would become her office. House plans, books, and magazines took up most space on the large desk. She grabbed the magazine on top of the others and turned to the pages she had marked. "Look at this."

"Wow, that is fabulous, Georgia." I leaned closer to view the outstanding stained-glass double door with rounded tops. Full-length matching sidelites ran up and circled above the doors.

"I chose this one because the curves throughout it remind me of my roses."

"Lovely." I knew her plan was to cover much of the front yard with knockout roses she admired so much. "And are you going to use a satin nickel trim instead of black?"

"Absolutely." She gave me a bright smile. "Now I need to go."

"I love your choices," I said, and she waved and rushed out. I closed her magazine and walked outside to see how the men were coming along in the garage.

"This looks like a whole new room," I told the foreman. "Great job."

"Yeah, the guy that bought this place loves what we got done in here. I told him don't put his stuff in here, but he's been doing it already. He says he feels like he has a brand-new house."

"If you don't mind, I'll check it out."

"Go ahead."

It was a garage, after all, but at first glance, didn't look like one. While the foreman and crew continued their work, I looked closer, satisfied that Eve and I had suggested they start in here, something we had done because when we went to their current house, although it was large and in a great neighborhood, the garage was a mess. Theirs had been built for three cars, just like this one, and held their pair of top-dollar cars and his motorcycle and absolutely anything else they could jam in there. Boxes and devices and tools scattered alongside ice chests and buckets and folding chairs that jutted into a walkway. I'd bumped my leg on a barbecue pit that had been shoved right beyond a large box.

The workmanship here pleased me. Eve and I needed this business of ours to survive, so while I was under doctor's orders not to perform any carpentry work yet myself, I was satisfied that for the time being, my sister and I could work with house plans to help people remodel their homes, and others could do most of the actual labor.

There was no mess in this space. These workers cleaned up after themselves as they worked, which I admired. The beauty of this garage began with something I had suggested that the couple hadn't known about. Instead of harsh, cold concrete, they had used this durable floor finish that would resist chipping or stains. They could wipe away any spills from the floor that was now mauve. Georgia had chosen the color, which blended beautifully with the cabinets. Light-paneled floor-to-ceiling cabinet doors with slim perpendicular handles covered most walls.

"Great job," I called to all the workers who thanked me and continued their chores.

At home, I made sketches with ideas that might work in their new home and looked over their existing plans. After a while, my mind shifted to Eve and to Dave. Conflicting emotions wore me out, so I got to sleep earlier than normal.

In the morning, I focused on helping others. I set a large pot on the stove and pulled out ingredients for a seafood gumbo. I sautéed onions, garlic, bell peppers, and celery, added smothered okra from my freezer, a fresh tomato, shrimp, three quarts of water, a pinch of Worcestershire sauce, and salt and pepper. I let that simmer while I put eggs and potatoes to boil and fixed myself a tasty breakfast of cinnamon-laced lost bread with milk. Once I showered and dressed in slacks and casual moccasins, I added a pint of oysters and two pounds of crabmeat to the mixture on the stove, got the rice ready, made the potato salad, adding sweet relish to the mixture, and swiped mascara across my lashes and pale pink lipstick on my lips.

With everything prepared, I drove the meal and two loaves of crusty French bread out to our community center. The building was small and old, but had been donated and lovingly spruced up by volunteers. Now the walls were painted bright white instead of the dull finish they'd had before, and cheerful posters with positive quotes lined the walls. This was a soup kitchen of sorts that had become more of a gumbo kitchen since that's what most of us contributed and the needy enjoyed. No one sat at any of the long tables yet, but it wouldn't be long. Ladies in the kitchen took my offerings and set them near pots and bowls of others that emitted the most enticing aromas.

My high school friend Amy Matthews ran the kitchen. "Yum, girl, I smelled that gumbo when you walked in." Her skin was cappuccino and her clothes vibrant. "Thank you."

"No problem."

She stepped out of the kitchen with me. "So tell me about your love life with that guy." Her big eyes widened.

"I just met Dave a handful of times at the coffee shop downtown."

"Yes, and...?"

"I've told him how I felt about not hurting my sister. He won't try to advance our relationship until I'm ready."

"Sunny, you deserve a good relationship with a man."

I sighed. "I know. I want to be ready. But I wanted Eve to find somebody else—she always has before—and you know...."

She learned farther back. "I do know—your sister who died. You won't cause this one anguish."

"Not if I can help it." I gave her a hug around the neck and trotted out of the building.

In the afternoon, I showed up at Eve's house, afraid I would need to convince her to get out of her nightgown and dress in regular clothes. She surprised me. I pressed the doorbell once, and she opened the door and came out. My identical twin wore light makeup, no frown, and a pale blue knit dress.

"Let's go," she said.

Not getting any conversation from her, I drove to what would become Dave's fishing camp. I told her I'd seen an alligator in the bayou, but she didn't look for one. She showed little reaction when I pointed out an eagle that swooped low to the water. They were fairly rare here, but did build nests along some bayous. Reaching Dave's camp, I was pleased to see his truck pulling into his drive ahead of us.

"Thank you for coming," he told Eve, who gave him a tight smile. "Since y'all are guests, I'll let you in through the nicer entrance." He unlocked the front door and stepped aside for us to go in first. "The place doesn't look like much, and it doesn't need to for me to use it for relaxing. But I will want to fix it up some and hope you and Sunny might help."

Eve mumbled something and didn't try to get close to him, which was so unlike her.

Maybe if I took myself out of their space a couple of minutes, she would perk up. "Dave, you might want to show Eve around. I'll just check out some things over here." I scuttled from the living area, and he guided her toward the hall.

I stepped into the utility room. It was small with only enough space for the old white washer and dryer that must have come with the place and might or might not work and the water heater. A large black garbage bag that looked almost full leaned against it.

Plastic and heat don't mix well together, I would tell Dave after he and Eve finished their tour. In the meantime, I grabbed the top of the bag to pull it away from the heater. The thing didn't budge. I opened the top to remove some of what must have been chunks of wood or maybe plaster, judging from the wide shape at its bottom.

"Jingle bells," I bellowed, spewing more lyrics.

"Sunny, what's wrong?" Eve ran in ahead of Dave, knowing my unwilling song stemmed from fright.

My arms quivered and mouth dried as all three of us stared at the slumped body in the trash bag. Even though blood matted her hair, it was easy to see this was Eve's neighbor Mrs. Wilburn. The odd twist of her neck assured us she was dead.

Chapter 3

Eve and I rushed from the utility room, my heart pounding so hard I heard it thrusting into my head over the sound of my carol and almost missed hearing Dave say he was calling 911.

My twin and I stopped in the kitchen, both shaking. We held each other's hands, my eyes surely as big as hers had become. A mask of fear gripped her face. My feet quit moving, but my heart slammed my ribcage as if it were a power drill.

Dave stepped into the room with us. "Police are coming."

Eve flung herself against him, circling his neck with her arms. His arms came around her. I knew she clung to him for support, and I wanted it, too.

"You two stay together." He pulled away from her. "I'm going to hurry through to make sure whoever did that isn't still around."

"Do you have a gun?" I asked.

"Yes, but it's in my truck. I won't leave you in here to go get it."

"We could wait outside," Eve offered, but immediately reconsidered. "No, the killer could be out there."

Dave shook his head. "I don't think it just happened. The blood doesn't look fresh enough. Wait there."

I stood in place, not wanting to think of what he would do if he discovered a murderer.

We were with Eve's neighbor yesterday. How could she be dead now? And why here in the little building down on a remote bayou where Dave wanted to make his relaxing fishing camp? What about her poor motherless son?

"There's no one here." Dave's words competed with the cry of the sirens that I first thought was the electric saw from the next camp's wharf. He strode outside and car doors slammed. Moments later, he returned with two deputies, one I recognized and one I didn't. Both were real young and with solemn stances and faces, one of the faces wearing freckles. The one I'd never seen before stared at me. At Eve. And at me again, certainly registering that, yes, we were identical—except, Dave had told me, for the gold flecks that the sun picked out only in my clear blue eyes.

The deputy we'd seen before stayed in the room with us and began asking questions and taking notes while the unfamiliar one moved to the utility room. Sirens again swamped the air outside, and more men and a woman in uniform rushed in. With gloves and cameras and a gurney, they swarmed the building that grew tinier while I tried to pay closer attention to all of the questions and to Eve's and Dave's answers.

Thick black brows and lips so full they would put most women's to shame gripped my attention. The man owning them stamped to us on stubby legs.

"I'm Detective Wilet with the Landry Parish Sheriff's Department," he announced to Dave. His gaze grabbed us. "You two, again."

Eve and I offered tight-lipped smiles. We couldn't help it if we were involved in previous murders. We hadn't committed any, then or now.

"We've answered a lot of questions already," I told him as though I believed that should end the discussion and the need for any query from him.

"We didn't do it." Eve wiggled her finger between the three of us who had been there.

"And we don't know who did." I gave him a shrug as though that would put his mind at ease and send him off elsewhere to locate a killer.

We didn't throw him off, though. While a woman snapped pictures around us, I tried to focus more on what this detective asked and said, and heard him in a disappointed tone ask Dave if there wasn't a place to sit.

"Only the floor," Dave said. "The previous owner left a couple of appliances, and I wanted to get opinions from the twins before I put anything else inside."

"Like a body?" The detective lifted his chin.

"Absolutely not." Dave grimaced.

"Detective Wilet, Dave didn't kill her and neither did we. Dave showed me around in here yesterday, and I can guarantee you Eve's neighbor wasn't here."

The detective's stance stiffened. "I'll need you three to answer more questions at the office." He tilted his head toward Dave. "Officer Bennings will give you a ride."

I bustled forward. "Wait. Are you arresting him? He didn't do anything. He needs an attorney. He needs his rights read to him." All of these words swirled through my mind and probably rushed from my mouth. And then bits of words I'd heard registered. Dave had told him he'd gone home after we left here yesterday. No one could attest to that fact. He had been at work earlier today, arrived right before we did, and nobody else had a key to this place.

The freckled-face officer walked us out with Detective Wilet following. "I'm going to inspect in here and meet y'all there later," Wilet said.

Fearful that Dave would go to prison for something he didn't do, I fought to stop the carol that tried to rush from my mouth, biting down on it while I glanced toward the wharf at the camp beyond. The man on it was no longer working but standing and watching all of the commotion over here. Yes, the police would question him, and if we were lucky, that man had witnessed the killer getting Mrs. Wilburn inside here.

My eyes skimmed Dave's carport. Something looked amiss. "Wait," I said, and the officers stopped walking. The detective's dark brows tightened into one, letting me know I had better come up with something good. "I saw all your people coming in the front door."

"And?"

"Look back there." I pointed inside the carport.

"There's wood he's going to use for this place." Wilet swept his arm toward the stacks.

"The stacks were neat, but if nobody came in here, all of the wood should have stayed like it was. That two-by-four is tilted over." I pointed at the top one that was now on its side. "That's what first caught my eye."

The detective let out a loud huff and reached for Dave's arm. Would he cuff him?

"No, look." My words got their attention, although Wilet hardly glanced at the floor where I indicated. "Is that a key?"

The metal tip was barely visible beneath the edge of the wood that had slipped down. Wilet went there and pulled the object, a key, out from under the wood. He tried it in the back door.

The key fit.

Instead of thanking me, he stepped into my space. "How did you know this was here? It was so hard to see, you must have known about it."

I shook my head, protests slamming through my mind.

Eve stepped closer. "She notices details, Detective. My sister used to work for years at Fancy Ladies"—which he would know was the only nearby upscale clothing store for women—"and she fitted women for their undergarments."

When Wilet's eyes blanked, I continued the story. "So I learned to notice things, like I could tell in an instant if a woman was a double D or E, and I knew about panties or not and—"

His raised hand told me to stop. He held up the key. "And this?"

"I was born dyslexic, sir, so I might not always get numbers or words I read pronounced right, but I do know how to spot something others might miss. I saw that wood stacked yesterday. I didn't look at it when I came inside today, but I just spotted the top piece out of place. That led me to wonder why, and I checked out the space below it." I spread my hands as though a jack-in-the-box would jump out. "There was a key."

"You said nobody else had one," Wilet told Dave.

"No one does. Yesterday I wanted to give Sunny the extra one."

That comment drew an unpleasant face from Eve. Her eyes went hard toward me.

Dave reached into a pocket of his slacks. He drew out a key ring that held a number of different sized keys, flipped through them, and pulled one up. "This is the one I used to get in here today through the front door. Sunny and I walked out of here through the carport."

"And we sure didn't knock down any wood," I said.

Dave tilted his head toward the key Wilet held. "The one I took off the ring and tried to give her must have slipped down without me noticing."

"You would have been pretty distracted when you left not to have noticed," Wilet said.

I recalled the moments Dave and I shared before I left. Was it only yesterday?

Dave swung his gaze toward me, making me think he also recalled our time on the driveway.

Eve kept her lips tight. Her eyes didn't soften.

"Okay, I'll need to check out your story more," Wilet told Dave. "You can drive yourself to my office and wait for me to finish up here."

"I certainly will."

"You know where my office is?"

"I've seen it."

"I'll get you two to come by to answer more later, maybe tomorrow."

Eve and I had gone to his office more than once. We both nodded.

The tensed muscles in Dave's face relaxed. "Thank you so much, Sunny," Dave said once the detective went inside. From his body's shift toward me, I thought he might give me a kiss, albeit a light one. Then his eyes shifted toward Eve just like mine did. He stayed where he was.

All sorts of emergency vehicles were parked on the road in front of Dave's place and beyond. Seeing them pulled my thoughts back to Mrs. Wilburn, now the dead person inside.

Neither Eve nor I spoke when we climbed into my truck, and while I drove. I didn't want to think about what I discovered in that bag and tried to focus on the slim road. I steered us back toward her house, shaking in my shoulders intensifying when I needed to turn down her street. My jaw grew rigid when I rolled past Mrs. Wilburn's house.

Only after I'd parked in Eve's driveway did I let out a breath it felt I'd held since we left *the crime scene*. That term slid into my mind like poured concrete.

A hand gripped mine. I tightened my fingers around Eve's and stared at her frightened eyes that balled up like blue marbles, knowing they reflected mine. The truck's cabin felt like a space I didn't dare say anything in now that we were so close to her dead neighbor's house. Both of us turned toward it. Although it was late afternoon, the days were so long it was easy to see no one was in the yard.

Eve opened her door and stepped out. I did the same, and we shut our doors without slamming them. I looked next door toward the first window in front that Mrs. Wilburn had so often stared out of, seeming to watch everything Eve did. The curtains hung straight. Not even a slit opened between them. Her pale face—the small dark eyes weren't staring out at us.

Eve unlocked her door, and we stepped inside.

"I miss seeing her there," I said.

"Me, too."

"She should be watching you, spying on you."

Eve was nodding. "And Royce should be standing right behind her, watching over her shoulder."

"Of course." I was also nodding and squeezing her hands. "Oh, my God, he probably doesn't know."

"His mother won't be coming home," Eve said as though I had left off the end of my sentence. "Sunny, can you imagine that? A boy learning his mother was murdered?" Tears sprang to her eyes, and I figured she was imagining her own new grandson losing his mother, Eve's daughter.

"But if anyone wanted to kill her, why would she end up in that little camp Dave's bought, of all places?"

"Yes. Who would have connected her and him together?"

My twin's eyes went blank, and I knew she was thinking, like I was, especially when she blinked twice, her present state seeming to register when she stared at me. "The link between those two is *us*."

I grabbed her hands. "And Dave. But he couldn't have done it."

"Absolutely not." Her gaze shifted aside and then back at me with a different solemn expression. "Why did he want to give you a key to his place?"

"Oh, just so you and I could go in and look things over while he was at work."

"Oh." Her shoulders lowered as she relaxed.

"Maybe we can do some digging around and find out more about why Mrs. Wilburn would have been dead in his camp." I gripped my purse tighter. "I don't want to be around here when the police arrive to tell Royce."

"I don't either."

"Let's go somewhere so we can think."

She shook her head. "I'm going to the gym to work this body out so I don't need to think."

"Good idea." I gave her neck a quick hug and walked out. Taking a breath, I glanced toward Mrs. Wilburn's. A squad car pulled up and parked out front. I drove off in the opposite way, not wanting to see her son's face when he opened the front door and found officers who would tell him somebody murdered his mother.

A murdered mother. A need struck to visit mine. I would stay around Mom and spend as much time as I could appreciating all of our time together. Another benefit to that plan—she had many cronies who heard lots of gossip about what went on in town. Maybe one of them would help us connect the dots from Eve's neighbor to our mutual love interest.

Chapter 4

Sugar Ledge Manor welcomed me as it would everyone who drove up. The crepe myrtles lent clouds of soft pink, and numerous palm trees gave an air of a tropical island near the pale blue stucco two-story building. I rushed inside, past sweet-scented roses growing next to the archway, looking forward to seeing my mother, to enjoy her comforting arms around me while that could still happen.

Instead of her sitting in the midst of her Chat and Nap Group, she and all the others were scattering from their normal places.

"Hey, Mom." I needed to walk faster before she and her buddies went off.

My mother gave me a soft smile and quick hug. "It's so nice to see you, Sunny." She pecked a kiss on my lips. "Now I have to go."

Some of the other ladies turned their heads back to me and nodded.

"What? Where? Is Bingo ready to start? I could play with y'all."

"No Bingo today. I'm getting my hair done," Mom said.

"And I'm going to the bathroom. My Metamucil started working," one of her friends told me while she shoved her walker toward the hall.

"Congratulations," I called to her along with a big thumbs-up since I knew of her lingering problem.

She didn't look back. "Thank you."

"I'm hungry. I'm going to have a snack," a gray-haired lady in a wheelchair said.

"Wait a minute. Do any of you know Clara Wilburn?" I needed to lift my voice to ask it since they were all scooting like sprayed red ants.

Two shook their heads as they moved off. The one using a three-pronged walker glanced back. "I might. I don't remember." Beyond her, two young women wearing the cotton navy pantsuits of many who worked here turned toward me. From their intense stares, I got the feeling they knew Mrs. Wilburn. Maybe they would come to ask what I wanted to know.

I hadn't thought about the consequences of having someone tell me they knew the deceased woman. What was I going to say—that someone murdered her? No, that wasn't my place. I couldn't announce Eve's neighbor's demise. Word would get out soon enough. By tomorrow, it would be in the local paper. Then I could come back and ask more questions.

Uh-oh, I hoped the paper wouldn't mention Dave's camp as the murder scene or any of us being there.

I would have offered to go upstairs with Mom to get her hair fixed, but at this point, didn't want anyone asking why I had mentioned Eve's neighbor. I called, "Bye," to my mother and rushed out of the building, not asking why she was having this done so late in the day. Residents had their hair fixed whenever the kind volunteers could come over.

In the parking lot, I sat in my truck, lowered the windows, and thought about Dave. What was his connection to Mrs. Wilburn? Why would anyone put her body inside his new place? He had probably seen her watching him through her window when he'd gone around Eve's house taking measurements and recording windows for the alarm system his company installed. He may have noticed her there at other times when he'd gone to Eve's—to carry out the work, to eat the rare meal she'd cooked so she could keep him there.

He had seen or maybe met her when she came over to Eve's front lawn to see the baby right before Noah's parents took him away to Houston. Dave said he didn't know her otherwise, and I believed him. There was no way I could imagine him killing anyone. But even if he had killed the dead woman in his new place, why would he keep her there?

Unless he planned to dispose of her body later.

I shook my head to push that thought out. What was I thinking? Dave couldn't kill anyone. I was sure of it.

"Are you okay?" A man outside my door leaned to my open window, startling me. "Do you need help starting your truck?"

"No, I'm fine. And my truck works." I shifted my shoulder away from the window and cranked the motor, telling myself this was not the place to sit in contemplation. "But thanks." As he stepped away, I checked behind and around, ready to back up and go.

"I heard you asking about Clara Wilburn," he said.

"Yes." As much as I'd decided I wouldn't speak about her until others in town knew she died, I cared and wanted to know all I could about her.

"She's my aunt." He stood about five-foot-six and wore a button-down shirt and pinched expression. Either he knew about her demise, or he didn't care for her.

I didn't back up. "She lives—uh, her house is next door to my sister's," I said, correcting myself but trying not to give away anything more.

He nodded, his lips tightening in a grimace. "I came to visit my grandmother. That's her stepmother, but she never comes here."

So he did not yet know Mrs. Wilburn died. I needed to find out more. "I really never got to know her very well."

"Hmp, and you don't want to."

"Why is that?"

"Nobody in our family likes her. I doubt if she has any friends either." He pulled an electronic cigarette with a thick base from his shirt pocket, started it up, and sucked on the thing. Smoke swirled in the air.

Who are some people in your family? I wanted to ask, but couldn't think of an appropriate explanation for why I wanted to know. If I pried, he'd get suspicious and ask why I was inquiring so much about his aunt. If she upset him so, he would probably spout about disturbances with her.

Instead, he shifted back from my truck, face muscles and shoulders relaxed now with his smoke.

"What's your grandmother's name?" I tilted my head toward the manor.

"Adrienne Viatar. Who do you have in there?"

"My mom. It was good talking to you." I took off before he could ask my name or hers. I wanted to know who might have a motive for killing Mrs. Wilburn, but didn't want to let him know she was dead or where she'd been found. Or that I was the person who had discovered her body.

I'd try to get more information about their family from Mrs. Wilburn's stepmother once that elder had time to learn and digest the fact that she'd died.

The phone in my purse rang. "Where are you?" Eve asked.

"Leaving the manor."

"Come over. I'm back home."

"What's up?"

"We need to go next door and give Royce our condolences."

Doing that was not tempting, but given the circumstances, it was the right thing to do. "All right."

"Good. And while we're there, we might be able to get some ideas about who could have wanted his mother gone."

My foot tapped my brake, an automatic reflex in response to what she was suggesting. "Don't you think the police are checking into that with him?"

"Absolutely, but when I'm questioned by police, I feel much more tense and concerned and don't always get my thoughts straight."

"I'm the same. Okay, be there soon." I'd wait to tell her what I learned here when we were face-to-face.

* * * *

As I pulled up to Eve's, I spotted Mrs. Wilburn's older model car parked in her driveway and realized I'd hoped it would be gone. That would mean Royce wasn't home, and we would not have to go over there yet. Guilt pinched my heart for my attitude, but I hated to face the bereaved child of a parent who just died, especially one who was murdered.

My finger was going for Eve's doorbell when she jerked her door open. "Let's go." She stepped outside. "This is a task I dread just like I'm sure you do, so let's do it now."

"Front door or back?" I gripped her arm. We both glanced toward the front of the house. Even though darkness had set in, the place was visible. My gaze ran along all the windows. Sadness crimped inside me. I couldn't believe we would never see her there.

"If we go to the front, he might think it's somebody trying to sell something or preach. In the back, he'll figure it's friends," Eve said.

I believed the same thing, so we walked past the large bushes that separated their backyard from Eve's and across the grass to the storm door. Taking a breath, I exhaled as Eve rang the bell. Who would speak first, her or me? What would I say? Certainly Eve was wrong about thinking we might question him so soon about possible people who might have killed his mother. This was a time of grief, not a time for us to thrust questions at him.

Sorrow shot through me when the wooden door inside opened. Royce stepped closer to the outer storm door that was glass with the bottom half screened, and I waited for him to open it. We could just stay in the doorway to express our sympathy unless he invited us inside.

"You!" Beyond the glass, he thrust a finger at me. "I can't believe you would come to this house!" His reddening face looked like it might burst into flames.

"Why not?" Eve asked, as I'd thought of doing, although I couldn't get words to shake out of my mouth.

"Or you either!" He aimed his finger at her.

"Royce, we are so sorry about your mother. She was a kind woman," I said, although I actually had seen no evidence of her kindness. And I didn't understand his fury although he was probably experiencing mixed emotions, sadness, and anger. "We wanted to pay our respects."

"Yes, and ask if there's anything we can do," Eve said.

His chest rose. "You've done enough. You helped." He thrust his finger back at me like a weapon. "But you're the one who killed her!"

Chapter 5

I shook my head, unable to wrap my mind around Royce's accusation. "What are you talking about?"

"We didn't do anything," Eve said.

He thrust his finger at one, then the other of us. "You are both horrible people. Don't ever set foot on this property again and don't speak to me." He leaned close to the glass. His stare speared my eyes. "I hope they give you the death penalty!"

As I muttered incoherent words, he slammed the wooden door. I stood in place trembling. Eve and I gripped each other's hands as we had done when we were young children, and stepped across the lawns, not saying a word until we entered Eve's house.

She got us cans of Diet Coke and Sprite, and we sat in her kitchen. "So the police told him we found his mother. Surely he might think we could have killed her," she said.

I took a big swallow of my soft drink, determined to shake off inner discomfort from the accusation. "Okay, here's what I've got. I went to see Mom, but she and her buddies were all going off in different directions so she didn't have time to visit with me. Right before they scattered, I asked whether any of them knew Mrs. Wilburn. None did, although I don't think they all paid attention to my question. But once I got in my truck, a guy came up and said he'd heard me asking about her, and she's his aunt, and nobody in their family likes her. I'm sure he hadn't heard that she'd died."

Eve leaned forward, eyes wider with interest. "So who in their family doesn't like her? Maybe there's someone with a motive to kill her."

"He didn't say." My words made her lean back. "But he'd gone there to visit his grandmother, and I found out her name."

"Maybe we can get information from her," Eve suggested the same thing I'd considered.

"It shouldn't be hard to find her in there. First we'll have to give her time to learn about the death and start to process her grief."

Eve's phone rang. She looked at the caller's name and didn't change expressions to show whether she was pleased or dissatisfied. "Hello."

"Isn't this Twin Sisters?" The man spoke loud enough to be heard in the next town.

"Yes, it is. And I'm Eve Vaughn. May I help you?" A smile came to Eve's voice.

"Do both of you use sledgehammers and things to knock down walls?" The tone intensified.

Eve and I grinned at each other. "We do," she said.

"Great. I need y'all to do that by Thursday."

"Thursday." She lifted an eyebrow at me, asking if I thought that might be possible.

I answered with a one-shouldered shrug. Maybe my doctor would give me permission to start working again by then, but with the numbness remaining in my shoulder, I doubted whether I could wield a sledgehammer so soon.

Eve opened the door to the cabinet where she kept writing supplies. She took out an order pad and pen. "Would you want to give me your name and the location of the building you'd want work done on? My sister and I can go and check it out."

"And y'all can start now?"

"We can." Eve and I shared a look of relief. "We can't do the actual work with the sledgehammers ourselves right now, but we can use subcontractors who will do that." She pressed the tip of her pen down, ready to write.

"Wait." The word spewed through Eve's phone slammed across the room, making me draw back my head. "You've seen that show on TV where that little woman has a work crew, but she rams those big sledgehammers through people's walls herself?"

"I have seen it." Eve spoke with a nod. "So your address? And your name?"

Only a second passed. "Lady, I love that show and to see that tiny woman ripping out walls. I wanted to see you and your sister do that."

Eve and I shared a huff. "I can slam through a wall for you," Eve said. "But my sister had a little injury. She wouldn't be able to use both arms, but—"

"Oh, never mind. That was a stupid idea we came up with. We'll just go on to the Netherlands Friday and leave that wall the way it is."

Silence when the man hung up spread like a salve to my wounded eardrums and certainly to Eve's. She put her pen and pad away and sat at the table with me, my expression surely as gloomy as hers. I was to blame for us being unable to take on most jobs at this time. Thinking of that made my shoulders droop. Until I remembered I didn't cause any of that problem. The person who shot me did.

My mind raced to someone else. "I'd like to know what's happening with Dave."

"I know. I wish he'd call and tell me how he is."

Having her voice the same interest I had in him dulled my spirit, making me determine I needed to pull back from showing how much I cared about him since right now, having him free and not behind bars was our shared concern. We needed to keep the police assured that we weren't involved in that death either.

Eve checked the clock on her wall. "I sure wish it wasn't so late. I want to call Nicole and see how the baby is." Her sad eyes turned to mine. "I want to talk to him."

"And hold him." I stood and gathered her in my arms. "I'm holding you."

She pressed her head against mine, arms staying at her side. A minute later, they came up around me. We held onto each other, sharing inner pain that came from the same source and different sources. *Everyone needs at least four hugs a day*, I had once heard an expert on behavior say on a talk show. *If each person received four hugs, the world would be a much happier place.*

"I'm going home to eat," I said, letting her go.

"I didn't realize it was so late. You could eat here."

I grinned at that suggestion. She did the same. She wasn't the person who cooked in this family. I didn't fix big meals often since I lived alone and didn't eat too much, but my fridge always held more choices than Eve's did with her diet food. In my head, radishes and lettuce did not constitute food. This was the Deep South, by gosh, and I adored all of our southern dishes. Maybe that's why Eve stayed a bit slimmer than I did. She loved them, too, but didn't eat rich food as often as I did.

Suddenly ravenously hungry, I considered the small packs of leftover red beans and rice and sausage, a normal Monday meal down here, in my freezer. I would defrost packs of them in my microwave.

Promising to get to bed early so we might focus better in the morning about who might have really killed Mrs. Wilburn, we agreed to get together then, and I drove home. My thoughts swirled to baby Noah, Dave, and a dead person. They brought me back to that most horrible time in my life when my singing disorder began. I gripped my steering wheel and nodded, aware that I had held onto my sister really tight. I was fairly sure she also realized why. Soft words from a soothing Christmas carol came from my mouth and carried me back to the moment I was a child shooting hoops in our driveway near our older sister I adored when the unthinkable happened.

Reaching my street, I belted out a different song about what I wanted for Christmas, and changed it to *my sister Crystal*. Tears I wouldn't allow back then spilled onto my cheeks. I wiped at them, using the back of my arm and spreading warmth across my face like a rain-slick highway in summer.

Yes, I felt finally ready for a romantic relationship and really cared about being close to Dave. How much more did I want to stay close to my one remaining sister?

But would I really need to choose?

Chapter 6

Feeling my stomach empty once I rose after tossing in bed for hours, I dragged myself to my kitchen and remembered I hadn't eaten when I got back from Eve's last night but recalled what I'd wanted. I yanked the freezer door open and stared inside. Lots of quart-size zippered bags I could see through held shrimp and fish or crabmeat and oysters. Others held sliced okra, strawberries, and eggplant. I placed my hand on a frigid pack of rice, one of red beans, and another on smoked sausage. For breakfast?

Why not? I wouldn't be able to think straight about murder, romance, and suspects while I was so hungry.

I unzipped an inch or so from each bag, zapped them in the microwave with the defrost button, and soon sat with a tall glass of milk. I stirred the red beans and gravy in with the rice and sliced the smoked sausage into small pieces. If I wasn't in a bit of a hurry this morning, I would have baked sweet cornbread sticks to go along with the meal.

Ready soon afterward, I walked to Eve's. A humid breeze pushed in from the south. Even though foods didn't normally bother my stomach, I started to feel sorry I'd eaten so much with each step I took. I didn't need to think hard to know this discomfort came more from getting closer to the home of the woman I'd found murdered. She would no longer be in that house beside Eve's, but her son would. The back of my neck tensed when I recalled the fury in his eye with his assertion that I killed her.

He's feeling better now, I told myself, while I forced positive thoughts to my mind. Royce would have had time to consider and know that neither Eve nor I could be a murderer.

Since my street ran parallel to Eve's, I needed to only cross the road and walk through a two-foot wide space between fences to reach her place. Her patio held comfortable cushioned furniture and a burbling, bleach-scented water fountain. I rushed my final steps to her back door. Trying to remain positive but still fighting apprehension, I gave her doorbell only one ring and then used my key.

"Hey, it's me," I called out.

From the den, she stepped into her kitchen. "I know who you are, Sis."

"You're a much happier person this morning," I pointed out, pleased to see the spring in her step and hear the light tone in her voice. "You must have talked to your grandson."

The smile on her lips widened. "Nicole called. She put the phone to his ear, and I cooed to him. I think Noah might have cooed back to me."

I was fairly sure the little guy was still too young to let out many sounds except the burping he'd done when we were with him or the crying or expelling gas.

"He was probably trying to say your name." I spoke with a grin.

The sounds of someone close hammering intermingled with a whining noise. "Let's see what's going on outside," I said. "Maybe if we'd paid better attention, we would have noticed who went around Mrs. Wilburn."

We stepped out the back door. I glanced at what made the only current nearby sound—the angel pouring her clear water on the plastic goldfish in her fountain. In the yard to the left, Jake walked near the fence behind his place carrying a weed whacker. With a pale blue cap, snug T-shirt, and shorts, he looked appealing, especially once he noticed us and waved. His wide smile created dimples in his cheeks.

"Nice day, isn't it?" he asked.

"Very nice," Eve replied before he returned to slicing the tall grass edging his land.

If he still wasn't attached to another woman since his divorce, I wished he and Eve would get together. Or possibly she was already interested. I knew she had borrowed bread from him at least once. Maybe she'd borrowed other things, or he had borrowed from her. Surely she had gone back to return the items, not because he would need them but so she'd have an excuse to get close to a good-looking man again. The gleam in her eye when she waved back at him gave me hope that a relationship between them might be progressing. That would solve all of my problems about not hurting her if Dave and I started dating each other.

The pounding of a hammer came from the right. It sounded like it came from the front of the Wilburn house. We walked along the side of Eve's house toward the street, and she and I stared at each other, mouths open at what we saw.

HOUSE FOR SALE BY OWNER. The sign was large and the print bold and also held a phone number. Royce finished hammering it on a post in the front yard.

He straightened when he saw us. Lifting the hammer higher than his head, fury tightened on his face, and he seemed ready to throw that tool. A carol rolled up my throat. I grabbed Eve's hand and rushed to her front door.

Slamming us inside, she locked the door and we backed away from it. "He really believes we did it," she said.

"Or I did. What's wrong with him?"

"Well, I think he's frightening. I'm going to dread going out there when he's around."

"You could come and stay with me." Even before I'd completed the words, she shook her head. I wouldn't have wanted to run away from my neighbor like that either.

We stepped into the den. I glanced through the open doorway into her art room, where two canvases on easels displayed her earlier dark mood. At least now, with murder to distract us, she wouldn't submerge herself again in such deep gloom. Murder was horrible, and even if I hadn't really known Eve's neighbor, I was sorry someone exterminated her. I was sorry for anyone who loved her, and—"Wait a minute. I'll bet he killed her."

Eve pointed toward their house. "That young man out there who says we did it?"

"Yes. I don't believe he thinks we killed his mother. I think he did it." While Eve shook her head, I continued my thought. "We've learned that he's a big gambler, and he probably owes a lot of money he can't repay. He doesn't seem to have any kind of job ever since he's come back to his mother's home. He doesn't own a car and uses hers. Now he can sell her house and take the money." I ran out of steam and reasoning.

Eve's eyes pinched tighter, her expression sad. "Would you kill Mom if you needed money?"

"What a horrible thing to say." My chest pumped up with outrage. Just as quickly, it deflated. "I'm sorry. That was a wretched idea."

"Whether he owns the house yet or not, he's probably putting that sign out there to let us know he wants to get away from us. I can't blame him if he really believes we're responsible. After all, we did find her."

"So I imagine she didn't have any other children."

Eve shook her head and shrugged. "She and I never spoke enough for me to find out. She always seemed to want to keep to herself, so I left her alone. I just happened to be in the front yard that day a taxi dropped Royce off, so he asked me if she still lived there. I had only seen him go there about a year before but don't believe he stayed long then. When I assured him that was still her residence, he rang the doorbell and minutes later went inside."

"Let's check online to see if Royce owns that property now. If he does, and he can hurry and sell it and move, that would be wonderful." The thought of that happening anytime soon wasn't realistic but gave me great hope that we wouldn't need to be apprehensive with him so near. We hurried to the office down the hall, and she sat at her computer. She did a search on various sites that told who owned property in town. All of them showed Mrs. Clara Wilburn as the sole owner of the land next door.

"Did you ever know of a Mr. Wilburn?" I asked.

"No. I've gotten a few pieces of her mail, and all of them said Mrs. Clara Wilburn or Clara Wilburn."

"Nothing for Royce?"

"Not even one bill."

I pointed to listings on her computer. "And none of these sites show Royce or any other children she might have as co-owners of the property, so Royce might need to wait until a will is read or a succession is open that would pass the land down to him. Or his siblings, if he has any."

"Darn it." Eve's face pinched up.

I ran my mind through various scenarios. "She's probably listed in the obituaries today. That should tell us about any other children and also about her services. I'd like to go."

"Me, too. We need to pay our respects to her."

"We do." An ache sat in my heart for this mother dying. And she was murdered and stuffed in a trash bag. I couldn't imagine how horrible that would make her child feel.

Eve checked the online edition of our small local paper. The obituaries showed four people, none of them her and, thank goodness, nobody else that I knew. Eve turned off her computer and lifted her cell phone. Maybe she was calling a person who would know something about Mrs. Wilburn. "We need to see how Dave is doing."

Yes, I wanted to know.

"Hello, this is Eve Vaughn. Is Dave there?"

I watched, heart racing, while she waited and then spoke.

"How are you? Sunny and I are worried about you." She listened briefly, took steps away, turning her back on me, said a few soft words, and hung up. "The police told him he's under suspicion."

My heartbeat jumped a notch. "Where is he?"

"He's at work and really busy, trying to keep up with jobs and focus on them."

"But he's innocent, so they can't prove he did anything."

"Right." She placed her hands on the desk and pushed herself up. "Okay, I need to get my head on straight so I can think about trying to discover a killer." She looked at me. "We need to help find him, right?"

"Of course. Mrs. Wilburn was dumped at Dave's camp. She lived close to you. We were there and found her. The police are surely looking into what happened and probably getting a heck of a lot more information than we could, but we can't just sit back and do nothing about finding who actually did it."

Eve nodded, eyes hooded, face sad. "What can we do?"

I wasn't sure. "Don't you have line dance classes this morning? You could clear your mind there and might find out some things."

"I quit going to them." She walked toward her art room. In her state, she probably would paint. The color she'd use would not be a bright one.

"I'll let myself out," I called. "And maybe you'll come up with ideas while you're being creative." Before I stuck my head through the back doorway, I found myself pulling back. A carol grabbed at my throat, but I willed it to stay there. I anticipated that Royce could be standing right outside, hammer above his head, ready to slam it down on either of us who stepped out.

I peeked out and found no sign of him, locked the door from inside, and slipped out. *This is no way to live*, I told myself walking toward home. We, or more hopefully the police, would find the killer soon so that all of our lives could get back to normal.

A splash came from beyond the wooden fence on the right, followed by a woman's giddy laughter. The couple who'd moved in back there barely looked twenty years old. The woman must be enjoying a cool dip in their pool. That couple had surely been questioned about Mrs. Wilburn, but I doubted they or any other neighbors knew much about her. I wondered whether anyone did.

Mrs. Hawthorne, my friend and former customer from Fancy Ladies, was normally working with flowers in her front yard two doors down from me but wasn't out there today, so I would wait to question her about the death.

Making a decision about what I might do, I jumped in my truck and drove to the only funeral home in town. A one-story gray brick, it provided much parking space that I was pleased to see only partially filled. I hoped the only people inside worked there and weren't in mourning and wanting to inquire about their services. Possibly I would find Royce and a sibling inside making arrangements for his mother's funeral. Oh, but maybe that wouldn't work well. If he was there, he might yell at me and accuse me again of killing her.

That consideration made me pause. Perhaps I shouldn't go in.

I glanced back at the parked cars but didn't see Mrs. Wilburn's sedan. Maybe she would already be laid out. If so, I might learn more from someone who worked there. I pulled the door open and walked inside.

No one was in the wide foyer. The straight lines that crossed each other in the low-pile tan carpet let me know it was newly vacuumed. A fresh mint scent hinted that air freshener covered up the cloying smell of the many funeral flowers often displayed here on coffins. A paisley-print sofa and pair of chairs with matching prints waited for visitors to sit on them. The podium that normally held prayer cards and an open book for the deceased's visitors to sign held only a long white pen in a white holder.

The doors to the office I had been in once and also Viewing Room Two at the far end of the hall were shut. The door to the largest viewing room was left open. Perhaps they were setting up Eve's neighbor's casket in there.

I walked to the room, peeked in, and was disappointed to find no person or casket.

A hand laid on my shoulder made me jump. "May I help you?"

I turned to find a man wearing a gray suit with a sad expression that he probably always wore when a person entered his business. That expression quickly turned to annoyance. His lips and chin tightened. His eyes pinched closer together. I imagined, *"Oh, it's you"* ready to blast from his mouth when he saw me. What assuredly stopped him was an awareness that I might have a newly deceased that I wanted to have displayed here.

"Hello, Toby." I put my hand out to this undertaker who I'd had a run-in with.

He gripped my hand and placed his opposite hand on top of mine. Surely he did this with potential clients and not people like me who only wanted some information he wasn't always happy to give.

"I don't have a body to bury." The minute I said it, I squeezed my mouth shut. The words I'd used came out so wrong.

His hands pulled away. "But," he said, "you wanted to know more about burial vessels?" He drew his shoulders back. Veins in his neck stood out.

Yes, I had once come to ask him about adhesives for urns, which he didn't seem to appreciate. But now when I shook my head, Toby's shoulders relaxed. "I'd like to know if you have someone here who isn't laid out yet."

His jaw muscles worked and tightened. "You can check the newspaper to find out anything you want to know about deceased locals."

"Okay, here's what happened. I know someone from town who died yesterday, and I haven't seen her death listed yet."

He watched me and waited instead of filling in the information he must figure I wanted to know. When he didn't respond, I needed to ask questions. "Does anyone ever die around here and not have information about their deaths put in our local paper?"

"Yes."

His answer surprised me. He offered nothing else.

"Why wouldn't a family have the death of a loved one placed in the paper's obituary?"

"Some people can't afford to have the write-up."

"You're kidding me. It costs to have someone's death announced in the obits?"

"Yes, and the longer the piece, the more it costs."

"Okay, I can understand that. A lot more words take up space where other information could be written."

"And sometimes people close to the deceased really don't like the person."

This statement stunned me and also reminded me of what Mrs. Wilburn's nephew outside the manor told me. Surely saying nobody in the family cared for her couldn't be true.

While I stared at the space to the left of him as this idea sank in, Toby leaned forward. "Are you a close family member of a newly deceased person?"

"No, thank goodness I am not."

All semblance of sympathy washed away from his face and his stance. "Then I'll walk you out." He gripped my forearm and turned me toward the foyer.

I slid my arm out of his grasp and strode to the front door. "Thank you," I said and stepped out into air that didn't stifle. This time I purposely hadn't mentioned my friendly neighbor, his grandmother Mrs. Hawthorne, whom he had insisted was his *step*-grandmother, probably because his beloved Catahoula hound she'd been keeping in her fenced yard for him had gotten out and never found. His anger toward her said he held it against her, although that elderly woman would not have let a dog out where it might get hurt.

The urge to call Eve struck before I pulled out of the funeral parlor's long driveway, and I grabbed my phone from my purse. I knew, however, that she would have called me if she'd come up with something, and I hadn't found out anything worthwhile to report.

I left with thoughts scattered about what to do next. At home, I pulled out the plans for what Eve and I expected to do with Jeff and Georgia Andrews's house after the garage remodeling was complete.

Since the couple had contacted us for the job, we were the contractors and would hire as many subs as we needed, especially while my shoulder finished healing. Georgia wanted to widen the existing dining area, so we'd need to take down the wall to the bedroom on the opposite side of it. That bedroom could be made smaller, she'd said, since it would become their workout room. It was the only place they wanted carpet instead of hardwood or ceramic.

Although many larger builders had their blueprints drawn on computers, neither Eve nor I was proficient doing that. While our firm grew, we planned to learn. I stretched out the blueprints and set the ideas we had come up with for the project beside them. The small, drab guest bathroom left much to be desired, and I had proposed a pedestal sink to suggest more space and shelving built into the wall. Images of wall studs and locating electrical wires ran through my mind, along with hammers and electric saws. Those pictures turned into recollections of being at Dave's new place and the man at the camp beyond his using such tools. Probably most adults did use some of them at one time or another, I realized, my imaginings leading nowhere.

I took out my mixing bowl and ingredients I needed to bake angel food cakes to bring to the manor in the morning. While I put everything together and the kitchen heated and began to smell like the pinch of vanilla I added to the mix, my mind wandered, going after thoughts of death, finding Mrs. Wilburn, and protecting Dave. It wouldn't help to try and tell Detective Wilet anything since Eve and I had told him everything we knew while at Dave's camp.

I made three of the cakes and by the time my day ended, I had come up with more ideas for remodeling the Andrews' house but gained little insight into finding a killer. I looked forward to getting out and learning more in the morning. Maybe in the obits? Surely I'd hear gossip from the manor.

Chapter 7

First thing in the morning, I checked the online obituaries to try to learn more about Clara Wilburn. She wasn't mentioned. Four men, one woman, and a newborn had died in our area. I thought of all their families and others who loved them and wrapped all of those people in my prayers.

Doing that brought me back to Mrs. Wilburn and her son. Although it was especially difficult since seeing him in such a fearful manner with his accusations toward Eve and me, I sent prayerful thoughts around him. And then pictures arose in my mind of her nephew I had spoken with, his grandmother in the manor, and others who had loved her. Even though they might not have liked her? Or maybe that was only what her nephew believed. After he learned she was gone, he probably softened his attitude and realized how important she had been. I envisioned comfort wrapping around him and all of those other people in her life.

I showered, antsy because I wanted to know about Eve's neighbor and her family. I shoved instant cheese grits in the microwave and spooned them into my mouth and drank a tall glass of milk, barely noticing any of it going down. Getting the phone book from a drawer, I called the *Bayou Clarion*, figuring I had given them time to get more information.

When a woman answered with the newspaper's name, I asked to speak with the person in charge of writing the obituaries. It didn't take long for another woman to speak to me.

"Hi, sweetie, I'm calling to say I hadn't seen anything in your paper about a Clara Wilburn's death."

"Just a minute." She must have checked her files. "No, we don't have information about that."

"Do you think you might get something about it during the day?" I asked, immediately determining I'd asked a stupid question. How would she know what information she would receive unless she was psychic?

She must have thought the same thing since it sounded like a little snort at her end. "Ma'am, I'm sorry. I really have no way of knowing what kind of notices we might receive."

"I realize that. Just wanting some answers."

"I understand," she said, although I thought she did not. We disconnected.

My next call was to my sister. "How are you?"

"I'm okay." Her tone was dull again, so I didn't need to ask whether she had heard from Nicole again. The good news was that since she felt so down, she would be slapping black paint on canvas instead of going outside her house. And why did I keep thinking of Royce as being such a threatening person? We had only seen him holding up a hammer. And, of course, accusing us of murder.

"Any ideas about helping Dave?"

"Nothing yet."

Whatever caused my unease made me drive past Royce's house and Eve's once I left mine. No sign of movement at either place calmed my concerns.

I wondered about Dave, but figured he was busy with work, and if he wanted to call me, he would. As I drove the highway, I realized another reason Mrs. Wilburn's death might not be listed in the newspaper here. The name *Wilburn* was uncommon in our area. Her son was the only person I had ever heard of with the name *Royce*, although different and unusual first names were often given these days. If Eve's neighbor moved here from another place, notice of her death and her burial might be announced only in that city. Of course, if she had any relatives with her surname around here, I might learn about her funeral from one of them.

Sure, I could call friends and ask if they knew anything about her, but I had never heard her mentioned in conversation, and if I questioned friends of mine, like Amy at the community center, they would surely press for details of her death that I wasn't ready to give yet.

A gas station sat ahead. I whipped my truck into its lot, unbuckled my seatbelt, and got out. On the passenger side, I opened the door and took an older phone book out of its inner pocket.

The book was slim. Even though it gave listings from a few of the smaller towns around, more and more individuals were getting rid of landlines, and they weren't putting their cell numbers in a book. Would phone books and landlines become obsolete? I wondered and flipped through the pages. In our town of Sugar Ledge, more people than I'd thought had surnames that began with *W.* Many of them were *Williams.* Not even one was *Wilburn.* I turned to the next towns in the book and found the same thing. I replaced the book, threw myself back into my seat, and drove.

The people I knew of who could give me more information about Mrs. Wilburn were few. Royce would tell me nothing—except he hoped I rotted in hell for murdering her. Thoughts of him wielding that hammer made me shiver. A low hum escaped while I drove. The man I'd spoken to outside the manor was related to her, but I didn't get his name since I didn't want to give mine. Now I wished we could have exchanged them since he should know of her death by this time. Of course, he might have spoken to Royce, and Royce surely told him I killed her and then stuffed her in that garbage bag in Dave's new place. Royce might have figured I couldn't handle her body alone and had gotten Eve to help me get it inside.

I knew of only one other person connected to her, and I should go speak with that woman. I was pulling onto the main roadway when my phone rang. I rummaged through my purse and found it.

"Guess what." Eve didn't give me a chance to say a word before she yelled at me. "I spoke with my grandson."

I felt the smile break across my face. The thrill in her voice made me imagine my heart smiled, too. "Really?"

"Yes, indeed."

"And he spoke back to you?"

"Certainly. We had a long conversation. He is a really smart boy."

I laughed. "I'm certain he is."

"And he and Nicole and Randy are all doing well." She chuckled.

I loved hearing her joy. "Okay, now go and throw off that old ratty robe and nightgown and put on some clothes you can wear out of your house."

She said nothing for a second or two, in which I envisioned her glancing down at what she wore. "These things aren't ratty. They're silk and really pretty."

"Except for the black paint splatters. Hurry. I'm coming to get you, and then you can tell me all about your big conversation." I disconnected and headed for her house.

It didn't take long to reach her. She chattered nonstop. The joy in her face and body expression—arms waving and hands aflutter while she spoke of the baby and upper body twisting while she sat on the passenger side of my truck—all made me happy. I could barely keep up with her rapid-fire words about how Noah had made a sound while she talked to him. She was certain he had been trying to call her Meme. Nicole hadn't called too often because she was nursing, and the little guy was always hungry. They were trying to work out their schedules so both could get some rest.

Lifting her nose, Eve looked toward the backseat. "Your truck smells exquisite. You baked cakes?"

"Yes. I'm glad you spoke with Nicole. Now let me tell you what's going on on my end. I went to the funeral parlor to see if they weren't fixing Mrs. Wilburn up there."

Eve's eyes squeezed together. "Oh, Sunny."

"Well, they weren't. And I wanted to learn more about funerals that weren't announced but didn't get anything. There aren't any other Wilburns in the phonebook, either, but I did learn her stepmother lives in the manor, and that's where we're going."

"Great. She ought to be able to tell us a lot."

"Unless she does like Royce and starts yelling and accusing me of murder. I especially hope that won't happen in front of Mom and her friends."

Eve reached over and gripped my hand. "At least we'll be together."

Hmm, would that take the sting out of what could happen?

Chapter 8

Few cars sat in the parking lot of Sugar Ledge Manor. Those that belonged to residents rested in their familiar places—close to the entrance, near blooming crepe myrtles and rose bushes. I drove a little farther through the parking lot instead of taking one of the first empty places. When Eve looked at me, I explained. "I'm checking to see if I spot Mrs. Wilburn's nephew again."

"Do you know what he drives?"

"No, I left before he went to whatever it is."

She stretched her head forward and turned it one way and another as though trying to spot him, although she had no idea what the young man looked like.

When I reached the end to the right, I turned and spun back the other way. Two women who walked out of the entrance stopped and watched me. I nodded at them, getting no acknowledgement in return, and recognized them as the pair in dark blue shirt and pants of many of the people who worked here. One of them had long, tight curls I admired. They had eyed me when I was here the last time and had heard me asking Mom and her crew if they knew Clara Wilburn. A creepy feeling wormed along my shoulders.

"Do you know who those two women are?" I asked Eve, giving my head a small tilt toward them.

She exchanged stares with them. "No. I think I've seen them working inside, probably helping a person in a wheelchair or bringing a meal to someone's room." She turned to me. "Why?"

"They were together and seemed really interested when I asked Mom and her friends if any of them knew Mrs. Wilburn. That was soon after

Mrs. Wilburn was found murdered, so not many people would have known about her death yet."

"Do you think they knew something?"

"It's possible. Or it's possible that they just stare at visitors." I pulled into the empty spot where I'd parked before. Maybe the man I'd spoken to out here would come back and notice my truck here. Why that would matter, I had no idea, but I was searching for anything.

No one was in the foyer. What swelled inside it now was the rich aroma of roasted chicken and freshly baked bread. My nose led me forward, and I was pleased that I was here right now. I looked for Mom and her friends where they normally sat to visit with each other right beyond the foyer and wasn't surprised that none of them were there.

"They must be eating," Eve said.

"I don't blame them if their meal tastes anywhere as good as it smells."

"I agree."

We gave the angel food cakes to the young woman manning the sign-in counter so she could deliver them to the kitchen. She assured us diabetic residents would be thrilled. We needed to walk only a little farther and turn left to reach the large open area that held dozens of tables. Each table held four chairs. Residents lined up at the buffet with their trays. Servers placed food items that each individual asked for on their plates. Many people were already eating. A couple of staff members served those who required assistance to get their meals, normally those with walkers or wheelchairs.

Eve and I exchanged greetings with people. We knew some of them but definitely not all.

"Oh, you look just like her." A woman with deep wrinkles and puffy white hair pointed at Eve and then me when we stepped near her table.

"No," the gent seated with her said. He pointed at me. "She looks just like her." His index finger swerved toward my identical twin.

"I see that now. You're both pretty women."

"Thank you," we said at one time.

"We're looking for our mother," I said, seeing the table where Mom normally enjoyed meals now empty. "But I don't see her or any of the ladies she usually sits with."

The man nodded. "Those are some gambling fools."

Eve swerved her head toward mine as I did mine toward hers. "Our mother?" she asked.

The woman smirked at the gent and tilted her head. "No, she and the other Chat and Nappers just decided to go on the bus to a casino today. The Treasure, I believe."

They had done that a handful of times before, but certainly not enough times to worry about Mom being addicted to gambling. I glanced around, trying to pick out the person we were mainly here for. "Would y'all know who Adrienne Viatar is?"

"Yes." The lady pointed two tables over toward the serving line. "That woman who's got the mashed potatoes all down her chin, making it look like a fluffy goatee. That's her."

I had hoped we would find someone who appeared more alert, a person who could give us information about Mrs. Wilburn and family members who disliked her, who may have even wanted her killed, although I wouldn't mention that last part. We would need to be much more discreet. This woman slouched over, her shoulders even with the bottom of her breasts that flattened at the top and widened at the bottom like a ski slope. The wire-rimmed glasses she wore looked as thick as the bottoms of old soft drink bottles. Her hand shook while she carried a small piece of meat to her mouth.

No one else sat at her table, so now might be the best time to speak with her. Eve and I could each take a seat there and maybe help her eat.

"Thank you. We'll go meet her," I said to the pair who had returned to eating their meal.

"Oh, no." Our informant swallowed the food in her mouth before saying more. She gave her head a shake that made gold loop earrings that looked too large for someone her age swing in front of her hair. "She gets a bad upset stomach if she talks while she's eating. I believe she swallows too much air, and it cramps her up real bad." That wasn't a condition I was familiar with.

"Then we can just wait until she's finished and speak with her afterward," Eve said.

The woman's earrings again swung. "Uh-uh, right after her meals, she has to get her sleep. One of the workers comes and helps her to room, and she gets in bed for quite a long nap."

This idea wasn't going to work well. But the food I smelled and saw in their plates seemed delicious. Voices became louder as more people entered. The sound of chairs scraping back at tables added to the commotion.

"Maybe we could sit with y'all and eat dinner with you two," I suggested, tilting my hand toward the pair of empty chairs. We could possibly find out more and fill our stomachs at the same time.

The gentleman pulled his lips tight and back. "We have people who join us every day, although they sometimes get here after us." He stretched his index finger toward one and then the other empty chair. "Those are their seats."

"And did you pay for your meals?" the woman questioned sharply, to which we shook our heads. "You need to do that a day ahead of time so they'll prepare enough food for everyone."

We had been told that when Mom first entered the manor. "Thank you for talking to us," I said, and the two continued their lunch.

I couldn't help going toward Mrs. Wilburn's stepmother. She had cleaned almost every bit of the mashed potatoes from her plate so that the trace of white left on it was less than what she wore on her chin. She stabbed a postage stamp size piece of baked chicken, brought it up to her mouth, and held it there on her fork. Instead of eating her meat, she looked up at us. Her eyes did that thing I'd seen many times over the years—a person looking at me, swinging their eyes over to Eve, holding on her only a second, and then moving back at me. And then like I had witnessed often over time, the person who saw me and Eve next to each other took on a small smile with the realization that we were twins. We'd often been told that we were the most identical that people had ever seen.

While this lady stared at me, I was ready to speak to her. What should I say? Offer my sympathy? If I did that while she was eating, according to the woman I just spoke to, this one would probably choke on her food and turn blue and wind up exactly like her stepdaughter. What would be the point of that?

If I asked about relatives who didn't like her stepdaughter or might have had a reason to kill her, would that be more appropriate?

The chicken on her fork splintered, a slender part of it holding onto the tines, a larger portion dropping to her plate in the gravy that splattered to the front of her white blouse. The brown gravy created a pattern like a little map of Louisiana with its long toe aiming for her shoulder. One asset I was proud to possess was the ability to notice detail, that trait I'd acquired when I sold undergarments and had to measure and help fit bras and snug body-molding bottoms on so many women, I sometimes blushed when I saw those people in town.

"Sunny." Eve tapped my arm.

I was prepared to ask her if she also thought Adrienne Viatar's left breast resembled our state when reason took hold. I tightened my lips against my teeth.

Eve gave her head a strong jerk back toward the exit. Right beyond her, I couldn't miss the lady who'd spoken to us and warned us not to talk to this one now. She was shaking her head and wagging her finger at me so hard, she reminded me of my first-grade teacher, who didn't know about my dyslexia any more than the rest of us did at that time. Every time I read a few words or a group of numbers in class, she gave me that same hard shake of her head and finger wag as though I had been a really bad puppy. She would end this display of negativity toward me by speaking my name with a sharp tone and say, "No, you are wrong. Again." No wonder I hated my early schooling.

Only the smallest slivers of that chicken still held on to Adrienne Viatar's fork, making me think of the wishbone our mother used to remove from the whole chickens she cut up and fried. It was our favorite piece. Eve normally let me break off the smallest piece and then I got to make a wish, which was always the same: *Please don't let me be so dumb.*

Bless my third-grade teacher, who figured I was dyslexic and had me tested. Schooling became a little easier then since they discovered my problem and adjusted my classwork and testing to accommodate my disability. My gratitude really went out to that teacher who let me know about so many brilliant and talented people I had heard of who also dealt with the condition. That helped me hold my head higher, although the need to check myself with some numbers and words still remained. Eve helped with that in our business.

"Sunny." She hissed my name near my ear and tugged my arm harder, assuring me we needed to go.

I was so sorry to see the last slivers of chicken break apart and slide off Mrs. Viatar's fork and splash into the gravy. When I gave her a smile and a nod, she shared a tiny smile back, and keeping me in view, slid her empty fork into her mouth. I cringed. She pulled the tines out of her mouth and looked at that fork with a frown. Since we shouldn't be talking to her now, Eve and I scurried out of the dining hall before I lifted the elder's food and fed it to her.

"Maybe she would have spoken with us," I told Eve.

"And maybe she would have thrown up her meal in the process." She pointed toward a door with *Administrator* on the plaque above it.

Eve knocked with polite taps. Seconds later the door opened.

"Yes? May I help you?" A petite person wearing a long dress that swept the floor, she looked from one to the other of us with a smile. "Are you looking for your mother?"

"No, we know she went gambling," Eve said, and the lady in charge's smile widened. She didn't invite us into her office. "What we want is to know about Adrienne Viatar. What's the name of her grandson who comes to visit her often?"

Her forehead crimped. "I can't give you that information. It's in our privacy laws."

I stepped closer. "But I met him outside, and he told me she was in here. After I left, I realized he and I didn't exchange names."

She tightened her lips. "I'm sorry. Maybe you'll get to see him again." Behind her, a phone rang in her office. "If you'll excuse me, I have to get that."

Before she shut the door all the way, I noticed something interesting. The staff member behind the sign-in counter left that area and walked toward a door marked *Ladies* down the hall.

"Come see," I told Eve and bustled to that counter. Visitors were supposed to sign in on that thick leather-bound binder every time they came, writing their names and the dates and who they came to visit. Eve and I never did anymore, but I hoped some people in Mrs. Viatar's family did.

Excitement built as I flipped through recent pages. Our newfound friend that we had almost just gotten to meet had her name written four times in the last two weeks. How many more times had people come to visit her and done like us, not signing?

Enthusiasm raising my heartbeat, I pulled a small pad from my purse and not finding my pen, used the attractive white long-tailed one standing in its holder to jot down the names of each of her visitors and the date they were here.

Eve shoved my hand away and shut the binder. I was ready to give her a harsh retort but heard footsteps approaching behind before I noticed her head tilt in that direction. I pushed the items I held into my purse and walked with my twin toward the front door.

"I don't have a pen. Excuse me," the woman who'd passed by us called to someone. "I don't see the pen we usually use to sign in. Did it fall back there?"

Eve and I glanced at each other and rushed out the door. I was the one who felt like a thief.

"I'm starving," Eve said. "Let's go eat somewhere, and we can check out your list. Maybe it can lead us to a killer so we can prove it wasn't us or Dave."

Chapter 9

Eve and I chose to eat in Swamp Rat's Diner, a charming place that squatted partway over a bayou as though it might slide in. Lively swamp pop music and an inviting aroma of boiled and fried seafood called to me the second I opened the door of my truck. Cajun jokes in frames on the cypress walls and under glass on the tables entertained guests, along with photographs of swamp scenes and the ten-foot long locally caught and stuffed alligator that greeted everyone who came inside. I was pleased that we'd chosen this place since we always delighted in the food and atmosphere.

Today, though, the memories struck first of being in a similar place, although it was a place that normally didn't serve meals. The memory that flashed was of going inside Dave's rustic camp with a similar style and a gator swimming outside.

Eve and I exchanged greetings with people we knew slightly but didn't want to stop to talk with since we wanted to get busy with my names. We sat beside each other in a booth so we could study the list together. Knowing the menu well, we placed our orders without needing to look at one. Then I pulled out my pad and the pen I'd stolen. No, I borrowed it, I reminded myself, and forgot to put it back, but next time I would return it.

"This woman visited her twice in the last two weeks," Eve said, pointing to *Jessica Nelson*, the first name I'd copied. "And this man went a couple of times." Pleased, I looked at Eve. "I'll bet he's the one I talked to in their parking lot."

"And other people probably do like us and don't sign in at all."

"I didn't get to check most of the recent pages."

A nice-looking young man with a smile brought us our silverware and soft drinks along with frosted glasses in case we wanted to pour our drinks into them. "Your food won't be long," he said.

"Yum. I'm really hungry," Eve told me.

I saw servers carrying meals to tables and booths, and realized how empty my stomach felt. "Okay, I think what we should do after we eat is try to find contact info for the people who visited Mrs. Viatar."

Eve eyed me. "And then?"

"And then we can call them or go over or something." Out loud, my suggestions didn't sound foolproof. "What do you think?"

"I think my oyster po'boy is heading for me. That's all that matters right now."

"Right." My order was aimed at me, too, and we should think better after we were full.

She gave me a couple of delicious crunchy fried oysters from her sandwich with the crusty bread, and I shared my sweet potato fries and shrimp jambalaya. Lots of tasty seafood and seasonings went into the rice dish. Afterward, we shared a slice of creamy pecan pie with a flaky crust. Both stuffed, we paid for our meals and left nice tips. I waddled out behind my sister.

"Let's go to my house to check out the people on the list. It would feel creepy and cloud my thoughts if Royce was outside next to yours." Getting no argument, I drove to my place. There, we did online searches for the names, didn't find any of them listed locally, and didn't want to pay for advanced searches that might not even yield information we were looking for. Since I had received two phonebooks from different companies within the last couple of years, Eve and I sat at my dining room table with the list of visitors' names between us. Each of us took one book and had paper and pens.

"These are usually slightly different," I said, "so why don't we both look up each of the names."

We skimmed and double-skimmed our pages with the female name. We glanced at each other at the same time and didn't write anything.

"Let's check out the other towns around here, too," Eve suggested.

Because of my dyslexia, I need to concentrate to find words I wanted in the correct order, and it took me longer to figure some out. Eve, I noticed, had glanced at the list of names between us and started a new search from the beginning of her phonebook. I looked at her, and she patted my arm to let me know it was all right. I shouldn't be concerned. I had been bothered during most of my school years when almost everyone else in class finished work before me, but I surely wasn't worried with Eve.

She'd finished going through all the towns in her book again before I did mine. "The woman might be married and listed under their husband's names," she said.

"Or she might have an unlisted number or no landline."

Eve touched the name of the male I had copied. "Maybe we'll get lucky with this fellow, Andrew Primeaux."

"I hope he's the one I talked to. He sure didn't seem to care for Mrs. Wilburn."

It took no time for her to reach the *P*'s, so I waited and watched. Her finger slid right through the earliest listings that began with that letter. It stopped at *Price, Dave*. Eve's eyes crinkled with sadness that I knew matched mine. "He's got to be all right," she said.

"I know." My throat tightened. She looked at me, and I knew sadness showed in my face.

"They can't charge him with anything just because she was found in his camp, but they'll sure be trying to."

We stared at each other, both with unhappy eyes. "I'd like to call him to see how he's doing," I said.

"I know. Me, too, but he told me he's got a lot of work to catch up on right now. Let's not bother him. I'm sure he'll call when he can take time for a longer talk."

The phone book gave his number but not his address. We wanted to make sure his address didn't become the parish jail.

"Oh, look, there." I set my index finger on *Primeaux, Andrew*.

"Okay, now what are we going to do with this information? Do you want to call him? Maybe offer your sympathy for his aunt's passing?" She held her phone out to me.

I started to punch in numbers. When I got halfway through, I pressed *Off.* "I don't know if this is the man I saw outside the manor."

"Then let's go see if he is." Eve was on her feet.

I wrote the name and address on a slip of paper, double-checked what I copied, and stood.

I knew where Raccoon Road was and didn't take long to drive to his neighborhood. It sat in the middle of the older section of town where most houses were wooden and painted white with two-foot brick footings lifting them off the ground. Nearby a large Catholic church offered forgiveness, an elementary school tossed out knowledge, and old public swimming pool provided years of fun in the summer for countless people who grew up around here. I glanced at Eve, while she did the same to me, both of us with our lips lifted at the corners, probably enjoying pleasant memories from these places. I recalled the smell of chlorine that made my nostrils tighten even before I stepped out to the apron of the large rectangular pool and then the feel of buoyancy as I lay on my back, stretched my arms out, used my feet to push myself off the side, and then for the first time, floated. Amazing.

I felt my lip corners drop with one recollection from that church. I'd made my first communion there, an exciting time for us young children. But right after I received the blessed host for the first time and tried to regain moisture to my mouth so I would swallow but not chew it, I heard the boy behind me gag. He coughed and made a chocking sound, and I turned around just in time to see him throw up the blessed bread. It had touched the back of his throat that caused his gagging instinct, he told our religion class later, but that sound and the vomit smell came back to me these many years later.

So did the negative experiences from that school I drove past. One of the few two-story brick buildings in town, a couple of its rooms with dark-paneled walls taunted me even now. Those early teachers gave me little leeway for completing my work slower than most. Of course, they didn't know of my problem. My parents had no idea why one of their twins performed worse in classes than the other and whose self-esteem dropped because she couldn't do any better. It would take a while for all of us to learn from my favorite teacher who figured out what slowed me down in classes. She let us know the condition wasn't my fault, and extra assistance and studying would help me keep up. We discovered that many brilliant people had also been born with dyslexia and that twins often shared the same condition, but my sister and I did not.

"That's it." She pointed to the house ahead. Wiry grass was way past due for a cutting. The person inside it probably didn't own a weed whacker, or possibly something like an illness kept him from knocking down those weeds growing all around his house. The screen on one front window was busted, and large patches of mildew tainted the white paint. Eve and I figured this was the house owned by a man, the one who'd visited at the manor within the last two weeks. He mustn't have a wife who would be after him to take care of those things.

What would I say to him, I wondered when Eve stepped out of my truck and stood beside it, waiting for me to join her? Suppose he was the wrong person?

The side of his house held a narrow driveway with no garage or carport. The only thing it held was a new shiny maroon truck that looked out of place at this faded residence.

Before I lost my courage, I hurried up the three steps to the postage-stamp-size front porch. With Eve coming beside me, I pressed the doorbell near the screen door that covered the inner wooden one. The loud bell buzzed only once inside and then the front door was pulled open. A girl of about sixteen stared at Eve and then me and then Eve and then me before she cracked the slightest grin, making her appear more pleasant and two years younger than she had seconds before.

"Y'all both look the same," she said through the screen door with a voice that sounded much older than a young teen's. "I've never seen identical twins that look so much alike as y'all do."

With a pleasant smile, I leaned closer to the door. "Have you seen many identical twins?"

Her headshake made the tip of her blond ponytail swat her face. "You're just the second pair."

"I'm Sunny, and this is my sister Eve."

She gave us a spread-fingered little wave through the screen blurred with heavy dust. "Hey, y'all. I'm Jessica."

That was one of the names of Adrienne Viatar's recent visitors, although there had been no last name written.

I peered beyond her into the living room that wore an orange shag carpet from the seventies and hoped to see the man from outside the manor, but didn't see anyone. "Is your father here?"

She tilted her head. "My father?" Her pale eyebrows wrinkled when she frowned.

Eve and I looked at each other. Had this girl's father died? Was I wrong to come here?

"Who's that?" a man bellowed from a back room. "Some religious fanaticals? Just tell 'em you're spiritual enough and not interested in whatever they're selling." He stamped into the room behind the teen.

"That's him," I told Eve.

The girl glanced back. "Oh, you wanted my uncle."

Eve and I exchanged a look of apprehension. We'd both heard stories of *uncles* who lived with kids. None of those stories were pleasant.

"Yes?" His single word to us sounded like a bark. "What do you want?"

I wanted to grab that young woman and take her far away

from him. I wanted—

In once swift action, he popped the lock on the screen door, shoved the door open, and squeezed my arm.

Chapter 10

"Let me go!" I ordered and yanked my forearm away.

"Oh." He sounded calmer. "You're the one from the manor."

"Leave her alone." Eve shoved the screen door back against him.

He checked out her face. "Or maybe you are." He swung his head back and forth while he examined us, forehead wrinkling while he determined we looked alike.

I lifted my chin. "I spoke with you."

"Oh." His forehead smoothed. "You asked me about my aunt."

"I did. And that's why we're here."

"I'm sorry. I didn't know it was you." His tone sounded sincere. "Please come in." He gave a gentle push to open the screen door wider.

My gaze swung to Eve. The invitation from the male who lived here was the reason we came out to his place. Now that we were greeted so roughly, I wasn't sure we should go inside. The uncertainty in my sister's eyes mirrored mine.

I looked at the teen who now stood behind the man she called her uncle and knew we needed to go in, maybe to protect her. Maybe to lead to certain proof that neither we nor Dave Price murdered Eve's neighbor.

"Thank you," I said to the fellow holding the door open and walked inside. Eve stepped in behind me.

The girl's grin and eyes let us know she was pleased that we were here. "Y'all sit down." She swung her arm out to indicate that we were to take the sofa with a faded orange floral print and sagging center. "I can get y'all some coffee. Or would you want some tea? I can make y'all some."

"Neither, thanks," Eve said and looked at me, letting me make the decision of whether or not we should stay.

"Thanks for the offer. I don't want anything to drink either." I took a seat on the sofa. It sank a little but was surprisingly comfortable. Eve sat with me.

While our host and hostess took upholstered chairs with faded patterns that matched the larger piece we sat on, I used the moment to glance around. The gold drapes looked heavy. The size of the television that was the focal point of the room let me know that if our host liked baseball, he would have a difficult time seeing a batted ball on that screen. Maybe what surprised me most was even though the flooring and window covering seemed to have been here since the house was built, none of it carried a stuffy smell. The room actually smelled fresh, ultra clean. Maybe the girl sprayed air freshener right before she answered the door. Possibly, they just kept the insides cleaner than the yard.

"My name is Sunny Taylor," I said.

"And of course I'm her sister," Eve said as though finishing my sentence.

"Hey. That's cute." The teen gave us her small windshield-wiper wave.

"And I am Andrew Primeaux," the man in the room said.

"Yes, we met," I told him.

"I didn't remember that we'd exchanged names." He tapped the side of his head. With a small smile, he added, "I'm so forgetful."

The girl leaned toward him, although he sat diagonally across the room from her. "No, you're not." She spoke almost protectively.

"Well, I forgot that."

"Mr. Primeaux," I said, regaining his attention, "the reason we came today was to give you our condolences. We are so sorry your aunt passed away."

Wearing a sorrowful face with pulled-down lip corners, Eve nodded.

The girl in the room didn't change her expression. Her eyes swung toward her uncle and remained steady as though she were waiting to see his reaction to my words.

"I'm sorry for your loss, too, Jessica," I said.

As I'd figured, her expression turned grim. Her lips pressed together with her lower one pushed forward. All joy left her eyes. "Thank you."

With no change in his demeanor, Andrew Primeaux reached for a cigarette and lighter on the small end table beside his chair.

"No, don't," Jessica told him. "Use the electronic one. You don't want to light that thing."

"Yes, I do." He eyed her but stuck the unfiltered cigarette in his mouth and struck up a flame. The moment he did, he released a deep cough. And then another and another.

Eve started coughing, too. "I need to go." She shoved up to her feet. With another cough and a frown, she gave the others a small nod and rushed out the door.

"I'm sorry," the man smoking said between hacks. "I shouldn't have lit up."

Jessica stepped across the room to him. "No, you shouldn't. You know how bad it is for you." She yanked the cigarette out of his fingers and stubbed it out in a large seashell on the table that must have been her uncle's ashtray.

I walked behind her to the door.

"Tell your sister I'm sorry," Andrew told me. "I hope I didn't make her sick."

"I'll tell her," I said on my way out. Since they hadn't given any information that might help, I didn't imagine I should just ask who in their family hadn't liked Clara Wilburn, especially not in front of the teen. Before I had crossed the small porch, someone shut the wooden door, but not before I glanced back and saw the girl's hand locking the screen door and pushing the wooden one shut.

"Did they hurry and kick you out?" From the passenger seat of my truck, Eve watched me strap myself in.

I hesitated before turning the key. "Sure seems like it, doesn't it?"

"Sunny, what do you think is going on with that girl and him?"

"I have mixed feelings about that situation." We stared at the front door. I considered that possibly she might sneak outside to us after he left the room. Maybe she would ask for help. Maybe Eve thought the same thing. I counted down long minutes while we kept our faces toward the house.

When I gave up on anything happening, I started my truck and headed away. "At first I thought she might be a victim in there, but after the way she yanked his cigarette away from him and put it out and the way she spoke to him, I'm thinking she didn't act like he had power over her."

Eve kept nodding. She coughed one more time before she spoke. "I think it was pretty obvious that was the Jessica who visited the manor twice in the last couple of weeks."

"I agree. And none of the family liked Mrs. Wilburn, Andrew Primeaux had said. So possibly Jessica didn't either. But if not, why did she keep visiting her? I want to find out more about family not liking her."

Eve's fingers sped over the face of her cell phone while I drove a distance from Andrew Primeaux's residence.

"Sending a message to your grandchild?" I asked, a blend of pleasure and amazement mixing within me. I was thrilled for her having that little one in her life. At the same time, I found it totally confusing to believe my sister had become a grandmother.

She gave me a smile. "No. I'd like to. I can't wait until he's old enough to talk to me or play with me."

I grinned in return, trying to imagine that tiny baby growing old enough to speak but couldn't envision the scene. "Maybe wait till he can babble a little first."

She moved her gaze back to her phone. "What I did was a search for Mrs. Wilburn's name, thinking maybe a notice of her death came up somewhere." Her tight-lipped expression toward the phone let me know she still had not found any mention of the dead woman.

"So what do you suggest we do now?" I asked.

She lifted her shoulders and rolled them backward. "I have so many confusing thoughts. I want to be with my daughter and her baby, but it's too soon for me to be around them again since their family needs to bond. And I don't know what to think about the people we just visited."

"So you want to go and work out."

She gave me a small nod. "You know that'll help me clear my mind and think better."

"I do." I reached a corner and turned. Once I left the neighborhood, I felt my shoulders relax, letting me know how tense they had been. Seconds later, I noticed that even a musty smell seemed to leave my nostrils, the odor probably recalled from the old showers and changing room at that public pool that never seemed to leave the place. The tension, I recognized, stemmed from uncertainty about the relationship of the man and girl in the house and indecision about what I should do next that might help.

"Just promise me you won't go sticking yourself in dangerous places alone." Eve's words broke into my musing that had scattered all over the place.

"No, Sis, I definitely won't do that." I slowed right before reaching her house, disappointed to see the For Sale sign still in front of Mrs. Wilburn's place. Or maybe it really belonged to Royce now since he had set out that sign. Driving at a centipede's pace, I felt my heartbeat speed and eyed the visible area around that house. Not seeing Royce, I kept going past Eve's house, tracing my gaze all around her place to make certain I didn't see him trying to hide close to it.

She glanced at me with a pensive look, her eyes tighter than before. "Are you going to stop and let me out, or do I need to open the door and jump out while you're driving so slowly?"

"Just checking." I eyed the area beyond her yard to the beginnings of Jake Angelette's fence, his house, and yard. No sign of Royce or Jake around. None of Jake's tools remained on the grass. I backed to Eve's driveway. "Okay, you're clear."

With no hesitation, she opened her door, slid out, and kept the door of my truck open while she spoke. "If you keep doing this every time you bring me home, I'm not riding with you again."

I tightened my lips. Squeezed their corners back and watched her slam the door and rush into her house. I found myself waiting moments longer to make certain she wouldn't scream or come running back outside because she found a threat.

The parting drapes from her den grabbed my attention. She parted them more and stood where I was certain to see her frowning out at me.

I drove away. Where I would head, I wasn't certain. I didn't want to go home. I did want to do something worthwhile, but had promised her I wouldn't snoop into murder on my own. My mind began working into overdrive with whom I wanted to investigate to try to prove that no one I truly cared about had wiped out Mrs. Wilburn.

My gaze flipped away from the road and dipped to my purse on the seat. The white tip of the pen I had accidentally taken from the manor stuck up a half inch from the zippered opening. I touched its cool plastic and turned when I reached the bayou, knowing where I would go. I'd feel better after I returned that item I'd snitched to where it belonged. While I was there, I might find Andrew Primeaux's grandmother had finished her nap and was now refreshed, ready to give me all of the information I wanted about him and other relatives he had told me could not stand his murdered aunt.

Not wanting to take time to bake, I went into a grocery store and bought different cookies and cakes. I walked into the manor with one of the cooks and passed the goodies on to her, knowing many residents were pleased whenever they found something different to select. I took steps inside the building when my phone rang.

"Ms. Taylor?" a familiar man's voice asked.

"Yes, Detective." I quit moving.

"I'll need to speak with you again."

My pulse sped. "Now?"

A long second passed. "No, but soon. I'll let you know."

My breath relaxed a pinch. "Okay."

He clicked off. I wanted to know why he wanted me but had chosen not to ask. Maybe I wouldn't like his reply. In the meantime, I needed to rush for answers to whatever I could find on my own.

Inside, I reached the sign-in desk and saw that Jessica came to visit here yesterday. I had only signed in a few times after Mom moved in, something she chose to do. I wrote my signature with the pen lying next to the book, the kind of pen a person can buy in a pack that costs a dollar. In the column asking who a guest was visiting, I wrote: Adrienne Viatar. Maybe seeing that would make Jessica or her "uncle" contact me.

While I exchanged a pleasant smile with the woman seated at a desk behind and lower than the counter, I slid the flared-tipped long white pen up there, not in the stand where it belonged since she would know it was me who just returned it. Holding her gaze with mine, I slipped the pen under the edge of a binder a few inches away from the book and hoped other people would come and sign in before the woman eyeing me noticed the fancy pen was back.

"Do you know whether Mrs. Viatar is up from her nap yet?" I asked the staff member facing me.

"I'm not sure." She turned back toward her computer. Seeming to notice I hadn't moved on yet, she glanced up again. "Oh, there she is. I'm sure she'll enjoy getting to see you."

I had no idea whether the woman hunched over the walker she inched behind would like to have me around her. Shame pinched my conscience a second after I saw her when I was disappointed to find she no longer wore the small brown map of Louisiana on her bosom. Obviously, she'd noticed that gravy stain or someone told her about it, and she'd removed the apparel. She now wore a paisley-print dress.

Unlike some other residents with walkers who slid them ahead with ease, she bent way over hers and shuffled her feet. I wanted to go and help her walk. I wondered what might help her to move faster, and then decided it would be a wheelchair that would roll, but then her legs would lose most of their ability to support her body.

I intercepted her as she came down the first hall. She had nearly finished her walk toward any seating area when I moved in beside her. "Hello, Mrs. Viatar. It's so nice to see you again."

She stopped moving, lifted her head up, and looked at my face. With no recognition registering, she stared ahead and again puttered toward her objective, which I figured was a place to sit.

I wanted to sit with her. That way I could get information about people in her family.

I moved beside her. "Would you like to sit on that sofa?" I pointed to the nearest one. Only three feet ahead in the area where my mom normally sat, this resident could get there quicker and the seats would be comfortable.

She stopped again. Mrs. Viatar bent her neck back so she could look up at my face, waiting long minutes that must have made her legs tired.

I pointed ahead. "Look, the sofa on your left. Would you like to sit there so you can rest? We can visit."

This time she checked out the sofa. After some time in which she could have recited the alphabet, she moved her eyes forward and continued her stroll.

Would she talk to me? Could she even speak? I started to wonder if either was possible or probable and if I was wasting my time. Time, though, was what we didn't have. I wanted to discover who actually killed Mrs. Wilburn to take all suspicions off those of us who'd discovered her body. Hours and minutes spent in prison would feel much longer than they did out here.

Fewer residents than normal moved around. A younger woman wearing a dark blue shirt and pants that many wore here as a uniform took brisk steps along the hall facing us.

"Excuse me," I said. "Do you know when the bus that went to the casino today comes back?"

"No, I don't," she said in passing, and I recalled the riot of long curls on a young woman here. Since I saw so few natural curls on women now, I rather favored them. My long hair was wavy, but natural curls were nice. I also recalled this hair on one of the two women wearing these uniforms who'd seemed to pay unnatural attention to me around here twice. What was that about?

I glanced back at her and found her doing the same thing with me. Watching. Who was she? How did she know anything about me? Did she know something about Mrs. Wilburn and her killer? I would speak to her.

"Ooo," came from the woman I followed. While I was walking and looking back, I had run into her. She was pitching forward as though trying to take a dive over the front bar of her walker.

I grabbed her when she was partway across and set her upright on her feet—as upright as she could go—and hoped I hadn't broken any frail bones. "Are you okay? I am so sorry. I wasn't paying attention, and I ran into you and almost knocked you over." I glanced around, hoping to see someone in white. "I can find a nurse and get you checked out."

She lifted her hand at the wrist. "I'm fine. Thank you for saving me," she said, to which I released a sigh. "Now if you'll excuse me, I need to use this restroom I was heading for. After that, I will be happy to speak with you."

Relief. I experienced it and hope she did, too, after she went in that room. The lady could talk. And she would talk to me. The curly-haired worker was gone.

I leaned against the wall and skimmed inside my purse. Moving my wallet, phone, and lipstick aside, I located my pen and small pad and got them ready to record pertinent information. Grasping the pen, I automatically looked toward the counter where guests were to sign-in. I could see only the back of a man in a casual shirt standing there but was unable to tell whether he used the pen I replaced and couldn't see if it now stood in its base. I wanted it there since that was where it belonged.

Adrienne Viatar emerged from the ladies room much sooner than I expected. To my surprise, she gave me a soft smile. "False alarm." She pointed to the seating area we had passed. "We can go back there and sit awhile."

"Good." I moved toward that destination with her. Questions came to mind, but I chose not to speak to her yet in case my words made her stop to look up at me. One new question I wanted to know was the name of the young woman working here who'd checked me out and seemed to be interested in me. I scanned our surrounding area but didn't see that person again. Maybe, though, she would come around while this person and I sat and spoke.

After inching along, we eventually reached the nearest seating, the area where my mother and her friends often sat. My new friend got herself into position in front of a sofa, lowered her hips to it, and with a huff, edged her walked to the side. She looked at me. "Now."

I scooted to the edge of the sofa beside her. "Miss Viatar," I said but second thoughts pushed in. "Or it's Mrs. Viatar, isn't it? You're Andrew Primeaux's grandmother."

Her eyes opened wider. Her lips pressed together and created a firm pale line.

"Sunny," a woman called. The beloved familiar voice was my mother's. I stood, stepped toward her, and shared a warm hug with her. "How nice to see you today."

"You, too, Mom." Behind her, other cronies of hers and numerous people I didn't know swarmed in. The bus must have just dropped them off.

"That's my seat. You're in my seat." One woman from Mom's group who wasn't the most pleasant stood before Mrs. or Miss Viatar.

The latter scooped herself up and with moves much quicker than I had seen before, grabbed her walker and scooted off down the hall. The woman who'd chased her away remained on her feet and watched her go, and I got the feeling that if the intruder had turned back, this one would run behind her down the hall. After the invader of her place was no longer visible, the bully blew out a small exhale and wandered off down a different hallway.

"She didn't even want her seat. That was mean of her," I told Mom.

"Well, honey, I guess out here it's rather like a school playground. There are those who like to give others orders, and there are the docile people who are intimidated by them and follow every order they receive. Of course, there are quite a few who sleep most of the time just like I've heard some children do in their classrooms."

"And then there are special people like you." I gave her a one-armed squeeze. "Those would be the wonderful, kind people."

"That's nice of you to say."

Three of her friends who approached from the entrance told me hello and mentioned how much they had won or lost in the penny slots. One brought back eighteen dollars, while another lost the same amount. Most were tired and going to their rooms to rest.

"I left three dollars over there." Mom lowered her chin as though she had caused a major tragedy.

"Did you have fun?" I asked, and she nodded. "Well good for you. You were entertained, and it didn't cost you much."

Her smile came and went. "Sweetheart, I want to go to my room."

"Great. Then we can visit a little while."

"I got so sleepy on the ride I really would like to shut my eyes a few minutes before supper."

Okay, so my mother was brushing me off. "I understand. Oh, but would you tell me one thing first?" I asked, and she waited. "Do you know some things about Adrienne Viatar?"

Confusion flashed over her face, her eyes doing rare rapid blinking like they were some of those Haywire reels that went all kinds of ways in certain slot machines. Yes, I had occasionally been to a casino, too, since many had taken up space in our region.

When Mom's eyes stopped their dance, she looked straight at me. "I know a few things. What do you want to know?"

There were too many questions I wanted answered. The latest one came out first. "Is she Miss or Mrs.?"

"Oh, my goodness, if you talk to her, make sure you never ask her that." *Eek.* "Why?"

"Because she has children and grandchildren, but she was never married, and you know that's was an extreme no-no for older women of her time."

Well that goof hadn't been my first one and wouldn't be my last. I saw Mom's eyes wanting to close and gave her a good-bye hug before she went off to her room.

All of the spaces I could see here emptied of people. The main sounds came from the large area where residents ate. Chairs scraping the floor were being moved into place at tables. Pots and dishes clattered while the kitchen staff prepared for the early evening meal. Since I hadn't purchased one ahead of time, I couldn't stay to eat with some I might want to speak with. Another day I would. When I did, I probably could get a place at the table with my mother. I just wouldn't tell her it was too late for her to advise me that I shouldn't ask Adrienne Viatar whether she had ever married.

In the meantime, my sister might have discovered something important to the case. I could check that out.

Eve must have read my mind since she called me the instant I sat in my truck and pulled out my phone. Maybe that was an occurrence with a lot of people, but over our lifetimes my twin and I so often received the same vibe at the same time that our connection was hard to discount.

"Did you learn anything new about Mrs. Wilburn or anyone else?" I asked without the need for small talk.

"I was too exhausted from scattered thoughts and hardly spoke to anyone except to say, 'Hi,' or complain because some machines seem to be getting harder to use."

"I understand. My mind sometimes wears me out without my body doing any exercise at all."

"Yes, and that's the way I feel this evening. Anything you want to tell me?" She yawned. A second yawn came louder. "Sorry."

"That's fine. You're tired. Go put your body and mind to bed early. We can talk more tomorrow." I did a reflex yawn.

"Great. We'll get together then."

"Sweet dreams." I considered getting home and going to bed early, too, since the yawns set me to recognizing my weariness. As I clicked off, something I saw made me reconsider driving away.

From the exit at the far end of the right wing of the building, Jessica, the teenager we met earlier today, walked out. She moved without slowing, even to check to make certain no cars were coming into her path. Ponytail swinging, she moved into a vehicle I couldn't see since other cars and small trees blocked my view. I considered backing out of my space and hurrying to drive where she was but figured she would see me. Instead, I waited, hoping she would come out this way.

A maroon truck backed from the place where she'd gone and appeared to have two people in it. The truck swerved out of the lot through the far entrance.

Wanting to see whether she was driving or if she was with her supposed uncle, I threw my truck in reverse and shoved the accelerator. The *BAM!*

behind my truck gave me pinched shoulders and a tight neck and forced "Silver Bells" from my suddenly desert-dry throat.

Throwing my truck in neutral, I turned off the motor, swung my door open, and slid out, praying I hadn't injured or killed anyone.

Chapter 11

Uh-oh, even if the vehicle I slammed against didn't appear too badly dented, the white color and blue words printed on it told me it belonged to the sheriff's department. An officer of the law was probably not the ideal person to run into.

"Oh, my goodness, I'm so sorry," I blubbered while the uniformed driver stepped out of his car, and I felt relieved that he didn't look hurt. "I backed up without checking behind real well first, and—" I saw the dented corner of his fender. The glass from his left headlight was shattered into splintered pieces on the cement. "I am so sorry."

He pulled a pad and pen from his shirt pocket, began to write, and jerked his head up to look at my face. "You're the one that sings Christmas songs all the time."

I noticed I'd kept up the tune and forced myself to stop. At the same moment, I recognized the young man. "You came to Dave Price's camp."

"Yes, I did." He nodded toward my truck. "I'll need your license and registration please."

Just what I needed. My insurance would go up and probably wouldn't cover everything for his car and my truck. My truck. I hadn't thought of damage to that. I turned to check it and more lyrics tried to ring out.

The rear bumper on the driver's side hung like a broken arm without a sling. Its fender crimped like it was trying to become an accordion. That part of my truck was pushed up so that I wouldn't be able to open the rear gate. I hoped the deputy could still drive his car.

I'd often prayed that no hurricane would slam into our area soon since I already needed my roof replaced and hadn't been able to afford that. And now this.

74 *June Shaw*

"Ma'am, your license and registration."

I hurried into my truck and was pleased to find that under a few other items, my glove compartment produced my registration papers he wanted. From my purse, I dug my license out of my wallet and automatically took out my phone. Once I gave him the information he wanted, my first instinct was to call my sister.

Before I could do that, the phone rang in my hand. "Excuse me," I told the officer. "I'll just tell them I can't talk now."

He'd started to write on his pad, giving no indication of what he thought about my comment, but I was pretty certain he wanted my full attention.

"Hello," I said to my caller. "I can't talk now, but I'll call back."

"No, don't," a woman said. "Sunny, this is Georgia Andrews."

"Georgia, I'm kind of in the middle of something right now. I can get back to you soon or come over, and we can discuss the next phase of the job. Your garage looks terrific." Trying to keep my customer happy, I gave a small smile to the officer staring at me now, also wanting to please him, to let him know I was trying to get off the phone.

His eyes didn't tell me he liked my time spent with my customer.

"Sunny, I don't want y'all doing any more work for me."

Georgia's word came as hard as a slap, making my body tilt. I stared at the young man who kept staring at me. I turned away from him and gave my full attention to the phone. "What are you talking about? We've got so much to do there...unless you and Jeff aren't going to complete that other work now."

A silent pause came from her end. "We are having the remodeling done, and I'm sorry, but we won't be using your company."

Now I grew quiet. "Why not?"

"We read in the paper about that dead woman in a camp and heard you found her. I'm sure you didn't kill her....but you understand. Jeff wants to hire somebody else."

"Ms. Taylor." The deputy touched my arm.

I glanced at his hand and away from it, full attention still on the phone. "The newspaper said I found her? She wasn't even in the obituaries."

"No, a small article said a woman was found dead in a garbage bag inside a camp. More details would follow."

I hadn't read the whole paper today. "Did it give my name as the person who discovered her?"

"It didn't, but this is a small town. Talk in my Young Women's meeting first thing this morning was all about it. Your name came up."

"I'm sorry," the officer standing beside me said, "but you have to hang up so we can take care of this situation."

"I really am sorry," Georgia said in my phone. "Jeff and I will pay Twin Sisters for the work you've done so far, but—" A long painful pause followed. "Please don't come around our home again."

I pressed the button to disconnect, not certain whether she started to say another word. The ones she'd already said hurt too much.

The police officer's eyes shifted over to my face and toward my hand gripping the phone, making me realize I was holding it with my elbow bent as though I was trying to get it to reach my mouth but could not.

"You've never been in an accident before, have you?"

"No, never." And if my racing heartbeat was any indication of how the body responds to a wreck, I never wanted to be in one again. My heart would certainly blast out of my chest. Of course, Georgia's news hadn't helped.

The young man kept nodding, which I figured was a good sign. But then he spoke. "So you only get involved in murders?" He gave a little laugh as though he believed he had made a cute joke, and maybe thought I would laugh, too.

"That isn't at all funny."

"I know. I'm sorry." He tilted his head toward my phone. "What you should do now is call your insurance company and report this accident."

"Thanks. I'll need to check out my papers for that, too." I pointed toward the cab of my truck.

"I can help if you need more information to give the person you speak with."

I sucked a big inhale in through my nose, held my breath, and released it. "You are so sweet." Hope came with more important concerns reaching my mind. "Please tell me what's happening with the investigation into the woman we found dead at Dave Price's camp. Are y'all finding out a lot about what really happened or who could have done it? He certainly isn't a murderer. He didn't kill my sister's neighbor or anyone else, and we didn't either."

I'd gripped his forearm I noticed when he eyed my hand on him. The eyes he turned up toward my face weren't so kind. Maybe you weren't supposed to touch a police officer. I wanted information, and he surely wouldn't give it to me if I got him mad at me. I slipped my hand away.

His face relaxed from the tension it held. "Detectives take over the case after our initial contact with the perpetrator, so we deputies don't normally keep up."

"None of us is a perpetrator."

"This damage to my car might be more than I'd originally thought." His tight lips and chin, along with his stern eyes, led me to know I should back off with questions about the death and save them for another person and another time.

An additional squad car pulled into the lot. It parked next to this officer's, and another young deputy got out. He ignored me and joined his partner, both of them speaking about my crime and all the damage I had caused while I sat in my truck with the door open and connected with my insurance carrier.

Again, I considered calling my sister. Maybe I'd need a ride. I certainly could use moral support. My mother was inside that large building. But she would be eating soon and then going to bed for the night. Learning I'd been involved in a wreck might keep her from getting much sleep. Food might give me comfort. I could pick up a burger or po'boy on my way home. If my truck made it down the road.

I needed to check. Internally crossing my fingers, I turned my key. A smile touched my face when the motor turned over. The smile wiped away once I heard the rattles coming from my rear. The muffler? Bumper? The entire rear end swinging like a happy puppy's?

The deputy I had backed into appeared in my doorway. "What are you doing? You can't leave now." The other cop rushed up beside him.

"I wasn't trying to leave. I only wanted to see if my truck would still run."

"Well, it does, but it will probably have lots of rattles until you get this rear part fixed."

Motion beyond the uniformed men drew my attention and increased my pulse. The two women in dark blue who'd watched me before stepped out from the manor's main entrance. They stopped walking and looked toward us.

"Can I go talk to those women?" I pointed.

The deputy shook his head. "You need to stay right there."

By the time he had made his calls, gathered all the information he needed, given me a ticket, and told me I could go, I felt a slight drool from the side of my lips and realized I had fallen asleep. "But lots of broken glass is back there," I protested.

"It's been cleaned up," he said, to my relief. "Our department's insurance company will be contacting yours and then you'll see how things go from there."

They wouldn't be good if I had to pay for anything. I twisted my upper body to look toward the manor in case I had only dozed a second and those women I wanted to question were still around. I found no sign of them.

"Just be careful when you're driving," the deputy said, "and look around real well before you back up."

I replied with a small smile. Pleased to see his car capable of moving on past mine, I again started my truck. I looked both ways behind me and with a deep breath, took my time creeping back. It wasn't until I turned my wheel hard that I heard the clatter. Throwing the gears into neutral, I got out and looked at the back of my truck. The chrome that hung toward the ground still quivered from the motion. At least it wasn't quite reaching the ground, although the folded portion looked like it could never be straightened.

I threw myself into my seat, making sure to buckle up in case this thing stopped in the middle of traffic, and then I drove fifteen miles an hour to my house, hoping all of the back section of my truck stayed attached.

Chapter 12

First thing in the morning, I did what my insurance carrier told me I should do. I rattled along a few streets to a repair shop.

"Phew," the man wearing a heavy gray jumpsuit and name tag with Larry on it said when I drove up. "I could hear that baby coming two blocks away."

"That's better than three blocks," I said, trying to lighten my spirit he'd just dropped even further. "Could you give me an estimate on fixing it?"

"Are you kidding?" He lifted one eyebrow and stared at me. I hoped he wasn't getting ready to tell me it should be totally trashed. "Yeah, if you'll take a seat in the waiting room, I'll put it up on a rack and see how bad it is."

Great. I'd rather have him tell me he'd see how good it is instead. I preferred a half-full kind of person.

Four red plastic-covered chairs squeezed together inside the small waiting area that smelled of grease. Each one bore numerous cracks down the seats. An old sewing machine table held a tiny TV with a game show blaring. I found the remote and turned it off.

Taking the chair with the least splits, I made a small list of pending jobs that Eve and I might do fairly soon and said a silent thank you to all the people who would trust us and allow me time to heal. I shifted my left shoulder forward and back. Still no feeling came from that area of my body. The doctor who removed the bullet believed a sliver of bone he couldn't see in tests might be blocking the nerve endings, but the tiny piece of bone might soon shift so it could get better.

I hoped he was right. In the meantime, I needed to figure out what I could do with limited motion of that arm. I also wanted to determine how to get more information about people connected to the manor. I wanted to see Dave. Eve had called him, and he'd said he was fine but real busy with work, so I wasn't going to try to contact him. Rather, I hoped he would soon contact me.

The deputy I'd backed into didn't have any new information about what was going on with leads concerning Eve's neighbor's death. I called Detective Wilet. To my surprise, he answered right away.

"What can I tell you?" he asked. "Normally, not much, but since it's in today's paper, I can say this. We arrested her killer."

"Great!" My breaths came easier. "Who did it?"

"The guy that owned the camp, Dave Price."

My blood pressure spiked. I jumped off the chair. "No, he didn't. We were with him when you and the others came to see about her body, and you questioned him and us, and you let him go free."

"But then we found he'd been lying to us. He told me in front of you that he was home alone all of the night before you found that body."

"Yes, that's right." I paced the small room.

"But he was seen driving up to his camp during the night."

"It can't be. No. Give the person who told you that a lie detector test. Give—"

"I need to go." The line went dead.

Pulse thrusting in my scalp, I swallowed to get moisture into my mouth and was ready to call Eve.

Her call came through first. "Dave's in jail."

"I know. Oh, Eve, I can't believe it. We need to prove he didn't do it."

"Right, but first, let's go visit him. Today's visiting day at the jail. I've noticed that when I passed a few times. I'll come get you."

I glanced though the dirt-coated small window to the repair area and saw my truck up on a rack, part of its rear bumper hanging like a vulture's broken wing. "Let me direct you to where I am."

We agreed to tell each other about what transpired since we spoke last night, and within twenty minutes, she came for me. Larry wasn't finished inspecting my truck yet, so I told him I needed to go somewhere and would check in later.

I had passed the jail many times and glanced that way, hoping the prisoners inside it soon reformed. The wire fence was tall with spikes along the top. The yards on both sides of the building were small with dogs and guards making certain no one got out. I had never seen prisoners out in that yard and didn't know what they wore—orange jumpsuits? Or was that only in movies? I knew I dreaded seeing Dave.

"So you went to the manor after we agreed that we'd leave the investigating alone last night?" she asked while she drove.

I scrambled through my mind for a quick excuse. "It wasn't technically night yet. And I went to see Mom. And whoever."

"Come on, Sis, you could get hurt. Your truck did." She reached across the seat and placed her hand on mine, real concern in her tone. "I don't know what I'd do without you." She squeezed my hand.

I swallowed. I again felt the anguish I'd experienced when our other sister died beside me and didn't notice I had begun humming about Christmas being white until it grew louder. "I'll be careful," I promised.

With one more squeeze of my hand, she let go and steered us toward the jail, where we were about to see the man we both felt romantically drawn to, only she could easily tell him that, but I could not. At least a visit from us should bring him comfort.

Before we reached the parish jail, I said, "And I have other bad news."

"More than Dave being in here and you being in a wreck?"

"Fender bender," I said, believing that sounded more innocent.

"Okay. Get to it." She watched the road, tight lips pressed forward while she listened, and I gave her a summary of the call I received from Georgia Andrews. Once I grew silent, she turned her face my way. "I hadn't read the whole paper yesterday or today, but I guess our names are out there now. We are involved in a murder—again."

Both of us knew how word of what happened could affect our lackluster business. It could destroy it.

For a brief moment, I wondered if Fancy Ladies would even let me sell women's undies. Being the optimist, I said, "But we're going to get to see Dave again now. That's something, right?"

Her eyes remained stern.

Chapter 13

More vehicles than I'd ever noticed parked along the road around the jail. *The jail.* How hard it was to get the thought of Dave being behind bars in my mind. Eve parked. We looked at each other, both sighed, and after a moment got out. She and I ambled in one of the slowest walks I had ever taken until we reached the front gate. A large black dog that didn't look friendly followed us inside the fence like he was going to pounce on us the second we tried to get inside. He didn't plan to lick our faces.

My shoulders trembled while I walked. They tensed once we reached the gate. A heavily armed guard stood beyond it. He turned a steely eyed gaze at Eve, held it on her a long moment, and then turned it on me. There was nothing in his stance or expression that would invite us to smile at him. Obviously what he was doing was that initial oh-you're-identical inspection. After his scrutiny ended, he said, "Yes?"

My throat had dried so much I could hardly tell him our purpose here. Not so for Eve. She lifted her chin. "We'd like to visit Dave Price."

My whole body stiffened. I couldn't believe Dave was locked inside there.

The guard scanned us much quicker than before and then checked what resembled an iPad. "What are your names, and how are you related to him?"

"We aren't related," I said, "but—"

He lifted a hand. "If you aren't related, you aren't allowed in here."

Shoulders dropping, I looked at Eve. We could tell him, yes, we were related, of course that would be to each other, but somehow I figured he would find out what we meant and show us what his real unhappiness looked like.

"Can we call him?" I asked, aiming my eyes toward the entrance door to the place. I hoped it would open, and he would come outside.

The guard swung his head and held his pad up to show us. "This has lists of people who can call or visit our prisoners. That would be only their close family members."

Just hearing him call Dave a prisoner made my heart squeeze until it felt it would burst. "Thank you," I told the guard, and we walked away, the dog sniffing us and keeping us in view while he strode as quickly as we did.

"What now?" Eve hooked her seat strap.

I sighed. "Let's go buy him a card. At least we can let him know we're behind him all the way and working hard to get him out of there."

My suggestion met with Eve racing down the road. She seemed to remember we were still near the jail, probably not the place to drive way over the speed limit, and slowed. She headed for the nearest drugstore, only a few blocks away. We took our time poring over cards with just the right sentiment. We couldn't find one that mentioned jail and wouldn't have wanted it to, so we settled on one with words about caring about the recipient and friendship.

Eve wrote in it first. We sat in her car outside the drugstore, and she penned many words while I watched. My sister's face displayed one emotion after another when she looked up straight ahead, seemed to think of what else she wanted to say, and quickly wrote it. With her eyes lowered at their outer edges, her lips pulled tight, and after penning more words, she smiled. She handed the card and pen to me. "Would you like to sign it?"

What I wanted to do was write about how much I cared about him and hoped we could soon be together. My eyes flitted to Eve. "Sure." She watched as I wrote that we supported him and were working to prove he was innocent. She had signed it *Love, Eve.* He knew she wanted to go out with him or even much more, but now with my sister eyeing each word I jotted wasn't the time to express each of my feelings. *All my best, Sunny,* I wrote.

She took care to slide the card into the envelope and seal it. "He'll like this."

"I'm sure he will."

Back at the jail, we parked in the same place, had the same black dog sniff at us and follow our steps inside of the fence until we reached the gate. The same guard frowned when he looked at us.

"You still can't come in."

"We know," I said.

"But we can bring him a card, can't we?" Eve pulled it out of her purse.

"Sure. It's for Dave Price, right?"

"Yes," we said at one time.

He placed his hand near the small opening at the gate and bent his fingers like Eve should pass the card to him.

"He should be real happy to get that," Eve said to me while the officer took it, and I nodded.

"Sorry I need to do this." The guard yanked a knife out of a sheath on his belt and in one swift motion, slit the envelope.

My mouth fell open. Eve's certainly did, too, although I watched the officer in disbelief. "Why did you do that?"

"Do we look like drug dealers?" Eve grabbed the fence with both hands.

The dog rushed near, his growl and teeth warning her to move back. To accentuate that suggestion, he barked and jumped, slamming his front paws where Eve had just slid her hands off.

Beside him, the guard showed no sign that he even noticed an animal on his side of the fence. He was inspecting the envelope's glue, sniffing it, and pulling the now-cut card out of the envelope. He read the words we had written—did he think we had told Dave we were planning a getaway for him—skimmed his gaze over us, probably trying to detect which of us had written the most words and expressions of love. Returning his attention to the card, he checked the back of it and, just in case, shook the thing. Once nothing fell out, he jammed the card sideways into the cut envelope.

"I'll make sure not to bring him anything breakable," I said, anger heating my face.

"This is just how it is. Some people try to sneak in drugs and blades. We need to inspect everything."

Eve just shook her head and turned back to her car. "We have to get him out of there."

"I know." As we sped off, I wished we hadn't even gotten Dave a card. How bad would it make him feel to see that we'd brought him one and then watched a guard rip it apart? "I feel awful."

She kept nodding. "Okay, now we have to really go after a killer to prove it's not him or us."

"Right." My intense nods matched hers. "So where should we go first?"

"We might need to do some separate investigating. We'll go check on your truck right now."

It seemed a good idea although I dreaded what I might hear.

I had reason to. My truck was back down outside the entrance to Larry's Garage. Inside his shop, he bent over, inspecting under the hood of another truck. "Hm, I can give you an estimate and tell you what day I can start working on it," he said once he saw me. His item list and prices of all the parts and repairs stiffened my back and made my stomach pull tight.

"Thanks. I'll let you know." I took my keys from him, started my truck, winced, and hummed when the bumper rattled.

"We could leave it here and use my car." Eve walked up beside my door.

"I'm good. Let's go look for a killer."

She grimaced toward the rear of my grumpy truck. "While we're doing that, maybe we could start a job or two that wouldn't affect your shoulder much. Possibly we could help bail him out of that place after the judge sets bail."

"Okay, Sis." She could be optimistic about finances since she had accumulated some, mainly from previous marriages, although that was certainly not unlimited. I, however, had previously sold undergarments at Fancy Ladies before excruciating heel spurs made me quit the job that required me to be on my feet all day, so actually I couldn't work there even if they wanted to rehire me. Eve had started the remodeling and repair business with me but only after she'd moved back to town not that long ago, so we had little business cash in reserve.

"Suggestions?" she asked.

Her question made me feel good about myself. So many teachers and students from schools I attended hadn't understood or cared about my dyslexia that I'd often doubted my ideas. A special teacher and my sister worked to do the opposite. "We can check on jobs, but first I want to pass by Dave's camp and see how things look." I recalled the hammering and sawing that came from the camp not too far past his. "And maybe we can check out the people at the camp close by."

"Good idea. I'll meet you there."

She waited for me to lead the way toward Bayou Boogie Woogie, surely to see whether my truck would fall apart. I glanced in the rearview mirror, appreciating her even more than usual and hoping that when we reached Dave's camp, the police tape would be gone. He had wanted to give me a key to that camp, which again made me feel special. If the police tape was gone, maybe we could do a closer inspection of his place that might give us better clues as to what really happened there.

Chapter 14

The bayou felt like it went on and on, with the oak and cypress trees and thick palmetto beside it. The waterway and narrow road I drove on didn't get longer, I knew. It only felt like it now because the wind had picked up and seemed determined to shake the rear end off my truck. People in the handful of vehicles that drove past turned to stare while I approached. Probably my truck looked and sounded like an animal with a wounded backside that was desperate for a surgeon or for someone to put it out of its misery.

There were no buildings on either side of the road this far down the bayou. Only tall grasses and scrub bushes and scraggly trees that won out when hurricanes passed through.

A bald eagle swooped to the water and then up toward trees beyond the bayou when we approached Dave's camp, which would have been an enticing sight except it clashed with the yellow plastic still surrounding his place.

I pulled off the roadway and parked. Eve stopped behind me, and we left our vehicles. We were tall enough that we could easily step over the tape stretched around Dave's place. It was yards away from the building so that we couldn't get close enough to try to look in through the windows.

"Mrs. Wilburn was dead in there," I said, arms stiff and fists clenched at my sides. I didn't want to believe that really happened. Didn't want to relive finding her.

"I know. It all seems surreal. Her gone. Dave arrested…"

"Somebody killed her someplace else and brought her here."

"How would he have gotten inside? Do you think a man came dragging a garbage bag with her body here and happened to notice that key to the back door on the carport floor just like you did and used it to open the door and bring her inside? And then he replaced the key where it was?"

"Why would anyone consider bringing her here in the first place?"

I inspected the gravel driveway leading to the carport and didn't see any sign of something heavy being dragged across the shells or nearby dirt. The carport held the wood he'd had delivered still stacked inside. We both stepped aside and surveyed the areas we could see around the camp but had limited views because of wild bushes with trees on one side and a bayou in back. The slim plastic that protected this place said: Police Line. Do not cross. and repeated the warning numerous times in case anyone forgot.

"Somebody might come around if we do it," Eve said, reading my mind that held the intent to step across it.

"Yes, and that guy watching us from the wharf over there might even be a cop."

"Or a judge."

We stepped back to the vehicles we'd driven. I puttered ahead to the camp that was larger than Dave's and looked more like a fine house than a fishing camp. By the time we reached his place and got out, the man who I figured owned that place had left his wharf and was stepping across his yard toward us.

"Hi. Can I help you?" His face was friendly, maybe because it held so many freckles across the nose, and his pale eyes smiled and looked kind. He was maybe fifty and wearing jeans and an LSU T-shirt. Score one for him with the shirt. The top of his head came only to my breasts, and I was wearing flats. Not so with Sunny who wore heels. He had lots of really fine tools and other equipment in his yard and on the wharf beyond. I couldn't envision this guy being a murderer.

"This looks like a real nice place," Eve told him. "Did you build it?"

He pulled off his cap that advertised a tractor brand, ran a hand over his brow to wipe off sweat, and replaced the cap. "No, I wish I could do things like that." He swept his arm toward the structure. "I can only do minor work with tools."

"You have some good ones."

That got a smile out of him. "I like to get the best of things." He swung his eyes from one toward the other of us. "And you look the same. But I doubt that you're here to sell me a cleaning supply or your religious beliefs."

"No, neither," Eve said.

"Besides that, I noticed you two going to that camp over there and getting down. Something happened there."

"I'm sure the police came and questioned you and told you all about it," I said, and he nodded.

"But I don't know the guy who just bought that place, and I sure didn't know the dead woman either."

"I'm Sunny Taylor." I put my hand out and shook his soft palm. Strange that he owned such excellent tools if he obviously didn't do outdoor work often.

"Eve Vaughn," she said, shaking hands with him, her eyes flitting toward mine like she noticed the same thing.

"I'm Bill Hernandez. I live in Alabama, but I like to come out here with my wife and just chill."

"Except you've been working out here," I pointed out.

He replied with a tight smile. "So you've been around." His eyes widened like an idea was registering. "Oh, you're the two who were out there that day."

Eve and I nodded, our chins going up and down together like seesaws. "You were out here, too," she said.

His eyes swerved from one to the other of us, all friendliness from them gone. "I need to get back to work." He headed to his front door.

"It was nice meeting you," I called out, but his response was a door slam.

"Okay." Eve spoke while I took a breath. "I didn't learn anything useful."

"Neither did I." A splash from the water drew my attention. "Except there might be some good fishing out here."

We shared weak grins. Eve tilted her head toward the brown bayou. "I want to fish with Dave soon after he gets out."

I felt my lips droop. I didn't mind sharing a fishing trip with him and my sister, but I did not want to otherwise share him with her. And this feeling of attachment to a man was so unique I couldn't believe I was experiencing it. But I needed to admit to myself that I was.

My mind bounced back to Bill Hernandez. "He wears an LSU shirt, and he's from Alabama?"

"That does seem strange."

We stood staring at his place. There was no sign of his wife.

"Okay, before we do anything else," Eve said, "let's take your truck back to your house. I couldn't think too well while I kept watching your bumper shaking so much while I drove here that I was afraid it would drop off right in front of me."

"I guess I could think better without it rattling, too." We motored back up the bayou, passing a couple of more trucks the nearer we got to town. Traffic increased to its normal not-too-many cars and trucks as we reached

Sugar Ledge, many people inside them whipping their heads toward me. I guessed they thought my truck's rear end might drop. I feared the same thing.

When we reached our neighborhood, we parted ways. Eve turned at the corner and would drive down the next street to her house.

I drove down my street. In the yard two houses before mine, a plump figure bent over a flowerbed, looking like a thick beach ball except for the wide-brimmed straw hat on her head. Mrs. Hawthorne glanced up as I approached, surely my truck's noise calling her attention. She stood and waved at me with her small gardening shovel, and I waved back. Then noticed she wasn't only waving. She was flagging me down.

I pulled to the curb.

She came to my window and said the obvious. "Your truck has a problem."

"It sure does. It needs a truck doctor." I offered a pleasant smile. She probably only wanted someone to talk with a minute or two.

"I have a cousin who does that kind of work. Would you like his name?"

"Of course." This woman was probably as old as my mother, and her cousin was, too. Surely someone that age could not get rid of my mega-fender bender and solve my truck's woes.

I wrote the name and phone number she gave, intensely nodding like I was really interested. I actually wanted to get home and turn this motor off. "Thank you for this," I said, holding the pad up, ready to pull away.

"Oh, and Sunny, I thought about you and the police asking me if I'd heard or seen anything unusual before Mrs. Wilburn died." I nodded but knew she saw little of the world because she was always bent to the ground, working her flowers, the brim of her hat blocking the outer world from her view. "I did."

"You did?"

"Yes. I didn't see it, of course, but I did hear him yelling a day or so before she was found dead." She pointed at the house across the street from hers. The couple there was young and, as far as I knew, kept to themselves. I had no idea how this information could be connected to anything but paid attention.

"He must have been outside for you to have heard him. Did you see him?"

She shook her head, the brim of her hat bending toward her face. "No, but I looked since he was so loud. They must have been in their backyard."

Only a fence separated that backyard from the one that belonged to Mrs. Wilburn and her son. "Do you know who he was yelling at?"

"No. I'm certain they would have been in the back, and of course they have that fence."

A frightening thought occurred. "Mrs. Hawthorne, you didn't hear anything like he was making a threat, did you?"

She kept shaking her head. "I have no idea what he said." Her gaze moved lower as though she was thinking of something. She looked straight at me. "I believe a woman might have yelled back at him."

My pulse sped. "Could it have been Mrs. Wilburn?" Her home was right behind that young couple's.

She gazed across the street at the neatly kept lawn and tan brick house. "I never spoke to that woman, so I don't know what she sounds like." She lowered her head, lifted it, and corrected herself. "Or what she sounded like."

My phone rang. "Excuse me," I told her and answered.

"You're coming over?" Eve asked.

"Sure. I won't be long."

"Good, 'cause we just got a job! It's one that'll be easy for your shoulder."

I jerked my other arm back at the elbow, my hand making a fist like I was saying *yes*. "See you in a minute," I told her.

"You need to go. I won't keep you." Mrs. Hawthorne stepped away from the curb.

"Thank you so much for giving me all this information."

"I don't know whether it'll do any good." She glanced across the street and then back at me. "Couples do sometimes argue, you know."

My ex who had made me dread being romantically involved with a man came to mind. "They do. Thanks again." I accelerated toward my house.

"Don't forget my cousin," she yelled.

Pleased to put my wounded truck to rest under my carport, I walked across the street, moving slower while I passed through the slim area of grass between the fence she mentioned and the one beside it. The young couple's tall dog-eared fence retained a slight scent of cedar, although while I moved closer toward the rear section of their yard, a strong pungent odor of chlorine made my nostrils recoil. He had probably just added some to their swimming pool.

The white solid vinyl fence panels surrounding the backyard on the other side left no spaces between panels. This fence, however, had small spaces between the boards, in some areas slightly wider than others. Whoever built this wooden privacy fence could have used better professional help.

Hoping to see or hear the young couple out there, I pressed against the wood and got my eye as close as possible to a slender space.

Something pushed against the fence from the opposite side. A man's gruff voice followed. "What're you gonna do about it?"

Chapter 15

I jumped back, heart jammed in my throat. Glad he hadn't been eyeball to eyeball with me, I scrambled to Eve's yard. Words from a young woman trailed from their side of the fence, but the drumming in my head wouldn't let me make out what she said. I was satisfied to realize he hadn't been questioning me.

"Good Lord, who's chasing you?" Eve asked when I dashed near. She leaned forward from the patio chair she sat on and glanced behind me.

I caught my breath and spoke. "No one. I hope." I looked back, hoping nobody came rushing behind, his fist flailing in the air.

"Sit down, Sis. Take it easy. I'll get us some tea so you can chill. After that we need to talk."

I wanted to protest but wasn't certain why. Apprehension jumped around in my chest and my eyes swerved to the wooden fence. I'd thought the guy who lived there may have run after me. If he did, how would I explain that I was peeking through their fence because the elderly woman across from him had heard him yelling at someone? While I considered that idea, it seemed ridiculous. My pulse slowed when I determined how foolish it was for me to have been concerned about what Mrs. Hawthorne told me. I sat on a cushioned chair beside Eve's. Probably, I was only digging for anything that might get Dave out of jail.

Eve came through her back door carrying our drinks. The tea was icy cold and did wonders for my formerly tight throat. "This is good." I raised my glass to her. "I'll tell you about it after I relax a bit more."

She nodded, smiled, and glanced to her left, where Jake in jeans was out in his yard. With a few tools scattered near, he bent over opposite us, doing something low to the ground.

"Nice view, isn't it?" Eve asked.

I tapped her arm. "You wicked thing." I watched him moving and made up my mind that she was correct. Remembering my mission of getting him and Eve together so she wouldn't be hurt when I paired up with Dave, I made a suggestion. "It's pretty warm out here. Why don't you offer him some tea with us? I'm sure he could use a break."

"That's a great idea." She turned toward his lawn. "Hey, Jake," she called, and he straightened and looked our way. "You look too hot working out there. Come join us for some tea."

My sister certainly had a dual meaning for telling him he looked hot and surely wouldn't mind if he knew it. I didn't mind her telling him that either. It was a good start for bringing them together.

He ran his fingers back through his long, wavy hair and took long strides toward us, his smiling eyes aimed at my sister. "That's a great suggestion. Thank you."

"No problem." She scrambled to her feet and stood chest-to-chest with him, her flirtatious smile matching his. Maybe I wouldn't have to do anything. Possibly something already started with them.

I felt my smile widen.

"And you know my sister Sunny," Eve said, waving a hand toward me like an introduction.

"Of course. Hello, Sunny."

"Hi. Have a seat." I nodded toward the empty chair close to my sister. "And she'll get you the most delicious iced tea." I lifted my glass.

Eve rushed inside, and he lowered his hips to a chair.

"Jake," I said, "you're home a bit during the day."

"Yes, I'm fortunate. I can do a lot of work from my house."

I hoped he wouldn't suggest I let him advise where I should invest all of my excess income, which was nil. "What were you doing?" I tilted my head toward the edge of his yard.

"I still haven't gotten that permit for a fence yet, but I imagine I'll be getting it soon. In the meantime, I'm taking measurements for the stakes. What have you been up to?"

Trying to find a killer. Trying to prove it isn't the man I cared so much about. "I've been visiting my mom and trying to heal up from this shoulder wound." I shifted my left shoulder up. It still felt numb.

He shook his head. "I hope it gets better soon." The back door let out a little squeak, and he looked toward it with a smile. Eve handed him a tall glass filled with ice and tea, and he took a large swallow. "You do know how to treat a man." He gave her a little salute of approval with his glass.

"I try." She wiggled her hips back down to her chair.

If I didn't want them to get together, the back and forth flirting would annoy me. But then I've never been one to get gung ho about the male and female trying to mate thing. They shared eye contact both with lips pulled back a little at the corners, their looks suggesting they liked being together. That was fine. I almost suggested that Eve might help him once he got his fence going but didn't believe a suggestion was necessary. Their icy glasses might have steamed up from the eyes they were giving each other while they held their glasses to their lips.

"Jake," I said, getting his attention back to me, "the police must have questioned you about the woman who lived over there." I pointed toward the tall shrubs that separated Eve's backyard from the one that belonged to Mrs. Wilburn, and Jake nodded. "What did you tell them? Did you see or hear anything that might have seemed suspicious?"

He shook his head. "I said I didn't really know the lady. I'm really sorry about what happened to her, but I'm not even sure what she looked like. I saw her son drive away from there a couple of times. I never noticed her out in front of her house."

I thought about the people behind her house on the opposite side of that fence. "What about noise? Had you heard any shouting or anything not long before Mrs. Wilburn was killed?"

He dropped his gaze toward the cement, appearing to concentrate. He looked up at me. "Not that I can recall." He crooked his finger toward his place. "But the people who live on the other side of me keep having parties. I seem to recall lots of noise and cars at their place around that time."

"I noticed all the cars out there, too."

Eve swung her arm out. "Okay, you two, we are not here for the inquisition. I invited Jake over so he could sit and relax." She stared at me. "You are not letting him relax."

I tightened my lips. "I'm sorry," I told him. "It's just a concern."

"I understand."

"Now I'm alive, and I want your attention." Eve had no hesitation with getting males to notice her, and that was fine with me, especially with her getting it from him.

"You've got it," he told her. The hint of romance their smiles suggested toward each other told me I needed to set down my glass and leave them alone. They might not even notice I was gone.

I put my drink on the glass-topped table, about to stand when Jake's phone rang.

"Excuse me," he told us and looked at the front of it to check the caller. "I need to get this." He stepped away from the patio and spoke, his tone sounding all businesslike. A moment later, he lifted his hand toward us. "I have to get to my office inside. Thanks for the drink."

"Anytime." Eve kept her eyes on him while he moved across her lawn and his and stepped into his back doorway. Finally, she breathed a long exhale.

I let her have a moment to extend her enjoyment of the man who wasn't Dave before moving on with other matters. "So we have a job?" My enthusiasm returned. "And it's something I can do?"

"Yes. First tell me why you were so out of breath when you got here. I doubt that you were having a romantic interlude." That thought seemed to really sink in. Eve's eyes widened and brightened. "Or were you?"

I was tempted to blurt that the person I wanted such an interlude with was sitting behind bars. Admitting that to her now would serve no purpose and might hurt the relationship between us. As we looked at each other, I knew we needed to work together on a job now and help prove Dave didn't commit murder. The time it took us to perform both tasks would offer a longer period for a romance to develop between her and Jake.

I shrugged and smiled innocently with my eyebrows raised higher.

"Oh, Sunny, you were messing around with a man?" Her excitement expressed how much she wanted that to happen.

"I didn't say that." Of course I'd suggested it. And then I told her what Mrs. Hawthorne said about the yelling she'd heard not long before Mrs. Wilburn wound up dead.

Eve smirked, shaking her head. "So if somebody yells in their yard, they're about to kill someone? That poor lady does need to get out of her yard more. Or at least take off her hat and see what the real world looks like."

"But she did help the police once."

"True. Okay, here's what we're going to do if you want to earn some money real soon."

"I *need* to earn money."

"I got a call from a woman who wants some remodeling in her kitchen. She told me she would pay us double what we would normally charge if we can get it done."

"What? That sounds terrific." I leaned toward Eve and spoke softer. "Why would she do that? And why would she choose us? Or even trust us?"

The enthusiasm in her tone dulled. "She did admit she tried other companies, but they all had work lined up. Okay, here's the thing. She wants the work finished before she has a big party at her house."

"That shouldn't be a problem."

"The party's in ten days."

I shook my head. "How could we do that?"

"It won't be that much work, and of course she won't need to wait for a permit since she wants us to remodel her kitchen."

"I still don't understand why a person would want to pay us twice what we'd ask for. We haven't been in business that long." I lowered my voice even more. "And we're still associated with murder."

"She's married to one of those new young doctors in town. Her grandmother lives at the manor. It seems Mom and a couple of others in her Chat and Nap Group brag about us. Mom was talking to this woman, who mentioned she needed some work done really fast, and Mom told her how wonderful Twin Sisters Remodeling and Repairs is."

"Bless our mom's heart."

"Yes, and that woman wrote our names down and said she might give us a call. She did." Eve hopped up from her chair with her glass that now held melting ice and glanced toward Jake's yard. "Let's go inside. It's too distracting out here," she added with a grin. "I'll let you know what she wants us to do, and we can make plans to get started."

I glanced toward the wooden fence to make sure the young man from the other side still wasn't coming for me. Satisfied that he wasn't, I carried my own glass into Eve's house and wondered how in the world I could start working with my still-wounded shoulder.

Knowing we might discover more about Mrs. Wilburn's relatives who often went around the manor and hadn't liked her gave me more incentive. I wanted to learn more about people who might have disliked her enough to want her dead. Earning money would be a big bonus.

Chapter 16

Our new customer was Cherry Cleveland. She had given Eve an idea of what she wanted done, and Eve had assured her and now me that we could do it. Inside Eve's kitchen, she got Cherry on the phone. "I just checked with my sister, and yes, we'll do it." Eve listened and nodded, then she handed her phone to me.

I gave her eyes that questioned what the heck. With no response, I pressed the phone to my ear. "Hello. This is Sunny Taylor."

"Hi, Sunny. Eve and your mother and all of her friends tell me you are terrific with details."

I felt my chest puff up with her praise. Anyone who made me feel special gave me an affinity for that person. I even felt my cheeks color. "Thank you so much for saying that."

"They're the ones who said it. I just look forward to seeing your work."

Okay, now she had me. I would need to prove myself to this person who sounded barely old enough to be out of high school. "I mainly learned to pay special attention to women's bodies and underwear."

Her laughter bubbled up. "Whatever caused it, it's a good trait. Could you and your sister come over and see what I have? Then we can discuss what I'd want and, of course, the price."

"Yes. Is now a good time?"

"Sure. Let me give you the address and my phone number so you'll have it." She did, and I wrote it all to make sure I got everything straight. "See you soon," she said, and we clicked off.

"She sounds really nice." I handed Eve's phone back to her. "Let's go check her place out. Here's her address." I held up the sheet that I'd written the info on.

Eve grabbed her purse and headed for the door to her garage without looking at what I held. "I know where she lives."

I slid into the passenger side of her car, while she started the Lexus and it purred. Even with the comfort of the pillow-soft seat and the recent praise I'd received, my mind wasn't at ease. "Did she know you were already aware of her address?"

"Look," Eve said instead of answering my question.

I did look to my right where she tilted her head as she backed to her driveway. Royce stood on the grass right next to Eve's yard staring at us, his face mean and eyes hard. I felt he would have thrown something at us if anything had been available close to him. When Eve pulled off in front of his house, I noticed he slid into the driver's side of a sassy black sports car. The license showing it was brand-new sat in the rear window. His mother's five-year-old sedan that he had used while she was alive was not parked in front of the new vehicle.

"He got rid of his mother's car," I said.

"I guess he did. He's not waiting for much."

"Except for us to be arrested."

"He must know that Dave was arrested. Even if we know he's innocent, Royce doesn't."

Once she steered us out of the neighborhood, my tense shoulders relaxed. "Since we were with Dave and found her, he might still believe we were involved in her murder." I shivered and added, "And he looks like he might like to make sure something happens to us."

Eve showed no reaction but faced straight ahead and drove. In no time, she reached the bayou and drove along it until she crossed at the first bridge. She followed the greenish-brown waterway and after a quarter of a mile, turned onto a long driveway.

The breathtaking lawn was one of my favorites that always called my attention when I drove past. Many striking large live oaks draped lawns along highways down here. This place held some of the most spectacular massive trees with their branches like powerful arms that reached toward the ground, a couple of them resting on it and then dipping up again. Chemical crop-dusters that once sprayed the area's sugar cane fields had destroyed many pests that harmed the crops but did the same to most of the thick Spanish moss, which appeared dead hanging from branches like long gray beards. Actually, the moss was alive.

It swayed like a welcoming wave of fresh air when we drove in. The house was barely visible from the road since it was set back from the trees and had been there a long time. I'd heard it once belonged to an attorney.

The house was brick and not large, not nearly as imposing as its entry at the main road.

Its bubbly owner greeted us at the front door, swinging it open the minute Eve used the knocker for one strike. "Hi, I'm so glad y'all are here. Come on in." She was almost as tall as we were although her voice on the phone had made me believe she was tiny. I was right that she was young.

We followed her into a house with a dark look and old musty smell that made me imagine food fried in reused cooking oil sitting on my tongue. She took fast steps and stopped and turned so quickly I had to hold myself back to keep from running into her.

"Let me guess," she said and pointed at one and then the other of us. "You're Eve, and you're Sunny. Am I right?"

"You are," I said.

"I usually am." Her smile looked so genuine it was hard to dislike her, even with that little bit of bragging. She kept speaking while she resumed her fast walk. "As you can see, this is an old house, and that's okay. This living area is big so a lot of people will fit in here. We're going to have a house warming for our families to see the place, so I just mainly want a little done to spruce up this kitchen."

The room we sped through was nothing fancy, but it was spacious. I only had time to scan the overstuffed sofas and rugs and pictures of magnolias on the cypress walls. A shelf held many small framed photographs. I stepped toward one.

"Who is this?" I pointed to the elderly woman.

"Oh, that's my grandmother. She is the sweetest lady."

I glanced at Eve and forced myself not to frown. "We've seen her. She's at the manor." She was anything but sweet. She was the woman I spoke with who sat to eat two tables before the one for Adrienne Viatar.

Cherry lifted the picture and kissed the woman's face. "She'll be coming here for the first time when we have the party." She set the picture down and swept off out of the room into a hall. "I go see her almost every day." She stopped moving in a fairly small room I saw was the kitchen. I paid little attention to it except for the more pronounced odor of rancid cooking oil since my mind remained with what she'd just said.

"So as you can see, not much had been done in here." She kept speaking and sweeping her long arms toward walls and spaces, and I wanted to focus on remodeling but could not.

"Do you know Andrew Primeaux or his niece Jessica?" I asked before her words wore down.

"Yes. I met them awhile back when they were visiting at the manor while I was. They really are sweet."

Maybe *sweet* was her favorite descriptive word for a person.

Eve gave me a look with wide eyes, like *What are you doing?* And then she swung her eyes toward some cabinets like trying to remind me of what we were here for. Of course we were supposed to do a job, but finding a killer was most important. It was for Eve, too, but she seemed able to focus on two things at the same time better than I could.

"What about Mrs. Wilburn?" I said, "Clara Wilburn."

"Sure, I met her one time she went to the manor. She seemed real—"

I blanked my mind out from the next word she would use. "Did you ever see her and Andrew Primeaux or Jessica there at the same time?"

She placed her long index finger across her lips while she thought and moved the tip of it back and forth against them while the toes of her right foot tapped out a marching rhythm on the white ceramic floor. It was as though the woman could not keep all of her body still at one time. What did she do in bed? Surely she had restless legs and probably her whole body jumped around all night. Her lowering chin let me know the answer before she lifted it and said, "Yes."

I was ready to ask more questions when something in the room buzzed.

"Oh, that's my timer." She stepped across the floor and made the noise stop. "That's to remind me I need to get going to my meeting. Look, here's an idea of what I might like done in here." She handed Eve a two-page section that appeared to have been removed from a magazine. It showed an attractive modern kitchen done up in a teal color I liked. "So just take this and see what you think you can do with what I've got in here."

"I'll snap a few pictures real quick, okay?" Eve said, lifting her phone while our hostess did her head-bobbing thing.

With pictures snapped, Eve and I followed behind Cherry, who scurried to her front door. "Y'all are so good for coming on such short notice," she said and clasped my hand. "And your mother was right. You are so good at noticing things—like recognizing my sweet grandmother in that photograph."

Once the door shut behind us, I kept still and sucked in a large gulp of air. "Good grief."

Eve let out a long sigh. "I know."

It was as though both of us needed to stand in one place. For a long moment, we kept silent. I didn't even want to look at the moving moss when we rode past the oaks on our way out of her yard and had an idea I would never look at this place as serene again. The woman inside would scramble my mind and make my insides feel jumpy.

"So what do you think?" Eve asked.

I needed a new deep breath. "I'll have to look at the pictures you snapped to know exactly what her kitchen looks like since I was so distracted. We'll need to study the picture of what she has in mind to figure out what we can do with what she already has. But I'm most interested in her grandmother and people who visited the manor."

"Right. This isn't a good time to go there, but let's go check it out tomorrow."

"Yes, indeed."

She faced the road ahead. "You know who I've also been thinking about?" I smiled and waited for her to mention her new grandchild. Instead, she said, "Dave," making my emotions again swing around.

"I've thought about him a bit, too," I admitted.

She grabbed her large leather purse from the seat and handed it to me. "Get my phone and call his company, would you? They're listed in my contacts."

"Do you think they've gotten more information from the police than we have?" Our information counted as zero.

"Let's find out. Put the phone on speaker so I can hear, too."

Somehow, I didn't want the speaker on. I would have preferred my conversation with anyone connected to Dave to be private. I found that a strange idea but then determined it was caused by wanting a personal relationship with him. Of course, first I wanted him out of jail.

I speed dialed the number.

"Downtown Alarm Systems," a cheerful voice answered. "This is Alana. We would like to take care of your home's needs."

"Hi, Alana. Listen, I don't really need any alarm systems now." I heard what sounded like a small sigh of disappointment. I knew that feeling. "This is Sunny Taylor. Your company did some business for my sister, Eve Vaughn."

"Right. She isn't having any more trouble with her unit, is she?" This time her voice sounded almost panicked.

"No, it's fine," I rushed to assure her and could hear what seemed a relieved sigh. "Actually, it never really had a problem." The difficulty, we'd realized, was me and my pride. "Alana, my sister and I are concerned about Dave. Have y'all gotten any information about him?"

After a pause, she spoke. "What do you want to know?"

"Sweetie, we were with him when he found that lady's body." Saying the words brought back horrible memories of that moment and sent a shiver along my thighs. "We haven't been able to find out anything about him. Have the police let y'all know something?"

"No." Her tone dulled. "They won't tell us anything, either."

Both of us took a moment to let out a long sigh. "What about business there?"

"Absolutely nothing. Ever since news got out that he was arrested for murder, nobody wants to do business with us. We've been getting calls cancelling all the jobs that were scheduled."

"He didn't do it," I assured her.

"I know. He's not the kind of person to do something like that."

I kept nodding. "Correct."

"Of course, you never know what a person will do. Look at all the stuff you see in the news all the time."

Okay, she did not know her boss well if she believed him capable of such a thing. I felt a frown tighten on my face. "Thank you, Alana. If you do learn anything about him, I'd appreciate it if you'd let us know. You could call back at this number."

"All right. But who knows? This place might not even be open much longer. And then I'll be out looking for another job."

Eve and I exchanged looks that expressed our unhappiness with this girl and Dave's plight. "Good luck," I told her and clicked off. I slid Eve's phone back into her purse without saying a thing.

Back on Eve's street, I was relieved not to see any sign of Royce outside. Eve pulled into her garage, shut it with the automatic control, and we walked into her kitchen.

"We'd better look at this first." She sat at her table and took out the picture of what the constant mover wanted for her kitchen.

I gave her a look that told what I wanted to check into first.

She lifted a hand. "I know. I know. I'll want to learn things about Cherry's grandmother and the people who went to visit there and try to figure out what connection they might all have to Mrs. Wilburn's death, but right now, let's try to focus on this project. I thought you were almost desperate to earn money."

I sat. "I am."

"You know I want Dave out of jail more than anyone." Her words made me ready to protest. I didn't. She gripped my hand. "I want what's best for you, Sis. You need money much more than I do, so let's work on getting you some."

The outer edges of my eyes warmed. I squeezed her fingers. Yes, I still had this sibling. She and our mother were the most important people in my life. For the moment, I did need to concentrate on gaining immediate income.

The magazine layout of what Cherry wanted her kitchen to resemble looked appealing. I liked the colors and shapes and extra touches. I hadn't paid close attention to what hers looked like but had a strong notion it wasn't anything like the one facing us from Eve's table.

"Okay, I need to show you these, and we'll see what we can do." Eve opened the picture app on her phone, handed the phone to me, and I scrolled through snapshots she had taken.

I rolled my eyes toward her and began looking at them again, this time checking them slower and enlarging each one for a closer view of what was available and a thought about what might be possible to change or fix. The homeowner hadn't told Eve exactly what she expected we might do or what she'd want to spend. Since she lived in that home with a doctor and mentioned she would pay us double our usual price if we could start now and do it fast, she wanted whatever we could accomplish in a short time.

Eve and I checked out pictures and discussed what we might accomplish. Since she was more proficient with reading, she made the lists. Once we had put together various suggestions, she phoned Cherry to offer them. I watched Eve's hand—the one not holding the phone—swirl around as though she were painting her descriptions of what we thought about doing with the room, her expression brightening while she spoke. Hope grew inside me while I saw what might have been almost a castle taking shape in Eve's descriptions. She kept eye contact with me and nodded, her smile becoming one of the widest I'd ever seen.

"Well, thank you. We will," Eve said and clicked off her phone. "Yes!" She punched the air to accentuate her excitement.

"Which of our ideas does she want us to do?"

"As many as we can manage."

"Wonderful." We sat poring through more ideas for what might work best in the space she had in her kitchen, my physical limitations, and our time constraints. Our thoughts, as usual for work, were in sync. We hoped they would work. Lumberyards and a couple of big box stores in towns along these bayous were few, and their wares limited. Most could order items we might want to use. We made some calls and found out it would take longer for a couple of those items to come in than we had available.

Through online searches, we discovered products that would satisfy our needs in different establishments in New Orleans. We shopped locally whenever we could, so our first order of business the next morning would be to jaunt around town, gathering things here.

"Okay, now I need to do this." Eve placed her fingers over mine. When my lifted eyebrow asked the question, she said, "You'll see."

I watched while she slid her hand away and leaned back in her chair, hopeful eyes staring off into where she hoped someone in a certain place would soon answer the call she was placing.

"Mom," a voice on the other end said, Eve obviously using speakerphone so I could hear, "how are you?"

A satisfied smile relaxed on Eve's face. "I'm wonderful, sweetheart. And y'all?"

"We're all good. I just fed him."

Warmth spread through my chest. I knew it did the same to Eve's.

"He's up on my shoulder. I'll put the phone by his ear, and you can talk to him while he's waiting to burp."

Two seconds later my sister was babbling and cooing and calling out his name as though she were speaking to a baby doll. She used a finger to call me to get closer to the phone. Noah couldn't speak yet, of course, but just knowing that tiny bundle of flesh and small fingers and ears was at the other end of the line brought with it remembrance of the warmth of him in my arms while I'd rocked him.

"Hello, Noah," I said at the edge of Eve's mouthpiece.

"Oh, hi, Aunt Sunny," Nicole called to me.

"We miss y'all," I said. "Tell him I love him."

The loud explosion of gas he expelled could have shaken the lines. Eve, Nicole, and I all laughed.

"He said he loves you, too," Nicole said.

We all laughed again, the good hearty laugh that sooths the ribs.

Noah started to whine. "Oh, he's jerking his legs up and getting ready to wail. I'd better go. Love you both."

We assured Nicole of our love for her and her husband and baby and sat smiling at each other. "That was a great phone call," I said, and Eve kept her lips spread wide with her nods.

This wasn't a time to be concerned about planning work. "I can take you home now, and we'll get together in the morning," Eve said, and I concurred. "You know we might need to use your truck to run around and get some of those supplies."

I nodded. I dreaded what my truck would sound like and how much negative attention we would get inside it, but couldn't afford to have all the work it needed done yet. I hoped that would work out after our next job was complete.

We sat in Eve's luxury car. I felt totally at ease in it while it barely whispered as she backed it out of her garage, and it slid to her driveway.

Racket from behind shattered our serenity. A rider wearing a mean-looking black helmet revved up the motor of his mean-looking motorcycle behind us, making the air reek and blocking us from getting out to the street.

Chapter 17

"What's wrong with him?" Eve slammed her brakes so hard our heads bounced forward. She had almost backed into this person. We looked back, waiting for him to move.

He didn't. Instead, he revved up his annoying clatter and remained in place. Why? The stench of his exhaust grew worse. When we turned our upper bodies to look behind, he pulled up the part of his helmet that had covered his face. It was easy to recognize his sneer, the one he had given both of us, but especially me, when we'd gone over to express condolences.

"Royce bought a motorcycle?" Eve asked.

"And he won't let us leave."

He kept revving his motor, his furious face a threat.

I'd had enough of him. I grabbed the knob of my door, shoved the door open, and stood beside Eve's car. "I did not murder your mother and neither did my sister or our friend Dave!" I yelled.

He might not have heard all my words because of the racket his bike was making, but while I hollered, he slowed the noise to an idle.

I thrust my index finger toward the street. "And if you don't hurry and get that thing out of our way, my sister will slam back against it and then we'll see how much of a bike you have left!"

Plunging myself back in the car, I punched the door lock and strapped myself in. We might be in for a bumpy ride. Only then did I glance at my sister. Her mouth was wide open, her face white with shock from my outburst. Had I put her in a precarious position?

"All right, Sis." She lifted her hand and slapped her palm against mine. Eve raced her motor that previously purred, giving Royce's bike motor envy.

Faces toward each other, we then looked back.

Royce slammed his face shield down and roared away, leaving a rooster tail of smoke in his wake.

My huge exhale felt great. So did the exhilaration of telling him off, even if we'd certainly had no intention of running him over. Poor baby, he had just lost his mother. And if he had stayed there two minutes longer, Eve might have pulled her car up, and we'd have slammed ourselves into her garage and locked ourselves inside her house, not tried to hurt him or his bike.

I kept my gaze lowered as we rode away from her street and hoped no one around had witnessed my outburst. After all, the only thing Royce had done was sit on his motorcycle right behind Eve's driveway.

"He seems to have unlimited funds now," Eve said. "He's gotten a new car and now a top-notch motor bike."

"Right. I doubt that all of his gambling in Vegas suddenly paid off and delivered him a windfall. He's surely getting his money from his mother's funds."

It didn't take long for us to ponder his new wealth before we rounded the street and turned onto mine. When Eve pulled her Lexus behind my wounded truck, I felt the air suck out of my chest. I needed cash to repair that soon.

"Okay, thanks. I'll get you in the morning," I said and hopped out of her car with a jaunty air I didn't feel. "Eve, be careful out there. Look around before you open your garage door."

"I will. I'll be fine," she assured me, and I knew she hoped her words would be true. I only hoped that her neighbor would be riding his new motorcycle far away by the time she got home.

* * * *

After a restless night, I dragged around getting myself ready and tried to shift my mind to a more positive outlook. At the appointed time, I went out to my truck. The rear end clattered and shimmied so much, it seemed in a fight to push itself off the rest of the vehicle.

There was no way I was going to sneak past Royce's house to pick up my sister. I was grateful not to find him or her opposite neighbor Jake out in their front yards. Royce was a threat, and Jake probably wouldn't become so fond of Eve if he thought of her as riding around in what sounded like a junky old piece of metal.

The minute she climbed in, I rushed away. We rattled down roads around town to find items we wanted to use in Cherry's house. People in a few cars we passed turned back to stare, and a couple of drivers tooted and pointed behind my truck to let me know what was happening back there in the slim chance I didn't know. On city streets that were fairly quiet except for a few people outside, we were the eyesore, the call to look at us while we traveled in my noisemaker.

Eve glanced at me some of those times when my noisy truck called attention to it and then hastily turned her face away as though she felt guilty for noticing. After a while, I silently vowed I would quickly earn enough money to have my truck repaired, even if I had to beg Fancy Ladies to let me sell a bunch of way overpriced brassieres that had been created to hoist objects that many older women thought made their sagging breasts as perky as those of most slim teens. I visualized thick gobs of boobs. *Eew*!

Pulling in front of the only paint store in town, I turned off the key. For long seconds I sat in place, waiting while my rear shimmies settled. "Now," I said, looking at Eve, who also hadn't unstrapped herself yet.

She seemed to know I didn't need any more words than that. It was just that we'd finally experienced a moment of peace.

"I can back you on that until you're able to take care of it. No rush to repay me." She gave her head a small nod toward the rear as though she didn't want to mention all that we'd heard. In that moment, I also realized how my body had just calmed. While I'd paid attention to the racket and stares as we rode, I had not done the same with my body. It was only now settling down, as though the hanging bumper had shaken everything, including me and her.

"No, thanks. I'm good." Once we strode into the store away from my truck, she probably experienced the peace I did just to get away from that thing outside.

We had done business with Andre, the middle-aged manager, quite a few times. He greeted us with a grim smile. "Got a little problem out there, huh?"

Ignoring his words, Eve and I grabbed buggies and hurriedly went in search of items. We gathered drop cloths and the painters' tape that would create crisp lines between colors. Shying away from cheaper rollers, we selected short-napped ones with synthetic fabric since Cherry's walls weren't textured. While we moved on to other areas, I pulled the wrappers off the rollers and gave each one a good rubdown that would prevent lint from coming off these new items and staying on the walls. I did this as we walked so I wouldn't forget to get it done, and we would be getting to the job so soon.

We bypassed the paints with matte and flat sheens since what we planned to use would go in a kitchen, and kitchens picked up too many stains. Self-priming paints worked best. Moving past budget paints, we reached the color swatches of our favorite brand.

"If you ladies need any help, let me know." With no other customers, Andre remained where he'd been seated at the sales counter. He kept his fingers running across the front of his phone, probably playing a game. Eve and I chose a pale teal shade for the walls of Cherry's kitchen and a darker teal that would become an attractive focal point in the room for the stove's long hood. While Andre began mixing the colors, we picked out the white we liked best.

He helped us load our purchases that we charged to the Twin Sisters Remodeling and Repair account that I hoped would soon have a bit of extra cash in it. With everything in my truck bed, he walked around the rear of my truck, glanced at the bumper, and swerved his eyes toward and away from mine. Business was never booming in his store, and he surely wanted to keep his job, so wisely Andre only thanked us and walked inside.

"Now," I said, turning a smile on Eve, "that was good."

"Yes, it did go well."

At the lumberyard, we hoped to find what we planned to use on the side of the kitchen's island to give it pizzazz. Even though they didn't carry what we needed, they could get it in two days. Perfect. We made more charges to our business account.

After a morning filled with accomplishments, we stopped for a quick lunch at a burger joint. From there, we would make our trek to New Orleans, only an hour and a half away, so we could see samples of granite in person to select the one we liked best. We had already checked them online, but nothing beat seeing them under the light.

"Wait, these new shoes are pinching my toes." Eve pointed to the red sling-back heels, which she never should have worn in the first place. "Let me run in my house and change to a more comfortable pair before we go to the city."

In front of her house, I waited in my truck. She was taking longer than I'd expected. I turned off the motor so it wouldn't clatter up her neighbor.

Stillness of the house to the right snared my interest. I stared at the window nearest the front where Mrs. Wilburn used to watch Eve, and later Royce perched right behind her, also keeping Eve in view. Curtains there were straight with not even a breath causing one to stir.

The driveway was empty that I could see, but who knew? Royce might have taken her money and bought himself something else he could ride— maybe a golf cart. Many people in the neighborhood owned them.

Okay, I was curious, and Eve would be out again in only a minute. I could slip out the door of my truck and take a quick peek into the rear of his driveway hidden from view by the tall hedges that separated his backyard from hers.

I eased my door shut so as not to get his attention in case he was outside where I couldn't see him, although I didn't believe he was home. I took quick steps behind my truck to its opposite side and rushed to the edge of the tall bushes.

No new vehicle stood in their driveway that I noticed. What I did see was Royce. His bent pose on the ground did not make me believe he was trying to take a tan.

"Are you okay?" I yelled, running across the yard to him. "Royce...."

"Sunny! Sunny, are you out here?" Eve's frantic call came from the front area of her house.

"Here. Hurry!" I managed to get the words out my mouth as I bent to the crumpled young man with his eyes closed on the grass. "Call an ambulance," I urged since she came rushing across, purse in her hand, and my purse and phone remained in my truck.

"What's wrong with him?" Eve asked a second before she started responding to the person who answered her 911 call.

"I don't know, but he doesn't say anything." I moved around to the other side of him and started to kneel so I could get closer to feel for a pulse in his neck. Blood on the grass and back of his head told me he had not had a heart attack or seizure.

While Eve told the person she spoke to the little she knew, she placed an index finger across her lips to tell me to tone down the song that swirled out of my mouth.

My fingers that felt the young man's neck shook once they felt no sign of life in him. Whatever or whoever caused his demise had done a terrible thing, snuffing out his last breath. A cold helplessness seeped through me. It started from the pit of my stomach and ran through my legs. Along my chest wall and into my pinky fingers. I experienced such an icy feel that I threw my arms around myself and held on, trying to hold myself down while I shook. What had happened to this young person who'd lost his life? My gaze drifted to the back door of his house, where the woman who had given birth to him had also once thrived. Now she, too, was gone, although not deceased at this place.

I'd also found her.

My song came out as a soft hum while Eve came close and hugged me. The same carol sounded peaceful to my ears as the sirens whined. More drew near.

We were on our feet while the medics ran up with their gurney and medical gear. Eve and I stepped away, and these trained people checked her neighbor for any sign of life. Without hearing any words, it was easy to tell from their demeanors that they found he was beyond help. They didn't place him on their gurney but began taking pictures.

Police officers were running up, and we knew to wait. We would be questioned, me especially since I had found him. The detective in charge in our little town would not be pleased to see us at a murder scene once again. He was not the only person who would not find our experience a pleasant one.

Why us? Why me? Why would anyone kill Royce?

Voices barked orders and more doors slammed. This whole experience made the day feel surreal. A soft breeze found its way across the lawn and reached me. It gave me a strange thought. Low humidity. How nice. How pleasant on the skin.

My idea was so inconsistent with the whole scene it made me recall being near our sister Crystal when someone shot her next to me. While Eve spoke to the deputy who had been the first police officer to arrive, and Detective Wilet came stomping out from the driveway toward us, the neighborhood could surely hear me recall how a really bright red nose led Santa through what would have otherwise been a horrible night.

Chapter 18

Detective Wilet questioned me and Eve right in the deceased person's backyard and wrote answers we gave him and possibly other notations in his pad. I tried to focus on everything he asked Eve, and what she answered, but found it most difficult with all of the people around us snapping pictures and making drawings, and all the while poor Royce remained dead on his grass.

No, it wasn't his anymore. Or was it in the first place? He had posted that For Sale sign out front. It didn't matter now.

"Huh?" I said, seeing the detective face me with his mouth moving. His words seemed aimed at me instead of my sister.

"When did you see him last?" Our inquirer's tone and frown let me know he wasn't pleased that I'd been so distracted while he started speaking to me. Or maybe he just didn't like me at all. I knew he didn't like to find me around murdered bodies. I didn't like it, either.

"Oh, Royce," I said, looking down at the young man on the ground. He seemed so youthful and innocent, and I could almost imagine his mother wanting to rock him when he was a babe. "When I last saw him alive…?" Uh-oh, I didn't like where my mind went.

"Yes," the officer said with a hard nod, "I want to know when you last saw the deceased alive."

"Uh, that would have been yesterday."

He nodded more and wrote. "What time yesterday?"

"Early evening, I think. Right, Eve?" I asked, and she nodded, her hooded eyes telling me she was reliving that experience as vividly as I was, and it wasn't a good one.

What had I said to him? Yelled at him? Had I shaken my fist at Royce yesterday when he stopped his motorcycle he had roaring behind Eve's car, blocking us in her driveway, revving up his motor while he wore that frightful helmet that made him look fierce. But I had shown him. Instead of backing down and singing a carol and hiding inside Eve's car in her garage, I'd shoved out of her car and hollered at that boy. Yes, I did. I felt my chest swell with pride for not letting fear get to me yesterday. Right, it was yesterday evening, and I might have threatened him. And neighbors might have heard.

Thick, hairy fingers snapped in front of my face. "Ms. Taylor, are you still with us? Did you hear my question?"

"Mm, yes. What is it again?" I wasn't going to be too specific if I didn't need to.

"What time yesterday did you last see the victim?"

"Victim? So you think he was murdered?" The question seemed stupid even as I asked it. Like why else would anyone be lying around with his head bashed in?

The detective's jaw tightened, indentures making their way into it. His eyes drew so close together, he now displayed a thick unibrow. His neck moved with his swallow before he spoke to me. "Not only do I think he was murdered, which is quite evident by his bashed-in head. I also believe you might have been involved."

"Me?" A jolt ran through me with his accusation, although it wasn't totally unexpected. "Why would you think I killed him?"

He slammed his fisted hands to his hips. "You found him and also discovered his murdered mother at someone's camp." As he obviously saw the question start to form on my lips, he said, "No, we haven't discounted you from being a participant in that crime."

I shook my head. Eve did, too. Protests left our mouths, but he shushed us.

He faced me. "The coroner will give us the approximate time of this man's death, and once he does, you and your sister will both be answering a lot more questions that will need corroboration."

Oh my gosh, they would be questioning people who lived around here. Had any of them heard my encounter with this dead man?

I tried to find words that would prove I didn't do it and neither did my sister. My gaze flew wildly around this rear area then settled on the back fence.

"Look at that." I pointed to a space I noticed.

The detective glanced there and stared at me. "So it's a fence. All right, young lady—"

"Wait. I'm not trying to distract you. Please look closer at this section of the fence."

Even Eve gave me a skeptical glance, and I would have felt that way myself, only I had spied something that didn't seem right.

The three of us walked closer to the tall dog-eared wooden fence that surrounded the backyard of the young couple who lived right behind the Wilburns. I had walked beside that fence and noticed the panels and that some of them fit snugly against each other while a few others did not. Probably the people who lived there had it for privacy around their swimming pool, where the curvaceous wife liked to sunbathe. A rumor I'd once heard mentioned it was sometimes in the nude.

The detective, and even my twin, gave me inquisitive looks.

"Check this out." I placed my finger beside the spot. "You see this little empty circle? It's not a natural knot in the wood. The inner part is fresher than the rest."

Again, the pair gave me strange looks. The hole was tiny. I hoped I was correct.

"Place your eye against the opening." I used a pleading expression with the detective. "Do it please? It'll only take you a second."

With a huff, he placed his eye close to the space. His body's posture lost its tension as his shoulders relaxed. He tilted his head a little and pushed his face against the wood.

The phone in Eve's hand rang. Its noise blasted the silent moment, startling me and her and possibly everyone else back here. She shook her head like she wasn't going to answer it but glanced at the caller's name.

"I can't talk now, Nicole," she said once she answered. "I'll have to call you back later."

With the speaker on, my niece's words carried. "Why? What are you doing, Mom?"

Eve's eyes swung toward mine, the worry in them evident. Should she tell her I was being investigated for a murder?

Of course not.

"Just something I can't stop right now."

"Listen, Mom. He just started babbling!" Baby noises came from the phone, the sweetest unclear sounds I had ever heard. They dragged the tears that wanted to hide behind my eyes over my lower lids. Hot water touched my face.

I placed a finger on my sister's cheek. Her happy tears could've steamed an oyster.

"Hey, baby bumpkins, how are you? I love you. I want to hold you and—yes, go ahead, keep on talking," Eve told the baby who continued to make unintelligible sounds.

Detective Wilet drew his head back from the fence. His demeanor was no longer up tight or angry. He looked at Eve's phone and held up a hand in a signal to stop. "You'll need to get off now," he said in a quiet tone.

She nodded and held on a moment longer. "Nicole. Nicole, if you can hear me—I need to run now. Call again. I love hearing him. And I love all of you."

"Me, too," I called out.

Once Eve clicked off, the detective did something surprising. He smiled. It was a crooked smile, a little one that showed only three of his narrow teeth, but it looked real. "Congratulations," he told Eve. "Having a baby is a wonderful thing."

Oh, obviously he had one, maybe more of them.

He didn't want to discuss babies anymore. Instead, he told me, "I could see what you wanted me to look at. It looks like somebody drilled a tiny hole in the fence so it wouldn't be noticed, at least by most people." He almost smiled at me. "By putting your eye right against the wood, you can fairly easily see into that other backyard and their pool and its apron with an open lounge chair right inside."

"I hate to say this, but I'll bet Royce drilled that hole so he could watch the young woman sunbathing," I said.

The detective stared at the dead man on the ground. "You may be right."

No obvious weapon lay on the grass anywhere near Royce that I could see. Of course, if a person came into his backyard and struck him on the head with something, that person would not want to drop that object where it would be easily discovered.

"Detective Wilet," I said, still not dismissed to go anywhere else, and my idea blooming, "I believe his mother was also killed by being struck on the head." He didn't respond to what had seemed obvious, so I continued. "Do you think the same object that was used to murder her was used here, kind of like mother, like son? And then that would mean the same person killed both of them, right?" My thoughts that blossomed seemed frightful, too awful to fully consider.

A stern face replaced his sweet-baby attitude. "Is that how it happened?"

"Wait, you don't believe I really could have done this?"

"You're kidding, right?" Eve faced him, evidently figuring he believed I committed double homicides.

Before he could say anything—if he was going to say anything—the silent seconds were broken by the tinkling of a text coming in. Eve glanced at her phone. The frown on her lips gave way to a trace of a smile.

"Nicole wants me to come and stay with them awhile," she told me.

"That's wonderful."

"And where is Nicole?" the detective asked.

"In Houston." Eve appeared ready to send a text back to her daughter.

"That will have to wait." He thrust his hand toward her phone, letting her know not to text now. "I don't want you going to another state."

Frown lines reappeared in Eve's forehead. She pushed her free hand toward his as though she was about to shove it away. Was my sister ready to fight? And with a cop?

"Texas is right next to our state, and Houston is just right there. I wouldn't be far," Eve insisted as though he wasn't aware of those facts.

His gaze remained firm on her face, a pulse ticking along the side of his forehead.

She released a breath and lowered her phone.

"You two can go home for now," he said. "I know where you live. Stay close. We'll talk again." He turned away from us.

Eve and I rushed to her place, slowing only to duck beneath the yellow police tape that now cordoned off another death scene.

Inside her house, we stood for long minutes, sucking in breaths. Avoiding words and even each other's gazes allowed us both time to start to process what we had been through.

"What's happened to them is terrible," I said, "so I sure don't want to feel sorry for myself."

"Right. It's awful." Eve held her phone up near her face. She reread Nicole's text and lowered the phone with a grimace. "Let's drink. Then we'll think."

"Good idea." I stepped with her to her kitchen, knowing not being able to join her daughter's family now that she was invited would be a horrible punishment.

She pulled a nice bottle of merlot out of her wine rack and raised an eye, asking if that one was okay. I nodded. Anything that might take the edge off what happened would be fine. She used her electronic opener to lift the cork out of its snug place, poured two stemmed glasses, and set one in front of me. The rich aroma took a pinch of the bite off the moment. She sat with the other glass, placing the bottle between us. We both took big swallows. Mine took a little more of the sting off.

"Okay, our plans for this afternoon changed a bit." She smirked at her sarcastic statement. "Let's see what we were going to do...." She put an elbow on the table and tapped a finger against her cheek.

"We were all happy and had picked out paint and other items for Cherry's kitchen," I said, "and then we were going to take a run to New Orleans to select the granite we'd want to use."

"Let's do that tomorrow." Her eyes swerved toward the Wilburns' place. "The detective doesn't need to know every movement we make."

"Good idea." Another swallow of the warm dark red liquid assured me things would work out. What things, I wasn't sure yet, but we would work on it. My mind jumped to the items in the back of my truck, and I recalled the rattle, the noise, the income I needed so I could get the thing fixed.

Eve sipped her drink. Her face brightened. "Oh, maybe now that someone killed Royce, and that was almost certainly the same person who murdered his mother, the police should let Dave go free."

Her idea gave me hope. We tapped our glasses together.

"But the only person who was with both Royce and his mother when they were found dead was...." My enthusiasm dulled. My shoulders slumped, but my heartbeats raced. "Eve—" What did I want her to say? That she knew I wasn't guilty? That she had grown up with me, even in our mother's womb, and knew the kind of person I was, and that I'd never do such a thing?

That she had been at both murder scenes with me, although she had shown up at both immediately after me?

That we were not women who went around murdering people?

I stared at her, and she stared at me, her thoughts surely running around the same places mine did. If I were an outsider and not either of us, I would be certain I had done it. Sure, I had no motive, but who did? How long would it take for someone to find out?

We swigged our wine in sync.

"Who'll want to hire us after word gets out about Royce's death and us being there to find him?" she asked, nicely including herself in with the finder—me.

"Right, and if people don't notice that police tape around his yard or hear about the police questioning everyone in the neighborhood...." I poured more wine into my glass.

"And if they don't read about it in the paper...." She chugged her drink, motioned for me to dump more from the bottle into her glass.

By the time more worries flowed to the forefront of my mind—some I shared, some I did not—the bottle had emptied. Eve offered some concerns and suggestions, to which I might have concurred but couldn't think too straight.

"We really didn't do it?" I asked my twin once I finally stood, but swayed back, and grabbed the rear of a chair to steady myself.

Her smile was weak. Grim. She shook her head. "But it sure seems like it. We'll get to work on proving we're innocent in the morning. Let's eat a quick sandwich. Stay here to sleep."

"Oh, no. I'm fine." I plunked a kiss on her lips. "Thanks for everything."

"Come on. Sleep here. You can't drive."

"Then I'll walk. I'll come back for that noisy thing outside in the morning." Considering the racket it made, I didn't want to call attention to myself or it when I left here. Probably the police were still asking questions to people in the neighborhood.

I glanced out a window and saw it was dark. I didn't want to walk between those fences to my street. "Let's have a sandwich." I plunked back in my chair.

Eve had had a little less to drink than I did. She put together plain turkey sandwiches, which we chewed on and drank water. Once we finished, she had me go into her bedroom with her and select nightwear. I didn't feel like fancy negligee, which was most of what she owned, but I grabbed a long nylon gown and carried it to the next bedroom.

When I woke in the morning, I found I hadn't taken my clothes off or put her gown on. I recalled that I sat on the edge of the bed to remove my shoes. From then, I imaged I leaned back to rest a minute. That minute lasted all night.

Somebody coated my tongue with sandpaper while I slept and poured a vial of tartness across it.

I met Eve in the kitchen, where she looked much spryer than I felt. She had already showered and dressed.

While she looked over my wrinkled clothes, I held out her nightgown. "Thanks. It seems I didn't need this. The sheets are still clean, too." I brushed back at my wavy hair that had fallen toward my face. "I'll need to go clean up."

She pulled two small bowls from a cabinet. "Want some grits first?"

"No, thanks. I'll eat at home. I really want to get out of these clothes."

"And you'll come back after that, and we'll see what we'll do?" She dumped a pack of bacon-flavored instant grits in a bowl and measured water into it.

"I'll be back." I heard the microwave coming alive and zapping her mixture while I let myself out the front. I locked that door and stepped toward my truck, still parked in the circle beside her entrance.

My gaze drifted toward the side, but I wished it had not. Yellow tape out there called my attention to what I could have missed finding if I had only done as I'd planned yesterday and kept myself in my truck. Then I wouldn't be a main suspect in Royce's murder—or possibly I still would have. If I hadn't discovered him back there, who would have? How long would it have taken for someone else to enter his backyard? Nobody ever went over to visit that I'd ever known of, not to see Mrs. Wilburn when she was alive, and certainly not her son since he'd been there.

The morning held a dull hue. Pale bluish-gray clouds stretched like a light blanket that promised to be covered in the not too distant future by heavy, darker ones. The image of Royce lying for who knows how long in the yard in the heat and now the upcoming rain loomed and began to swell in my mind. Hot rain fell, and I rubbed my cheeks to buff it off, determining the slick wetness came from my eyes.

Outside the truck, the day kept still. The sky hadn't cracked open yet and probably wouldn't within the next hour. I stepped into my vehicle and shut the door as quietly as I could, not wanting to call attention to myself. Who knows how many of these people in nearby houses had been questioned last night concerning Royce's death?

Deciding not to make noise with my truck, I left it parked while I hustled behind Eve's house and through the small pathway between the two fences back there. Reaching my street, I saw Mrs. Hawthorne busy at work in one of the flowerbeds in her yard and hoped she didn't see me. I bolted into my house, stripping off my clothes as I swept through. I turned on water as hot as I could stand it and stepped into the shower, letting it wash over me while I hoped to clean images of what transpired yesterday evening from my mind. My fingertips began to prune before I gave up and got out.

Although it was a warm day, and the shower had been extremely steamy, I felt chilled. Envisioning Eve's grits cooking made me want some. I prepared my own with a cheesy, buttery base since I needed all the comfort food I could get. I ate it with lots more butter and a pile of bacon bits and thought about Dave. He was locked up in prison. What would he do there? Why couldn't we get him out? Would I get locked up beside him?

I wanted to be near him, but not there. The police surely weren't doing much to find him not guilty of Mrs. Wilburn's murder that I knew of. I had felt compelled to get him released before. Now that I experienced more inner pain, I wanted the comfort of him even more. What needed to be done was prove Dave didn't kill anyone. Considering that fact gave me instant relief. Eve and I could help do that. Except the only alternative to his being a murderer seemed to be me.

I let myself out and rushed on foot toward the street.

"Hey, Sunny!" Mrs. Hawthorne hollered from her yard and gave me a wave with her trowel.

I returned her greeting but didn't slow.

"So your sister's neighbor was really murdered, huh?" she called out.

I twisted my shoulders toward her and shrugged. "I guess."

"Did you call my cousin yet?" she continued, but I chose not to respond to anything else and rushed on my way. I darted between fences, getting to Eve's yard, where I hit the doorbell in back, and unlocked the door.

"Hey, it's me," I called out.

A little rustle and then footsteps hitting the hardwood floor from the area of her bedrooms came nearer. She looked refreshed. Tall and all made up although it wasn't showy but more like her natural appearance plus a slight enhancement that brought out her clear blue eyes and fair skin. She made me so glad I looked like her, although my appearance felt duller. And murder was what we were all about this morning, so the way we looked had no bearing on that. It was just that looking all right lifted the mood a little.

"Where do you suggest we go first?" she asked.

"I thought of a lot of things, but where I would like to start is with seeing Mom." I gave a slight shrug. "Maybe to get some comfort before we race after a killer, or maybe to get some news from her or others there. Then maybe we can sneak out to New Orleans to see about the granite for Cherry's kitchen."

"I think that's a great idea." She led the way to the front door.

I started my truck I'd left in the driveway. Eve and I glanced at each other when the noise began, first accompanied by a small, different kind of vibration, but as I pulled through the circular drive onto the street, a rattle intensified.

I drove in front of Jake's house instead of the Wilburns' since I wanted to avoid horrid memories. We spoke little during the short ride to Sugar Ledge Manor, and I was relieved when the rain began. Fat drops slapped my truck's roof and hood, causing enough racket to drown out the cacophony of sounds my truck made. We grabbed the umbrellas I kept in the pockets of each door.

Rain bounced from the concrete walkway toward the covered entrance, the day's temperature immediately having dropped at least five degrees. The fresh smell of the air also lifted my mood. This, I told myself, would be a better day.

We shook water off our umbrellas and stood them upside down out of the way to the side of the entrance. While I placed mine, the motion of a person rushing from the building caught my attention. It was from the exit at the far end of the right wing. A woman wearing navy pants and top became instantly drenched. Her hair stuck to her scalp and neck like a tight hood, and clothes clung to her body. She moved so fast it was rather hard for me to see her face, but I did believe she was one of the two that had lately stared at me. She drove a small white car out of the far exit.

Eve watched with me. "Maybe we can find out who she is."

"Yes, she and the other one. And what their interest is in me. Or us."

We stepped into the building, the entrance as always appealing with potted palms and framed floral prints, and not many steps later found our pleased mother with her friends in their normal grouping. As usual, we hadn't signed in.

"Eve, Sunny." Mom spread her arms, and both of us swept in, taking turns to get powdery-scented squeezes from her. "It's so good to see both of you at the same time."

"Hi, Mom," we said and acknowledged the group.

"Oh, now I know how to tell y'all apart," one of her buddies said. She pointed at Eve. "You're the one who uses more makeup."

"And she dresses better," another one pointed out, both of them messing with my emotions.

"She's also the one that keeps marrying and divorcing men."

I grinned. This was making me feel better.

"Yes," the previous one said, "you are a smarty." She nodded at Eve. "Get 'em and get rid of 'em and make 'em pay for it."

"Oh, no." Eve gave her head a hard shake. "I would never have a man pay anything once we divorce. We all just stay friends."

I felt kind of sorry for her to have to explain to this group and certainly wouldn't tell them how most of her exes still showered her with fine gifts. She must have made each one of them an extra-good wife. That thought made me pleased—until I recalled that's exactly what she was hoping to do with Dave Price.

A momentary thought made me consider it could be better if he stayed on jail until—until what? We proved his innocence? He would get out and then... Eve would go after him like a momma gator gunning for an intruder who tried to get between her and her babies.

"And, Sunny, you poor thing. You still can't get a man, can you?" Ida, the plumpest woman with bluish hair who sat on a sofa adjacent to Mom, recalled.

I lifted my shoulders and felt the edges of my lips lower. "I believe I can. It's just...the time isn't quite right. But it's coming."

"Oh!" my mother said, her smile forming.

"Oh!" Eve said, clasping my hand. She looked at Mom with her own smile wide. "Maybe my little sister is finally going to put some excitement in her life."

I glanced at her, my lips tight. She wouldn't want to hear about my plan with the man she was after. And she called me little, probably because I was wearing sandals, and she wore heels. Also, I shot out of Mom's birth canal minutes after she did.

Our mother, of course, kept retaining hope at all cost, although she'd never say it, that I would also shoot out babies that she could cherish.

"Ladies," I said, swinging the topic away from me, "we need your help."

That silenced everyone. How often did these elders hear those words anymore? White-haired ladies on sofas and wheelchairs leaned forward. Mom's sofa was full, but with small spaces on the two adjacent ones, ladies there scooted over. Those on the ends patted for Eve and me to take seats on the ensuing empty spots. We did, and the lady who always wore three strands of pearls started fooling with the back of her ear.

Seeing me watch her, she said, "Just turning up my hearing aid, sweetheart. I don't want to miss a word of this."

A couple of workers in navy passed by and glanced at our group. Eve and I exchanged nods with them. I wanted to wait until they were out of sight before speaking again, and the eyes of the elders in our gathering led me to know these wise women figured they would also keep quiet now. When no others were near, two in the group let out loud breaths.

"Phew, that was close," Grace said.

What she thought it was close to, I had no idea. It was a good thing we had come before lunchtime. Most should have minds refreshed from the night's sleep and not too cloudy from a noonday meal and the need for a nap soon afterwards.

"Here's the thing," Eve said, getting their heads to swing toward her, faces alert with anticipation. "Someone was murdered in town."

"Aw, we know that," one of them said.

The one seated beside Eve touched her shoulder. "Are you talking about when the latest man you like killed your neighbor?"

"No. He didn't kill her."

Of course they would know Eve cared about Dave.

The women shifted their eyes toward each other, this action and their serious faces suggesting that wasn't what they'd heard and seemed to believe.

Our sweet mother nodded. "I'm glad to hear it, Eve. I'd like for you to settle down with a nice young man."

"Right, and not a killer, huh, ladies?" Ida asked, to which the others concurred.

The one seated at the opposite end of my sofa leaned even farther ahead and rubbed her hands together, using a sotto tone. "Ooo, I love this detective snooping. It makes me feel like what's her name."

"Esther what's her name?" one blurted.

"No, she was that pretty swimmer," another one said. "It was, uh…"

"It really doesn't matter." I hoped to stop what seemed ready to become an argument. "But as Eve said, we need your help." A quick run through thoughts made me decide they hadn't heard anything that might help us prove Dave's innocence. If they had, one of them would have mentioned it. I needed to move on to the most recent. All of them watched me in anticipation. "There's been a more recent murder in town."

Heads nodded. They knew something. Great. I hoped it might help.

The one who'd raised her hand the first time shot it up again. "I know. Your dead neighbor's son," she said, facing Eve.

More head nods assured that they knew of what happened.

"But I told everyone you didn't do it, hon," my mother said to me, making tears squirt from my eyes.

"Thank you, Mom."

"That's right. And no matter how many people say you did, we tell them otherwise. We believe in you, Sunny. You, too, Eve." The speaker rubbed her pearls.

Light picked up the moisture that lit the bottom rim of Eve's eyes. She mouthed a thank you.

"Okay, wait," I said, raising my voice, "none of y'all need to agree with our mom just because we're her daughters, and she's your friend. We didn't do it. Either of those killings."

"Golly." One wheelchair-bound woman had almost nodded asleep, but lifted her head and faced Eve and then me. "I missed that. So you both got the mother, too. It wasn't Eve's boyfriend?"

The sound that left my throat sounded more like a squeak than a sigh. We were getting nowhere. This gathering was not bringing out new angles or other suspects. Most of these ladies had family or other visitors and possibly staff members who passed on news from town. Although some still had good enough eyesight to read a newspaper with glasses, most of them had told us they preferred not to. People who ran newspapers seemed to think the only things worthwhile was the bad stuff, and in waning years they preferred cheerful thoughts—like who'd win at bingo and the casino, and who did everyone think should be crowned king, queen, maids, and dukes of the next Mardi Gras ball here? Also, whose birthday would be celebrated next month, and what local band might be coming to play, and who might dance at the party?

I concurred. Those thoughts were best. Still, we needed more information that might help clear our names. It didn't seem that would be forthcoming from these ladies.

"Oh, Sunny, you stole that pen from the sign-in, didn't you, and then snuck it back here?" That question from the woman with orangey hair stunned me almost as much as them believing Eve and I were killers.

"What makes you say that?" Eve asked, seeing I appeared tongue-tied.

"Somebody saw her take it," the accuser said, waving her hand like the theft was nothing. "So it figures she was the one who put it back."

"Well—"

I didn't get to reply since she cut in. "So it also figures that if she's a thief, people could easily believe she'd be a killer, too."

The woman who considered me a murderer gave herself a self-righteous nod, and my insides pulled tight like they had been struck by a crowbar. The air in my chest escaped. My accuser turned to Mom. "No offence, Miriam. Maybe she didn't kill anyone."

All faces in the crowd aimed at me. In that instant, I imagined the dry mouth and dread someone looking at a firing squad might experience. I sucked in a deep breath and then another and still waited so my voice wouldn't break. "I did not kill anyone. Neither did Eve." Through the corner of my eyes, I saw our mother smile. "Somebody else killed both those people, and we are trying to prove who that killer was."

"Ah." One of the ladies tapped her index finger across her lips, reminding me of an action Cherry did. "If the same person killed the mother, bless her heart, and also her son, bless his, too, then the murderer really mustn't be Eve's boyfriend since he's already in jail."

She looked around at the group and appeared smug. Many gave her a nod of approval.

"That's what we knew," I said. "Dave Price didn't kill Mrs. Wilburn. We certainly didn't kill anyone." I looked at Mom, wanting a sign that she still believed me, and she didn't disappoint. Her soft smile and nod felt like they gave me absolution and made me breathe easier.

"Ladies," Eve said, "Sunny and I really need to get more information so we can help prove who actually did kill those people. We had hoped y'all might have heard about anyone else who could have been involved."

Some gazes slid toward me but quickly pulled away. Heads shook no.

DEAD ON THE BAYOU

Disappointment lowered my spirit even more. We had come here for nothing. What we received, the notion that people in town were spreading the word that my sister and I were murderers, made things worse. It seemed the best we could hope for from this visit was one or two of them might tell others that none of us killed anyone.

Sound carried of people moving around. A young woman wearing the navy outfit of many workers here scurried down the hall. I didn't recognize her as one of the pair who'd watched us before but really didn't know much about what they looked like. A man with a cane walked past. Two other slouched gents I recognized as residents slowed when they reached our area and appeared to check out the group. The lips of the one with gray brows an inch and a half long tipped up on one side.

"Good morning, ladies," he said with a gravelly voice.

Some of us returned his greeting. As though the men gave some kind of signal, two women looked up at the large wall clock. One of the women said a couple of words to the other man, who didn't react, but the male residents moved faster than they had before, their postures better.

"Ah," Eve said, eyeing the ladies with a widening smile, "there's some romance going on around here. I love it."

Grins on a couple of faces aimed at the last one who'd spoken, leaving no doubt as to who might be involved in a rendezvous.

"Good, you're giving my sister a reason not to fear ever needing to come and live here," I said.

Eve nodded in agreement. My words brought out smiles from others.

"Okay, let me ask y'all something," I said but noticed some in our gathering growing antsy, more faces turning toward the clock. That's when I noticed the scent of roasting meat carrying from the dining area. It would have been an extra early for lunch for us, but not for them. I needed to hurry if we were to get any useful information before we lost the group. "Do any of you know someone who works here and has long curly hair and drives a little white car?"

Heads shook. Some faces turned toward the dining area, attention drawn there instead of with me. From the enticing aroma swelling toward us, I didn't blame them. I needed to talk fast.

"It would be one of the ladies who wears the navy top and pants."

"A lot of them do, honey," one said and heads shook. Eyes blanked. I had lost interest even of my mother who furtively sniffed toward where the food was about to be served.

"Enjoy your meal, ladies," Eve said and stood. "It's time for y'all to eat."

"It sure is." Grace pushed on her wheels and started rolling away. Others bid us good-bye and went off.

"It was so nice to see you both again. I'm sure everything will work out." Our mother stood and kissed Eve and me, and we gave her hugs. She strode off after her friends.

Frustrated, I shook my head at Eve. Her grimace matched mine.

Beyond her, Grace came rolling back. Once she reached us, she repeated an action we'd previously witnessed. She shoved a hand down into the top of her polyester dress with the large floral print, and part of her arm disappeared. Soon something bounced above her belt, her large droopy breasts doing a kind of dance. I was mesmerized.

"Look, I wanted to show you this," she said, and for a moment I wondered if she meant her lady part's pseudo-dance. "Ah, there." Her elbow came up first and then her hand. She held out her phone, making me recall that's where she kept it. Actually, she had told us she kept it in her bra, and sometimes it dropped lower and she needed to dig around for it.

As we'd seen once before, her phone looked damp.

"I forgot. This is the latest picture I took, and your mother is in it, and she looks wonderful. She had just had her hair done." She tapped the phone a couple of times, and a picture of Mom came up. She was seated with her regulars and did look nice, as usual. What caught my eye was the navy blue outfit of the woman standing near them. Her hair was long and wavy.

I took the damp phone. "Who is this?" I placed my finger on the staff member's face.

"I can't tell you that, honey. I really don't know. Getting kind of old. I can't remember names like I used to."

I showed the phone to Eve. She stared at the photo and nodded.

Grace grabbed her phone and dropped in into the top of her dress. No telling how far down it went. She turned toward the cafeteria.

"Thank you for showing us that nice picture of Mom and all the ladies." For a brief second I considered running up to Mom or some other friends of hers and asking if they knew this person's name. But they were in the midst of others now, and we didn't need our questions heard by the masses.

"Have a nice lunch," Eve said when our friend rolled on.

"I will." Grace pushed her on wheels and then turned back, covering the side of her mouth with her hand so she could tell us something in private. "I don't know that worker's name, but I can tell you she's a harlot."

Eve released a small laugh with her smirk.

"Yes, I know you've had many lovers, too," Grace told her, "and you married some of them. But you never got pregnant by any of them and then had an abortion."

"What? Who are you talking about?" I said.

"The woman you asked about. I don't know her name, but I know about her relationship. She had it with your neighbor." She pointed at Eve. "The boy that died."

"Royce?" Eve and I said together.

"Whatever his name is. The one whose momma was killed and then he was." She swung her gaze toward me. "And I hope you won't take offense because I thought you murdered both of them."

"None taken." I said the words automatically.

"Did he know about it?" Eve asked.

"That she was P.G.? I'm not certain, but I believe so." She looked around. "I'll need to ask my friends. I'm not sure if I even told them what I heard about her." She eyed a bent woman who was inching along. "She's always the last one in the cafeteria. I need to go before most of the best food is gone." She almost knocked down the slow woman rolling past her.

The scene returned to my mind of Eve's grandchild leaving Eve's home with his parents. Mrs. Wilburn had come into Eve's yard for the first time that I knew of so she could see the baby. A small crowd of us, including Dave, had gathered in the front yard and watched them leave. When I turned from the departing car, I noticed Mrs. Wilburn's window that she'd normally watched Eve from. The curtains were parted, and Royce stood between them. He was staring out, and something in his look struck me. I'd wondered then if he didn't want to have a child of his own, or possibly he had fathered a child that its mother kept away from him.

But suppose he knew his girlfriend—or possibly his ex?—had gotten pregnant, and he'd wanted that baby, but she got rid of it and then he found out?

Eve still stared at the final figures departing behind a wall toward the cafeteria, her mind certainly also trying to take it all in. A woman who worked here—pregnant by Royce? Eve turned to me, our looks telling each other everything. We would have a discussion about what we'd just learned here and decide what we'd do with that news. In the meantime, we didn't speak while both of us headed out the door.

Chapter 19

Eve and I grabbed our umbrellas and ran into the rain. The minute we slammed our doors, I said, "Someone got pregnant by Royce?"

"And plenty of people believe you killed him and his mom?"

I shoved my back against the rear seat. "Can any of this really be happening?" I sucked in breaths and blew them out. "Okay, let's go tell Detective Wilet." I started my truck and threw it in reverse. Remembering the police car I'd backed into, I inspected the area behind me. "Wait. Did we learn anything for certain? We knew some people believed I was involved with those murders."

Eve kept nodding. "And some think I was involved."

"Okay." Was her admission supposed to make me feel better?

"But the thing is—just because one person in there told us a woman who works in the manor conceived a child with my neighbor doesn't necessarily make it so."

"What do you mean?"

"I mean having that sweet lady who keeps her phone under her boobs telling us about a pregnancy doesn't mean it really happened." She paused, and I lifted one eyebrow in a question, wanting more of an explanation. "Sunny, she said none of the other Chat and Nappers are aware of that, so she wants to share the information with them. But for all we know, it's not true. I think we should wait. Let's go to the city to get what we need so we'll have time to sort out what we heard in there. "

I'd kept my foot on the brake as my mind wrapped around these thoughts. "You're right." I checked behind my truck again, especially the rear exit of the lot, thinking I might see the little white car. I did not.

Both of us were hungry since we'd smelled good food cooking in the manor. We would think better without craving food but didn't want a heavy meal or an order that would take too long. On our way out of town, we made a quick stop at a great Cajun diner with a southern flair. B&T's crabby burger was to die for, Eve and I agreed while we devoured ours. The soft patty made of tasty crab meat and wonderful seasonings dressed on a wheat bun left me licking my lips to get the last fleck of seafood from them.

We avoided mentioning the manor until we were snug in my truck. "If we tell the detective what we heard from Ms. Grace, what would that prove?" I asked while I steered us out of town.

"Mm." It appeared she had really put all thoughts of what we'd heard completely out of her mind while we were in the restaurant and now needed to call up that topic again. "It would probably prove that we were actually guilty and trying to put all the blame on someone else since we have nothing to back up what we'd be telling him."

"Yes, and then what? Let's suppose the young woman who works at the manor did get pregnant by Royce and then aborted a baby he really wanted. Why would she murder Royce?"

"Would that give her a motive for doing it?" Eve faced forward, and for a long while we rode in quiet, each deep within our own thoughts.

"No." My word came out of the void, making Eve's head jerk as she faced me. "If he had been angry enough after he found out she had done that, he might have had a motive for killing her."

"But not the other way around."

I shook my head. "I'm afraid not." I'd reached the turnoff at the 316 split and almost took it since that was the way I normally took when getting on the Interstate to New Orleans. Instead, I remained on old Highway 90. My truck seemed to make more noise from the rear when I pulled the wheel so fast to the right, and I realized I was getting used to the rattle. Maybe I wouldn't need to get it fixed after all, I thought, the minute before a severe racket in back made Eve glance there.

By the time I headed up the ramp for the Huey Long Bridge, we had begun exchanging concepts for how we would complete some fast remodeling in Cherry's kitchen.

Eve pointed out tugboats passing below and mentioned how swiftly the Mississippi flowed down there while I tried to watch the river and bridge and passing trucks, but became too distracted and almost bumped into a car that slowed right in front of me. From that moment on, I kept my eyes forward and attention focused on where I was going until I steered us down from the bridge and soon had us parked in front of one of the establishments that sold granite and marble.

Inside, we looked at large sheets from the samples we had seen online. They did look nice, but so did some others once we got to see them up close.

"Let's go with colonial cream for the countertops," I suggested to Eve, and she agreed. "And we'll do something more creative with the island."

She nodded, and we pored over other colors. "We'll need to measure in our customer's kitchen and let you know the exact sizes," Eve told the salesclerk, a middle-aged guy with a shaved head.

"All right. And you're sure this is the one you want?" He pointed to a color that was only a small sample. I shrugged, ready to double-check a large sheet again before giving him an answer.

My phone rang, and I glanced at it in my open purse only to see who the caller was. "Excuse me a minute," I said.

Eve's eyebrows lifted, letting me know she wondered who the call came from.

I scooted back from both of them, pressed the button to answer, and moved to another row of shelves.

"Ms. Taylor, this is Detective Wilet. I need to ask you a few more questions. Are you at home?" he asked, and my gaze swerved around the showroom. "I can come over there right now."

"Uh, no I'm not."

"You aren't out of town, are you?" That was gruffer than his first words.

"Actually, I'm in the midst of something really important right this minute." As soon as I said it, I knew he might protest that what he wanted was much more significant than anything I might be doing.

I heard his exhale, as though he was ready to tell me off or insist he was coming over.

"I mean, I'll wrap up the business I was taking care of," I said, "and I'll be there to see you as fast as I can. It shouldn't take long. What about if I give you a call when I get home?"

His hesitation made me fear he was spearing his unmarked car toward my house. After I arrived there, he would arrest me for sure.

While I waited for him to make up his mind, I waved across the showroom and mouthed, "Come on" to Eve and headed for the exit.

"Now?"

I gave her a big nod and rushed to the door.

"I'll tell you what," the detective said in my phone. "Just come to the office once you get through with your *business*." It didn't sound like he considered whatever I was doing too significant. "And you'd better not be long."

"No, sir. I mean, yes, sir, I will be there. And it won't take long."

"So which one did you want?" the salesman called to me since Eve only looked confused and came after me. The salesman stood a wide palette that held the various small samples that we had been looking at.

Yanking the door open, I glanced back. He was pointing at one of them, although I wasn't certain which one. "Let's go," I told Eve as she came to the doorway, and I nodded toward the area the man stood in, then rushed out to my truck.

"What's going on?" Eve barely got in and shut her door before I took off. She swerved to the side with my fast turn of the truck and needed to right herself before she could grab both sections of her seatbelt and strap herself in.

I realized I'd better do that myself, normally a must-do before I drove, but this minute I needed to get to my house. But a police officer was waiting for me back in Sugar Ledge, and I didn't want to get stopped by police here for speeding. Getting a ticket would take too long and add to the time Detective Wilet would have to wait for me, and I didn't have extra cash to throw away. While I drove, Eve helped buckle me in. "I'm thinking your phone call had something to do with a detective in town."

"I think you're right." I sped only a little to get to the stoplight we approached and barely made it underneath before the yellow changed to red. As I raced across the Huey Long Bridge, my mind conjured possibilities and concerns about what the officer wanted with me that was so imperative, and I found nothing positive.

Chapter 20

"So you completed your business?" Detective Wilet leaned back in his chair behind his desk.

"Yes, sir, we did." I included Eve in my reply since we'd arrived in town together, and I drove straight to the station. He had agreed that she could come into his office with me, so now we sat facing him.

"Murder is rather important, too."

"It is." I swallowed and scooted to the front edge of my chair. "What can I help you with concerning that?" The corner of my eye let me see Eve's knee jerk.

The man facing me pushed himself even further back against his swivel chair. "Did you do it?"

"What?"

He leaned way forward, his thick upper body over his desk. "Did you kill someone?"

"Who?"

"Sunny." Eve elbowed me.

I looked at her, looked at him. "Sir, no, my reply to you is absolutely not. I never killed anyone and would never do anything like that. Nothing could ever make me consider doing such a violent act."

"Yes, it could." He said it so matter-of-factly that I believed him, but then pulled my head back.

"Excuse me. Maybe you don't know me well enough, but I would never kill another person."

"Suppose someone was ready to shoot your sister." He pointed at Eve and left his words like a question in the air. The way he held his hand as though it were a pistol aimed at her brought back an image and reminded me all too well of when that happened. And if I had had a gun close-by when that took place, would I have shot the person? Like somebody shot at and killed our sister?

I hated guns, hated violence. I needed to swallow three times to get enough moisture in my mouth. "I would shoot him."

"Okay, now that we have that out of the way, we need to discuss the death of your sister's neighbor." He nodded toward Eve.

"Which one?" The second I asked it, I cringed. Why couldn't I have waited for him to go on before I opened my mouth?

"I understand your question since two of Eve's neighbors have perished, and you were the person who *discovered* both of their bodies."

Eve lifted her hand. "I was there, too."

I looked at her with gratitude and squeezed her hand. "You don't have to say that."

"Yes, I do." She faced the detective, her face solemn. "I was at the scene of the crimes when my twin was, so if you're going to do something to her, you need to also do it to me."

Her words melted my heart. A lover could never pull up such an emotional reaction.

"What can you tell us about what you've learned with both cases?" I asked the man who already found me guilty. "Dave Price didn't kill anyone and should be released. I can bet everything I've got on it." I hoped he didn't know how little that was. "Of course, Eve and I are innocent, too."

The detective gripped his hands together on top of his desk. They were so wide, they looked like insulated gloves. "I can tell you we can't let him out now, not yet anyway. If he didn't murder Clara Wilburn, we need to find out who did." He quirked his brow—maybe thinking I would confess.

After a moment of silence building pressure in the room, Eve spoke. "So y'all aren't really looking for anyone else since you already believe Dave did it." Possibly, that was a question, but it came out like a statement.

"Right now," he focused his attention on me, "I need to ask you about something concerning Mrs. Wilburn's son who was murdered." I waited during a long pregnant pause. "What were you yelling at him about the night before he died?"

I pressed back and sat straighter in my chair. "Who? Me? Yelling at him?"

"You most definitely were."

I looked to Eve for help. She had none. My mind rolled back to the evening before Royce's death. Did I yell at him? Mm, yes, I did. "I didn't really yell." I spread my hands. "My sister and I were getting ready to back out of her driveway, and he blocked us."

"Oh, he did? With what?" Now he looked sincere, interested.

"Not a car or his body or anything like that. It was only a motorcycle he had just bought—actually he's bought a lot of things since his mother died—that new bike and a fine new automobile." I caught a breath, giving him time to look shocked or surprised or something besides that straight face he kept. "Royce stayed there behind Eve's car, revving up his motor, and not letting us get out."

"So you think that was bad?"

"Of course. Why would you ask that?" Eve's eyes narrowed with righteous indignation.

He aimed his focus at her. "Did you ever think that quite possibly he was proud of his new possession and wanted to show it off to both of you?"

Eve and I glanced at each other. We shook our heads.

"So you were screaming at him in the driveway—in fact, you were so angry, you got out of the car and threatened to harm him." Wilet's neck turned red.

I sucked in a breath. "Who told you that?"

"Neighbors."

Eve and I did double-takes toward each other. I faced him. "You're kidding. Which ones?"

"Ms. Taylor, did you or did you not yell threats at Royce Wilburn?"

"Not to kill him." My words came out as loud as his.

Eve whispered, "Shhh," making me realize what I was doing.

My thoughts scrambled back to the evening with Royce behind her car in the driveway. I did yell something at him, fearing him, wanting him to leave us alone. I had feared him and knew he believed I killed his mother instead of just finding her body stuffed in a garbage bag at Dave's camp. I had been proud of myself for getting out of the car and hollering at him instead of letting the fear get the best of me. But what did I yell...? Yes, his bike might get smashed. Maybe his leg?

"I did tell him his bike could get hit if he didn't move it out of the way." I offered an innocent shrug. "I mean, of course Eve's driveway couldn't be obstructed for too long or she wouldn't be able to get to the street."

The detective narrowed his eyes, making his thick dark brows meet above his nose.

"We had seen his motorbike and had enough time to admire it," Eve said, pressing forward in her chair, "and we needed to leave. But his bike made so much noise, Sunny had to get out of the car and speak loud so he could hear her."

Seeing my sister make those wide innocent eyes and hearing her statement made me almost convinced that she told him exactly what happened.

We all sat staring, us at him, him skimming the air from one to the other of us, his harsh eyes wanting to suck an admission of guilt. To murder? The odor of burned coffee from the hall beyond the open door reached my nostrils. Voices of other officers sounded out there, males and females speaking. My mind scrambled, seeking anything that might help me not be thrown in prison. I could feel my arms pressed behind my back and cold hard handcuffs clinking around my wrists. His stare hardened on mine and his hands flattened on his desk, but with wrists raised. I sensed he was tensed and ready to shove up to his feet and come at me.

"Did I tell you a woman down my street heard the guy who lives behind the Wilburns' fence yelling at Royce?"

"At Royce Wilburn? Are you certain the young man was yelling at him?"

"That's what she told me." I felt sweat pop out on my forehead. Good grief, was I telling the truth? Was I so desperate that I would grab for lies to a detective? What if he hooked me up to a lie detector? My mouth dried, shoulders tightened. My mind brought up the *clang* of the jail cell door slamming behind me.

"And listen to this," Eve said, pulling his attention toward her. "Did you also know that a woman who works at Sugar Ledge Manor got pregnant by him?"

The detective's hands and wrists relaxed. "By Royce Wilburn?"

"Yes," I said, all too happy to pick up the story, "and she aborted the baby, but he wanted her to have it." Did he? His angry stare from his front window when he'd watched baby Noah leave Eve's front yard had told me he did. Although come to think of it, he normally had an angry stare.

The detective did something that pleased me. Instead of coming near to arrest me, he grabbed a pen and pad. But then he asked, "What's her name?"

I looked at Eve, whose wide eyes and blank stare I was certain mimicked mine. My shoulders dropped lower. "We'll have to get that information for you."

He threw down his pen and placed his hand over his lips.

"Okay, this is what happened." Eve sat so far up on her chair, it appeared she might tip over. "One of our mother's friends who's a resident there like our mom is told us that. She had a picture of the young woman who works there in her phone and told us all about it. We'll need to get the woman's name from her. That should be easy."

He stared at me. The fingers covering the detective's lips spread apart, letting his thick lips show through. Those lips pressed tighter together.

I felt blood thumping in the outer corners of my forehead. It struggled for my attention with the sweat covering it.

Finally, the detective spoke again, giving us his verdict. He slid his hand away from his face so he could do that. "I'll tell you what. You have until this time tomorrow to get me that information. And I had better not find that you're lying."

"We sure will get you that information. And no, we are not lying." I looked at his wall clock and then at Eve. She was looking at me. We stood at the same time.

"Thank you," she told him on our way out of his office. I wasn't certain what she was thanking him for, but guessed it was the extra twenty-four hours of my freedom.

Chapter 21

Since we were fairly close, the first place Eve and I rattled down to was my street, where, as I'd hoped, Mrs. Hawthorne knelt in her yard, weeding the flowerbed alongside the cement path leading to her house. The wind had picked up, I could see, since the wide brim of her straw hat that normally shielded her face was pushed up and shifting.

She stood facing the road before I even pulled close to the edge of the street, lowering the front passenger window. "You haven't seen my cousin yet, have you?" She spoke with a smile, not like an accusation but only as though she stated a fact. Her gaze, though, swung toward the rear end of my vehicle, which she must have heard.

I shrugged. "I really haven't had time to get it fixed yet." I left out the part about not being able to afford that work. Besides, if I got thrown behind bars, I wouldn't need to worry about a noisy rear bumper. The edges of my lips pulled up while I thought of this positive outcome.

Her sweet smile widened, and I could imagine her one day in the not-too-distant future becoming one of my mother's Chat and Nap buddies.

"I understand. Hello, Eve."

"Hi." Eve spoke through her open window. "It's nice to see you. I hope you're doing well."

"I am, thank you. Oh, except I get this pain right here above my stomach sometimes. Maybe it's something I eat."

Or that girdle I sold you way back while I worked at Fancy Ladies, and you were much smaller but still squeeze yourself into it even to eat and then bend over and work in your yard. I swung my eyes toward the clock in my dashboard. We didn't have time to chat. "Mrs. Hawthorne, I'm sure a detective came to question you about that young man across the street from you yelling at Royce Wilburn on the other side of the fence that separates their yards from each other." I pointed to make certain she knew exactly where I was talking about.

Her faint eyebrows furrowed. Loose dirt fell off the trowel she held. She studied the house across the street from hers and then looked at me. "You know one officer did come to ask me about that." She paused, and I hoped she had replied what I suggested. "I'm not certain he was a detective. He might have been some other kind of police officer."

We needed to finish this interview and get on to the manor. My eyes swung to the dashboard. I was certain the time display had jumped forward an hour. "Did he wear a uniform?"

"A uniform?" She placed her hand holding the trowel against her chin. Dirt from her fingers clung to her skin. Some of it dropped. I wanted to tell her about the rest and suggest she brush it off, but did not want to distract her thought process.

"Yes, you know," Eve said, "the kind of uniform all of the police in town wear."

"Ah." She appeared to know the answer now. "You know I'm not sure."

So much for certainty and helping us. Helping *me*, I realized. Yes, I was the one who'd get thrown in jail. Time raced down. I had no minutes to spare. "Mrs. Hawthorne, you told me you heard the young man who lives across the street yelling not long before Royce Wilburn was discovered murdered."

Her lips twisted.

"And it was Royce that he was yelling at," I suggested, or maybe I knew, especially now that I had discovered Royce drilled a small hole in the fence separating his place from theirs so he could watch the young man's wife. I was certain she hadn't heard me yelling at Royce on the next street, especially with that motorcycle making so much noise at the same time.

My elder neighbor stared at me long moments as though her mind was whirling. Finally, she swung a finger forward. "Yes, that's it. He was the person that man was yelling at."

"Thank you. And if an officer who says he's a detective—Detective Wilet is his name—comes and asks you, make sure you tell him that."

"I most certainly will." She stood, her posture straighter than before. She was going to perform her civic duty. I could imagine her saluting.

"Thank you so much. I'll see you again." I gave a small wave.

The wind pushed her brim so that it flapped over her face. "And don't forget my cousin," she called as I drove away.

I pointed my truck toward the manor, where we were about to extract the other information we required. I should be able to retrieve what I needed from my mother's friend and get back to the police station without waiting until tomorrow. I lifted my chin, confidence regained. I was about to have myself absolved from the prime suspect pool.

Most of the usual vehicles were parked in their usual places in the manor's parking lot. "Five dollars for your thoughts," I told Eve when I pulled in. Neither of us had spoken during the drive from Mrs. Hawthorne's house.

"Not a penny?"

"Inflation." I turned off the motor.

"I guess I'm like you, needing to focus on getting the information we need from here and hurrying it back to Detective Wilet."

"Then I should no longer be considered a killer."

"And we can hurry and find a way to get my man, Dave, free."

Her door slam right after she said those words couldn't have accentuated that problem more. It felt like an exclamation mark letting me know I would face a major difficulty with letting my sister know how much Dave meant to me and I believed I meant to him.

But doing that would need to wait. I had to make sure I wasn't thrown in a cell next to his.

We scooted into the building. Expecting to see our mother and her friends huddled not far inside, I felt disappointment swell. Not one of them was in sight. We were also looking for the woman who'd aborted Royce's baby but didn't see her either. By now, Mom should have found out about it and could tell us who that worker was.

An assistant administrator, a tiny woman of maybe mid-twenties and with the fastest gait I'd ever seen on a woman, bustled down a hall toward us.

"Hi," I told her. "We didn't see Mom. Would you know where she is?"

Without slowing a beat, she pointed back. "Right after supper just now, I saw Miriam head for that restroom."

"Supper already?" I asked, my mind registering that I had smelled cooked onions and grits while we'd hurried past the eating area. Maybe they had shrimp and grits together, a really tasty dish. But time was moving too quickly.

"They do eat meals early, you know." Spinning backward to reply, she pointed at us. "One day you'll both get old, too." She turned around toward wherever she was going.

Eve and I stared at each other. Was that a new crease in her forehead? How many wrinkles lined my face? Was I really worried about what a kid like her said?

The ladies room provided three stalls. The doors to two of them were slightly open. Our mother's most comfortable shoes, the white flats with straps that closed with Velcro were visible beneath the door of the third one.

"Hey, Mom," I said.

"It's us," Eve told her.

A minute passed. "Is this where you need to wait for me?" Her tone wasn't its most cheerful.

I pushed my hand out to Eve to let her know I had this. "No, but we've got a little situation and need to kind of hurry to get some answers. We were looking for that friend of yours who takes a lot of pictures with her phone." And darn it, why hadn't I sent the picture I wanted to my own phone or Eve's? Oh, because the phone dropped back into the woman's bosom and she took off before I had time to think of it.

"Yes, I know who you're talking about. Grace."

It felt so weird talking to her shoes. I didn't want to envision the scene behind the shut door. "Well, we just need to hurry and go talk to her. Would you know where she is?"

Mom let out a small huff. "She got to check out of the manor and go off with her daughter."

Gloom dropped inside me.

"So she's not here?" Eve's face leaned forward, almost against the door to Mom's stall.

"No, she is not. And if you two would give me a chance, I could try to finish up in here and then come out there and visit with you in a more appropriate place."

"Sorry, Mom." I was the one now placing my face inches away from the stall door. "We're in a hurry, and this is really important."

I heard her inhale. Heard her breathe. "This is concerning those deaths, isn't it?"

"I'm afraid so."

Eve did little finger taps on the stall door. "Would you happen to be coming out of there soon?"

"Not if I keep having all this company."

"We won't stay." I lifted my voice. "Did Ms. Grace happen to tell you and the others about somebody here getting pregnant by Eve's neighbor Royce?"

"What? Someone here did? Are you sure?"

"Yes. No. But your buddy with all the pictures on her phone told us that."

"Oh." Her tone dulled.

The outer door pushed open. An attractive woman I had often seen visiting her aunt here at the manor walked inside. "Good afternoon. I guess we all got the same idea at the same time."

Not actually. Did your idea concern finding a killer so you could prove yourself innocent? I nodded. "I guess so."

"Are y'all waiting?"

"Oh, no. We're done," Eve said and washed her hands as though to prove she had just used the facility.

Once the woman entered the stall two down, I asked Mom, "Please tell me you know where her daughter lives."

"I do. It's straight down the street from here to the left only two blocks away. The third house from the corner on the right. It's painted green."

"Mom, we love you. Eve and I will come back and see you real soon."

"Thank you. Love you, Mom," Eve said.

"I love you both. Good luck."

A surge of adrenaline made me rush down the hall and toward the exit, with Eve barely keeping up. Some people glanced at us, but at this point, I didn't care. I needed to get that photograph, needed to identify that young woman who worked at the manor and could have had Royce's baby but did not. And I needed to rush that information to the police station before a certain detective made cold thick silver cuffs the newest fashion bracelets I would be sporting.

Chapter 22

Eve and I sprinted to my truck and zipped out of the parking lot. Two blocks down, I would find my answer that I could then rush to Detective Wilet. A green house should be easy to find.

Brick and vinyl-sided finishes coated most of the houses around here. Sharing a slight smile with Eve, I pulled up in front of the wooden green one. A front porch, closed black shutters on windows, a huge azalea bush, one of my least favorite, in the front yard. No garage or carport at the other end of the empty driveway beside the house. My stomach jerked tight.

"Suppose they aren't here," I said to Eve the second she and I slammed ourselves out of my truck.

"They could be. Even if no car is here, they could be inside."

Pulling in air for positive thoughts, I determined she was right. The person I wanted to see might be inside. Actually, I wanted to see her phone, to send that photo she had of the woman from the manor to my own phone so I could bring it back to the manor and get Mom or one of her friends to tell me the woman's name. That's all the detective asked for. No, he didn't ask. He insisted I do it or else.

I ran up the steps to the front door, Eve coming behind, and rang the bell. Nobody answered, but I did hear the bell echoing inside. I rang it again. And again.

Eve pushed my hand aside. "You're going to tick them off if they're in there." Instead of ringing, she knocked. She knocked against the glass storm door. Then against the doorframe. Against the wood near the door.

"Maybe out back," I said and scooted down to the grass. We jogged to the rear yard, where a huge dog in a fenced area almost jumped over his chain link fence while he let out a tirade of rip-roaring barks at us and squirted urine straight at Eve's dress.

We moved back to my truck and climbed in, Eve wearing a frown. "Get me home so I can clean up and change clothes."

It didn't take long to reach her house. We went inside, and while she got ready, I walked out the front door again. Her neighbors had told Detective Wilet they heard me threatening Royce. Or had it been only one neighbor? Who would have done that? Who could have heard me when I hollered at him over the sound of his motorcycle that he kept behind us while we sat in Eve's car?

I stood in the sultry air on the circular drive. My throat squeezed up when I recalled here was the last place I had seen him alive. And I yelled at him? What a terrible memory.

I stepped off the driveway onto the grass and peered around. Since this street started the upscale section of the neighborhood, all of the lots were large, the houses big and fine and pushed back from the street and each other. People who lived here normally kept to themselves with their own employment and families and travels their main attention. The piece of property right across the street from Eve's remained empty. The owners planned to build one day but hadn't begun yet. Houses on both sides of that area were so distant from here I couldn't imagine my voice had carried that far. I had only yelled at Royce the short distance between Eve's driveway and the street behind it.

On one side of her yard, Royce and his mother had resided. I felt certain the families living beyond it had not been able to hear me. Jake lived on the opposite side of Eve's. I doubted he would have told on me even if he had heard me holler.

I walked along that side of Eve's house to the back, no sign of him at home. Behind Eve's, her patio fountain burbled with the angel in its center pouring a constant stream of bleach-scented water onto plastic goldfish that rolled when the water struck them. The older neighbors beyond the rear fence were so hard of hearing, they could barely hear each other talk, so I was fairly certain they hadn't heard me yell out front. Beyond the other close fence lived that young couple with the wife it seemed Royce had been spying on. With the sauna-like heat south Louisiana experienced much of the year, lots of people enjoyed their pools. Some liked their privacy surrounding them and occasionally took a dip in the nude. Or stretched poolside without swimsuits. Since Royce seemingly created that hole to watch the wife, Detective Wilet surely questioned them and possibly believed the husband had discovered Royce's voyeurism and put a permanent end to it. Whether he could prove that or not was another matter. One thing was certain. I was not going to their house to ask whether they had heard me yelling at Royce and told the police.

"Oh, there you are." Eve's sudden voice surprised me since I hadn't known she'd come outside. Still wearing the same dress with the dog's wet stain, she also wore a smile now and gripped her phone. "I'm talking to Nicole and little one."

I smiled back at her. "Go on. Take your time." I sat on a lounge chair to show her I was in no rush—although I really was. Otherwise, I would have wanted to talk to the baby, too. I needed to prove my innocence to Detective Wilet within twenty-four hours—no, I clicked on my phone and saw the time. Ugh, those hours were zooming by. A gray sky was creeping in, pulling darkness behind it.

The roar of a lawnmower sounded, making Eve return inside while she listened to either her daughter or babbling grandson.

The mower's starter, I saw, was Jake Angelette. I liked seeing a man push a lawnmower that was not self-propelled. His arm muscles bulged and broad chest looked nice through his T-shirt. The shorts he wore exposed more of his muscular build. I wished Eve would hurry and finish her business inside and get out here to see the man like this. I hoped it wouldn't be long before she'd totally fall for him and then once Dave got out of prison, I could have him without experiencing the fear of hurting her.

Simple? How nice that would be.

The long hours of daylight were coming to an end and would surely make Jake rush to get his work outside done. He cut a swath of grass coming this way and glanced up. Taking on a smile, he waved.

I trotted over there, grinning myself. "How are you?" I asked, although before I'd completed my question, he turned off the mower so that the last word and a half I said came out more of a yell. He and I both laughed at that.

"I'm great. And you?"

"The same." I nodded, aware that I needed to move away from this small talk and get down to asking what I wanted to know. I hoped he didn't answer in the positive.

He wiped his brow, making a strand of his hair stand up at an angle. My instinct was to reach over and pat it down in place. I needed to hold myself back from doing that action. The upturned section was rather cute.

"And your sister?"

I had to think of what he meant. "Oh, she's doing fine." I jerked my finger back toward her door. "She's on the phone with her new little grandbaby. What a sweetie he is."

Jake's smile widened.

"But I need to ask you something. I'm sure you know that the people who lived on the other side of Eve's house have both died—first the mother and now her son. Royce was his name."

He watched me and didn't nod or give away anything about his knowledge or lack of it.

"Of course neither Eve nor I would hurt anyone, but the detective in town called me in because he said one or more of Eve's neighbors said they heard me yelling at Royce and threatening him."

Still no reaction of any kind. No sign of shock. No lifted eyebrows. I would have to continue the whole thing.

"You wouldn't happen to be one of those people who said that about me, would you?" I gave this handsome man the best tight-lipped innocent smile I could muster.

"Yes, I'm afraid I am."

Well knock me out and call me a crayfish. I couldn't believe what he said. I certainly didn't want to continue to stand here in front of my accuser.

Jake spread his hands. "I'm sorry. I hope that doesn't hurt you, but the detective came over and asked whether I had seen or heard when Royce stopped his motorcycle in front of Eve's driveway."

"And what did you say?"

"I'm a truthful man. I told the officer I had just walked in front of my house to put my garbage out when I heard the bike being revved up at Eve's. Her car was partway out of her driveway, but the bike rider was blocking the exit to the street. That's when you got out of the passenger side and yelled at him."

Air left my lungs. "And then what?"

"And then Royce left. So did you and Eve. You drove off in front of my house, opposite the way he was going."

We stayed silent a long moment. "You said I threatened him?"

Jake shook his head. The attractive lock of raised hair looked silly now. "I said what I heard. You told him to get that bike out of your way."

"That's it?"

He gave his head a brief nod. "I didn't think there was anything wrong with me telling that to the officer. Nothing about what happened would incriminate you or your twin." He rolled his thick shoulders up. His eyebrows wrinkled. "I certainly hope I haven't said anything that would hurt either of you."

I let a long exhale escape. "No, we should be fine. Thank you for telling me about it."

"Please keep me informed about what takes place."

"I will," I said, walking away. Just as my mind was conjuring him to be a bad guy for squealing to the police, I decided otherwise. He would still be a good catch for Eve. He was a man that a woman could trust to tell the truth, even though I wasn't particularly thrilled with the truth he admitted to police.

Eve was coming out of her back door. She had changed into another nice dress and looked especially fresh since her happy phone call. "Ready to go?"

"Sure. Do you have any suggestions for where?"

"Let's go see if that woman with the phone and the picture went back to the manor."

Right before we left the backyard, I angled a finger toward Jake, again pushing his mower, this time away from us. "He asked how you were doing."

She stood a moment and watched him. Her cheekbones lifted from her smile of admiration. I was glad to see it but needed to tap her arm to regain her attention and hurriedly rush ahead out of her yard.

I drove to the manor. In the parking lot, I inched across to one end and then back toward the entrance while we looked at every parked car and truck, searching for any sign of Ms. Grace possibly exiting a vehicle with her daughter. As I expected, almost every one was parked in its usual place. Seniors were not known for doing many things out of the ordinary. I left my truck in the place I'd parked in earlier, a thought crossing my mind that I was becoming one of them.

We hurried inside. Eve and I turned our heads one way and the other to try to find the woman with the picture or the worker who might have gotten pregnant by Royce. Few residents remained in the common areas. One, though, almost ran into us.

"Mom," Eve said, catching her by the shoulders to keep from knocking her over, "where are you going in such a rush?"

"I need to get upstairs to see the movie from the beginning."

"What movie?" I asked.

"Oh, one where an older couple fall in love with each other. I don't recall the name."

The movie would be played in the much smaller common room used for various get-togethers on the second floor.

"Where were you coming from so fast?" Eve asked, and our mother just pouted and shook her head.

What was that about? She wasn't saying more, but I needed to know the answer to another question. "Do you know whether Ms. Grace came back here?"

"She did not." Mom glanced toward the way she had come from and quickly turned to us again. "And I need to go." She planted quick kisses on our cheeks and hurried toward the nearest elevator.

I glanced toward the hall where she had come from. An elderly gent wearing a small grin used a cane to make his way toward the space we stood in. With wispy white hair, pale blue eyes that looked washed by too much sunlight, and large gray hearing aids, he nodded to Eve and me as we did to him. He reached the elevator's door that had closed since Mom just rode upstairs on it.

My sister and I stared at each other. "Have you ever seen that man before?" I asked her.

Her eyes were wide, her lips formed an *O*. She shook her head, then did like I did and looked back down the hall where the male who might be a new resident had come from and right before that, our mother rushed from. She hadn't wanted to tell us anything.

"What do you think?" I asked.

Lips now pressed together, Eve mustered up a slow shrug.

Both of us looked at the man again. He appeared to be whistling now while he waited, and I battled with emotions. The first that flared up was fear. Why, I couldn't immediately tell but noticed I hummed a bar of a carol. Anger pushed up while I stared at him, but I quickly realized I was comparing him to our father, who had been deceased for almost six years. This man was clean-shaven and dressed well in khakis, loafers, and button-down shirt. He seemed patient while he waited for the doors to slide open in front of him.

"But he might not be Mom's new boyfriend." Eve's words shook me, startled me.

"So you think he could be?"

She lifted her shoulders. "Worse things could happen."

"You're right. And it might not even be what we're thinking." Obviously I knew my twin, and she knew me, and we were aware that the thoughts of one of us were often those of the other.

Eve's phone rang. The gent at the elevator looked back at us. Probably his hearing aids worked well. I smiled at him. He did the same back at me. Maybe he wasn't so bad I was figuring while Eve did her quick conversation that I'd thought would be with baby Noah again.

"We need to go." She grabbed my arm and pulled me toward the building's exit.

"Okay, but who was that?" I was almost running to keep up with her. We slammed ourselves into my truck before she took a breath and told me.

"The granite shop. They're about to close and need the measurements we said we would get them for Cherry's kitchen."

"Why such a rush?" I backed out of my space, barely slowing to check behind. Which reminded me—I would soon need to pay for that police car I had rear-ended. I let out a moan. I had been getting used to the sound of the rattle behind my truck from that incident, so even if I didn't get it repaired soon, it probably wouldn't matter much. Our police department wasn't that large and probably didn't feel the same way about one of their vehicles. I hoped the officer wouldn't call soon with the estimate for what it would cost to repair his squad car.

Eve had started telling me something. With all my concerns about repairs, I needed to catch up to the explanation. "...and if they don't install the granite top tomorrow, we would need to wait almost six weeks before they could get to it."

"Tomorrow?" My tone was weak. I knew what else needed to be done by tomorrow. My fate rested on it.

"Yes. Get Cherry on the phone and make sure she'll be home, and it's okay for them to install it then."

"And if not?" I knew the answer before I completed my question.

"You know." Eve turned hooded eyes toward me.

That would be too late for us to do the job at her house, and we would be without that much-needed money. The roof of my house, too, would soon need replacement, and a hurricane could come. I scrolled to Cherry's number on my phone. If she didn't answer, how would we know if it was okay to get the material installed there? I mentally shook my head.

Before I pulled out of the parking lot, I tapped in Cherry's number.

"Yes!" she said, answering on the first ring and hearing my question. "What time will they come here?" Before I could say I would try to find out, she blurted, "Oh, never mind. I'll be home. Ooo, I can't wait."

She was the only one of us who looked forward to getting that done by tomorrow. I flew back to Eve's house. There she retrieved the measurements we had taken and called them in to the granite store, letting them know the owner of the house would be there to let them in. Thank goodness, we wouldn't need to also be around when they delivered and did their installation, which should take only a handful of hours. Eve released a long breath and faced me. "You know I can't quite remember which color we chose to have installed on her island."

"Hmm." I ran my mind back through colors and textures. Detective Wilet had me on the phone during that time, and I'd rushed out the store. "Nope, I can't either."

"I'm sure it's pretty."

"Definitely." The uncertainty in my voice made Eve send me a concerned look that said she doubted my assuredness. I scrambled my thoughts again through samples in the place. I'd been running out the door, pointing back across the showroom toward... Nope, nothing.

I left her so we could each work on our own ideas alone. She would toss off her clean dress, throw on older things, and enter her art room. With paints, she would be able to let her mind ramble and possibly focus on what we needed to do next. We needed answers, we agreed before I drove away. As I did, I noticed that again I avoided passing in front of the Wilburns' house, the route I formerly almost always took before I'd go around the long block to reach my street.

My phone rang. "What's all that stuff going on with that guy you like?" my friend Amy Matthews asked.

Her question surprised me. It was one I didn't want to answer right now. "What do you mean?"

"Girl, don't kid me. I saw in the paper that he was arrested for murder. Are they kidding me? Did he do it?"

"Absolutely not. That's going to be proved soon, but right now I'm in a rush and can't talk."

Her silence let me know she wasn't certain she believed my response. "All right. We are going to talk really soon."

"You got it."

Sweat popped out at my temples, I realized once I hung up. I didn't know what to tell her or anyone else yet about the two people who died. Their deaths were haunting me. I needed to figure out what I might do about that and the woman who had aborted Royce's baby. Back in my own house, I locked the doors, drank milk with toast and a big bowl of instant grits, wishing I had smothered shrimp in gravy to put on them, and went for the shower. I stayed beneath it, letting the warm steamy liquid soak into my skin as though I were enjoying a sauna. Instead, I was forcing my mind blank. Whenever my thoughts strayed to one problem or another I needed to deal with, I forced them to back away. After I totally relaxed, I would deal with all the difficulties once again.

Hopefully, good solutions would come.

Chapter 23

Steamed, sated, and dressed for bed, I sat at my dining room table with a pen and legal pad, my mind clear and ready to work. I put on my glasses I didn't wear often enough and then wrote a heading: *Suspects*. I felt rather strange doing that, like who did I think I was—the police? But then I reminded myself I probably knew almost as much about or maybe more than some of them did about Eve's neighbors who perished.

Of course finding killers wasn't the only situation I needed to deal with.

On the second page, I wrote across the top: *Cherry's house*. That was another situation with a ticking clock.

Fix the police car headed the third page.

Mom has a boyfriend? As soon as I wrote the words on the next page, I scratched them out. That wasn't enough since I could still see parts of each word underneath. Besides, I didn't want to concern myself with this situation, if there was one, right now. Other major priorities came first.

I needed to get the name of the woman who had been with child by Royce. I looked at the wall clock. Too few hours left. I hoped the woman with her picture would be back at the manor by morning or maybe the employee herself and wanted to rush there first thing. Because of that, I wrote as number one on the first page: The woman in navy from the manor. Why I thought she could possibly be a suspect in Royce's murder, I had no idea, but maybe I would get another thought about that. Anyway, I needed to learn her name and get it to Detective Wilet before midafternoon.

Number two on my suspect list became the young man who lived beyond the wooden fence behind the Wilburn yard. If he had discovered Royce watching his wife sunbathing naked, he could have easily yelled at Royce that day Mrs. Hawthorne had heard him yelling at someone.

And he could have easily followed up by getting into Royce's yard and bashing his head in.

The thought of that happening to anyone, even Royce, a fellow I knew little about and who had not been at the top of my favorite people's list, squeezed a tear from my eye and tension into my stomach.

The police, of course, would already be looking into the possibility of that young man as the person who did away with Royce. Possibly, too, Royce supposedly gambled so much during the time he lived in Las Vegas that he could have lost a lot of money and owed someone. He couldn't pay it all back, so the loaner cashed in another way. That scene was only conjecture on my part, although it might have happened. I wrote that possibility as number three with a large question mark behind it. A quick rummage through my mind gave me nothing else, so for number four I admitted it easily could have been someone I knew nothing about.

Then what about Royce's mother? Dave was in jail for her murder, which he didn't commit. Then who did?

I wrote *Mrs. Wilburn* in the center of the page and beneath that began a new set of numbers. I thought back to that dreadful moment when I found her stuffed in a garbage bag in the camp Dave had recently bought. A new set of reactions hit my body. A giant cottonmouth seemed to swim through my stomach and carry chills down my arms and around my fingertips. Heat built up behind my eyes. I wanted to retch.

"Okay, who did this to you?" I asked out loud, which stopped the gagging instinct. Yes, who indeed?

Mind back at Dave's camp, I envisioned the man from out of state who owned the camp beyond it. I pictured the fellow using his fine tools out on his wharf and throwing Eve and me an ugly attitude when we went to speak to him. The deceased at Dave's camp had been killed by blunt force just like her son, although that didn't mean the same object or person had taken the lives of both. She had probably been killed somewhere else and then placed in the bag and brought there. Could she have known the man with the camp next to Dave's, and for some motive I wasn't aware of, he cracked her over the head and dumped her in the nearest place, Dave's camp next door? I definitely knew little about him but placed him as a suspect for Royce's mother's murder.

Of course, there was an alligator or two or possibly fifty in the area, but even if one of those would have pulled her underwater and done the death dance with her on the bayou's floor, it surely hadn't carried her back up and tied her inside a garbage bag.

Who else?

Royce I wrote immediately. Yes, I hated to think it, especially now that he was also deceased, but I, and I believed Eve, had begun to get suspicious about that possibility since right after she died, he began to make large purchases like the fine car and motorcycle. He'd also hurriedly put up a For Sale sign in her front yard, which still remained. The large phone number he had penned with a black marker was surely theirs. Was a phone there still connected? I imagined walking on that side of Eve's house and hearing a phone ringing from inside their home and needed to struggle to quell a new set of shivers.

There had been no notice of his death or funeral arrangements in the paper. Again, I did a quick check online. Nothing was said about him in the up-to-date obituaries.

How awful. There was no closing ceremony to remember the life of either he or his mother. Those two people had lived their lives, had touched other people. Hadn't they had any relatives?

Yes. For number three under Mrs. Wilburn's name, I wrote what I had heard from the fellow I spoke to outside the manor who'd heard me mention her name. He was her nephew Andrew Primeaux, who apparently had his niece Jessica living with him, and he'd let me know he was angry with Mrs. Wilburn because she almost never visited her stepmother in the manor. He'd shocked me by insisting that all of their other relatives couldn't stand her. This didn't give me an exact person's name to write, although I put down his and then penned the other things I knew or had heard from him.

My eyes fluttered, I realized much later when my lids pulled open, an ache in my cheek seeming to wake me. My head was down on my list, the back end of my ballpoint pen pressed into the side of my face.

I sat back and found all the lights still on. A sliver of drool may have caused the small blob amid the names on my list. Not wanting to think of that list now, I rose and went to bed.

Morning woke me with a ringing phone. The one next door to Eve's—the one still inside the Wilburns' house?

My mind scrambled and brought up the knowledge that this was a new day, and I was in my own house. A glance at the clock beside my bed told me I had slept later than normal. A quick thought between the ringing reminded me of the most urgent thing I needed to do this day—learn the name of the woman who'd gotten pregnant by Royce and rush that name to Detective Wilet.

I didn't believe the caller was ready to give me the name of the once-pregnant woman, and I didn't recognize the number of the caller. I sat up, deciding I might not answer and instead rush to get ready and out of the house, yet I grabbed it. "Hello."

"Hello. Is this Sunny? Sunny Taylor?"

The woman's voice didn't sound familiar. Was she going to tell me I'd won a trip to Hawaii? If so, I'd tell her to take it herself and remove my name from her list.

"It is," I said, waiting to hear my fake prize.

"Hi, Sunny. This Dave Price's sister Penny."

I shot up to my feet. "Oh, my goodness, how good to hear from you." I was ready to blurt about Dave but stopped myself. What if she didn't even know about his arrest? Should I be the one to break this bad news to her?

"Sunny, I went to see Dave."

"You did?" How wonderful. How awful to see him in jail.

"Yes. That was pretty tough, you know, going to visit anyone in jail. Especially your own brother. Especially him."

"I can't imagine." Although I wanted to. I wanted to be there to see Dave, to assure him things would be all right. To assure myself.

"He told me you were his friend."

I had only seen him a few times, but had gotten the feeling he wanted to explore a relationship with me, just like I wanted with him.

"And he's told me how close you are to him."

"He's a really great guy." An image came—him in a prison jumpsuit, him with few good meals to eat. "How is he doing?"

"He's doing okay. You know Dave. Or I don't know how well you really know him, but he can put up with lots of turmoil and negatives. He's sure he'll get freed soon."

The concept of Dave walking out from behind the bars of that jail strengthened me. The image of the horrible dog that walked back and forth, following us inside the fence came. He would not be around. Dave would be wearing his own clothes and look great. And I would be there to greet him and—

"He wanted me to tell you he's thinking of you. And he really appreciates the card you and Eve brought him."

The one the guard ripped apart.

"Wait, I remember he said you live in Shreveport. If you're here in Sugar Ledge and want to stay awhile to visit him more, you can come and stay at my house. I have plenty of room."

I imagined a smile crossing her sweet face, a face I never had seen but Dave had told me about. Actually, he'd told me what a wonderful person she was and that she continued to keep in touch with him almost like she would want to be taking care of him. But she was the one in the wheelchair.

"Thank you so much, but Stan and I already have a room rented for a few days at the hotel in town. You know I'm engaged to your sister's ex-husband, Stan."

He had been the second man Eve married and divorced, a pleasant divorce as they all had been. Stan seemed an especially agreeable person. "That's wonderful. I really like Stan. But both of you could come and stay here."

"I really appreciate the offer, but we have handicap facilities here, which are excellent. I need to go now. I'll let you know when I have anything else to report about Dave."

I thanked her again, asked her to give him an extra hug from me the next time she saw him, and we hung up. I stood clasping my phone and inhaled deeply, imagining Dave telling her those nice things about me. She hadn't quite said the same about Eve. Would she be calling her, too? Had she relayed a message to my sister before she contacted me? I dropped my hips to the edge of the bed.

My phone rang. Quite possibly it was her calling me back, remembering something else Dave said to tell me. "Hello." I spoke quickly, my voice cheerful.

"Sunny." Her tone was extra loud. "Sunny, this is Cherry Cleveland. Your sister's phone didn't answer, so I thought I'd try you." Okay, now what? "That granite you two picked out for our kitchen arrived. The installers are putting it in place." So that was the background noise.

"Nice." Except that would mean we'd need to get busy soon doing the extra work on our end.

She grew quiet a second, strange for her. She must have walked away from the kitchen since all of the voices and other sounds slacked off. "The white countertops on the back wall look fresh and lovely. I'm sure what you ordered for the top of the island will look great once it's all put together." Her tone sounded anything but certain.

"That stuff in there looks like crap!" This from a man in the background.

"Oh, honey, I'm sure it'll be all right. These women are professionals. They know what they're doing." That was Cherry. She wasn't speaking to me.

"Well, if they don't, they're sure as hell going to get that gross-looking stuff out of our house." A door slammed.

I remained silent, feeling my heart thump until Cherry spoke. "I'm sure you both have something wonderful planned," she said in a lower uncertain tone. "So I can't wait to see what it is."

Thanking her for believing in Twin Sisters, I assured her we would get a terrific job that she would love completed in her kitchen before she knew it. She agreed, reminding me of the approaching due date for completion, and we hung up.

Elbows on knees, I gripped my head. What color granite had we chosen for the island? Replaying the event in my mind, I recalled Detective Wilet phoning me. I stepped away from the counter with the display pieces the salesman had been showing us so the sales guy wouldn't hear. The detective had wanted to come over to my house, and I tried to stall, saying I would be at the station in an hour or so. I waved to let Eve know we needed to go, and the salesman called out, asking which one we'd chosen. I pictured myself rushing out the door and pointing back. And good grief, who knew what color I selected?

Okay, I asserted, getting up. That was another matter Eve and I would deal with, and we needed to do it soon so we would get paid.

First things first—I had to get to the manor to find out if the woman with the phone holding the picture of the woman whose name I needed to know would be there now. If not, I might soon be modeling the prison jumpsuit that Dave would be removing.

Chapter 24

I raced out the door as soon as I dressed. Without checking with Eve, I sped across town until I reached the manor. A couple of people I recognized as residents were walking to their cars, surely having finished the early breakfast. I wasn't concerned with them—only one person here who drew my interest had that phone and photo—unless I came across the staff member who had been pregnant herself. If so, I would ask a resident the woman's name or if need be, I would ask the woman. I could introduce myself, say something nice about her, repeat her name in my mind until I was certain of it, and get that name to Detective Wilet. Before noon, if I was lucky, because what if he went out for a long lunch and didn't answer calls while he ate? Matching orange jumpsuits sprang to mind as I ran toward the main entrance. Me and Dave, a nice pair. Only he would be getting out of jail. I would be going in?

Dave is really a prisoner. That thought slammed into my mind while I reached the entrance doors and yanked on one, but a moving large object to the far end of the building grabbed my attention. It was a bus, a fairly large one that had stopped and made a rumbling noise from near that rear door. A few people were streaming out of the building and getting on that bus. What if one of them was a person I needed to see?

I let go of the door and ran toward the bus.

"Ow!" a female's voice cried behind me, making me glance back a second to see a nurse who'd been entering the place obviously right behind me, and I had let the door go. It must have hit the hand she was shaking while she frowned at me.

"I'm sorry," I called to her and returned my attention to the bus and its occupants.

I stopped a woman using a walker while she exited the building. "Where are y'all going?"

"I'm going to my doctor," she said, not slowing. "And I need to go because I like to get a good seat." She allowed the bus driver, a large woman with tiny glasses, to take her walker and hold her hand while she gripped the rail inside and moved up the steps. The driver folded the walker and placed it with others in the open cargo holder. And then the driver looked at me, scanning the others who came out the building. "Can I help you?"

"Are they all going to doctor's offices?" I asked, although the answer to that question actually didn't matter.

"A few of them are. One has an appointment with his dentist."

I knew the manor provided this service to its clients. What I really needed to know right now was who was leaving here. "I'm looking for someone. Maybe she's going with you."

The driver lifted a pad with names listed. "Who is it? I can see."

"Sorry, right this minute I can't think of her name." The second I said it, she gave me a look. Did she think I was going to steal one of her riders? "I have to get on here and take a look." I scrambled up the steps, heard footsteps right behind, turned and saw the driver had come up with me. Maybe checking to make sure I wasn't going to plant a bomb or hurt any of the occupants.

I watched the news too much and wasn't thinking right. Rushing down between the rows of moldy-smelling seats, I didn't find either of the people I was looking for. I slowed to check each one again. There really were few people. Elderly men and women stared back at me. Two of them gave me a little smile.

At the rear of the bus, I spun around, ready to rush back to the manor and check in it. The driver was in my face when I turned. "Did you find who you were looking for?"

"No, I'm sorry. I really have to talk to this woman, and I can't remember her name. I'll just go check inside there. Didn't want to miss her and thought she might be going with you."

She pressed back against an empty seat to let me get by and then followed me out of her bus. As I moved away, I glanced back. She was still standing in the doorway of her bus, watching me. After I was a few yards away, the door to her vehicle closed, and she drove away.

I could have gone into the entrance on this far wing of the building but figured the person I wanted would go through the main door. Scanning vehicles, I didn't find the maroon truck. There were a couple of small white cars. I hurried into the building. Just as I did, my phone rang. Eve.

"Where are you?" she asked, and I slowed.

"Getting to the manor."

"Oh."

Her tone made me stop. She wasn't pleased for some reason. "Yes, I'm running inside to see if I can find the girl who got pregnant or Ms. Grace with her picture."

The pause kept me in place. "I'm in front of your house. I thought we'd go together."

Why hadn't I contacted her before coming out? Ah, I'd rushed off after I received a phone call, an important one. It came from Dave's sister. "I just wasn't thinking about us getting together yet. Figured I'd hurry and discover a name here and get it to Detective Wilet."

"I see."

Hmm, she and I had been together since we played footsies in our mother's womb. We normally knew when the other one wasn't giving the entire truth.

"Did anybody call you today?" I tried to make my tone innocent while mentally crossing my fingers about her answer.

"No. Why?"

Good. Dave's sister only phoned me. "Just wondering," I said, walking farther into the place and knowing she would doubt that fat fib. And then I remembered another call I'd received. "So Cherry didn't contact you?"

"Not if I didn't receive a phone call today." The annoyance in her voice let me know she still doubted whether I was saying everything.

Okay, so I wasn't. I'd left out the part about Dave and now scooted through the foyer and into the large central gathering area. Lingering smells of breakfast sausage started to be overwhelmed by stronger aromas that came from cabbage the cooks were preparing for lunch.

Uh-oh, lunch. The detective required info. I needed to find the woman with the phone but scurried around and didn't see her or my mother to ask about her.

"I'm still here." Eve's voice was cold. "So, what did Cherry say?"

"Ooo, she and especially her husband didn't seem too thrilled with the color—yes, I know that was my fault. I can't recall which color I'd pointed to while I ran out of that store, so we'll need to get to her house soon and straighten things out."

Another pause. "Is that all?" Again with a chill.

"No. There she is." I started to run but realized how that would look and slowed my speed to a walk toward the large room's distant wall.

"Who?"

"The person who could have killed Royce." I clicked off my phone, not wanting to speak into it while I accosted the slender woman wearing navy.

Chapter 25

Two female staff members in navy blue that I had seen together staring at me on previous days stepped toward each other. This was the first time I'd seen them up close. One was a bit larger than the other with short-cropped coarse black hair that probably wouldn't move if she were out during a storm. The one I aimed for with curly hair was really slim except for the little bump around her middle that the drawstring belt of her pants created. All of the staff members wore name tags, although they seemed to have a choice of where to place them. The larger woman had hers pinned to her chest. Her friend had hers hanging from the bow she'd made with her drawstring. It hung at an angle so I couldn't read the thing. The two were on the side of a table where three male residents played cards.

I stood next to their table and watched them play a little, trying to decide what I would say to both of those women. I had planned to compliment the one who aborted Royce's baby and introduce myself so she would tell me her name that I could relay to Detective Wilet. But now the other one was here. I could do the same thing with both of them. I just had to come up with nice things to say about the pair.

"No, I wouldn't discard that one." The female whose name I wanted leaned over a wrinkled man's shoulder. She flattened her fingers over the card he had pulled from his hand to stop him from throwing it away. "Do that one instead." She placed the tip of a finger on a different card.

He slid his gaze toward her and back to his hand. Then he did as she suggested.

"Darn it. That's not what I wanted," another player said, and she patted the one she'd instructed on the shoulder as though letting him know he'd done a good job.

The larger woman moved away, and I stepped closer to the person I wanted.

"You did a great job there," I told her, tilting my head toward the group of card players.

She backed away from the table a little. "Thanks. We try to help our residents." An endearing faint blush touched her cheeks. Maybe she had a difficult time accepting compliments. Her gaze darted to the side, to the path her friend had taken. Her pale eyebrows folded in crinkles when she let her gaze sweep over me. Was I staring at Royce's killer?

I swallowed hard and wished it weren't so. Second thoughts struck—the accused might be her—or me. I put out my hand. "I'm Sunny Taylor, by the way."

Her small handshake was weak. "Rayne."

I grinned. "Excuse me? Rain?"

"I know, it's unusual. It's spelled R-a-y-n-e, not like the rain outside." Her gaze shot away from me almost like she was seeking an escape route.

Moving closer to block any movement in that direction, I said, "That's a lovely name. Unique. But what about your last name?" She couldn't get away without giving me that.

"Adams."

Okay, *Rayne Adams. Rayne Adams.* I needed to remember the whole name. Surely I could. My dyslexia sometimes caused me to confuse written words, but these were not. Her name was all I needed.

"Sunny. Hi, Sunny." It was my mother walking with a couple of her friends toward me.

"Hey," I called out and waved. I glanced at the woman in navy now starting to scoot away from me in a different direction. "That's my mom," I told her, also recognizing other residents or visitors I wanted to place but could not. This was much more important at the moment.

Rayne might have been a gazelle the way her lithe body did its swift move away from me. She knew who my mother was and who I was. Therefore it was easy to figure out the reason she and her fellow worker had stared at me and Eve before. She must have known Royce lived next door to Eve. If Rayne murdered him, she probably was frightened that Eve or I might discover her connection to him. And report it?

That's exactly what I was about to do.

"Hey, Mom." I stepped up to my mother and gave her a kiss.

"Hello, sweetheart. How nice to see you here again."

Her buddies and I exchanged greetings and then I leaned closer to my mother and hugged her, placing my lips close to her ear. "I really need to go."

When she withdrew from the hug, she gave me that tight-lipped small smile with deeper creases outside her eyes that had saddened. "Come again later, okay?" she said, not knowing the reason I'd rush off but accepting it.

I placed my fingers around her gnarled hand that the rheumatoid arthritis had taken over and gave it a slight thank-you squeeze. With another kiss on her cheek, I was gone.

Surely Mom was getting hit with questions from her cronies about why I wouldn't stay to visit with her, but that didn't concern me. Our mother was proficient in letting her daughters do what they needed to do. She had long ago stopped asking where we were going and what we were up to unless there was something she felt she needed to know to protect us. My time for being able to give birth was quickly depleting, but if I were ever fortunate enough to have a child, I would want to raise him or her the way Mom raised us. Maybe I could help do that with Eve's new grandson.

That thought brought a smile to my lips as I rushed toward the main exit, a couple of administrators glancing at me while I went past. I didn't concern myself with them but hurried outside, away from everyone, my fingers hitting Detective Wilet's number while I moved.

"Wilet," he said on the second ring.

I came to a complete stop. "I found out her name." I was so excited, my voice sounded thin.

"Who?"

Enthusiasm dumped out of me like a cement mixer. "That woman. The woman at the manor who got pregnant by Royce but didn't let him know until after she had an abortion and he really wanted that baby and she probably killed him."

"You know all of this for sure?"

"No." My body calmed. Eve came trotting from her car toward me. She would hear this conversation, which was okay, but I didn't put my phone on speaker since I wouldn't want anyone who worked here or visitors to take note of my accusations. "But I really believe that's what happened." The pause on his end was long, so I said, "This is Sunny Taylor."

"I realize that. So give me whatever information you have."

"Okay, first, here's her name. Rayne Adams." I saw Eve's lips quirk to the side in a questioning frown when she came next to me. "The woman's first name is unusual. It's Rayne." I spelled it for him and repeated that and her last name.

"Right, got it. Now what else?"

I let my mind run to a scene I'd envisioned before and hoped it was true. "Probably they were in his backyard when she told him about the whole thing, and they got in a big argument, and he was furious with her because he'd always wanted a child. And things got rough. Maybe he pushed her around or hit her. And she saw something hard out there— maybe a shovel or whatever—and grabbed it and struck his head." I ran out of breath. And the story.

Eve watched me. Her eyes widened while my tale had unfolded. She looked at my phone.

"I'll check on it," Detective Wilet said in a curt tone.

"Wait. What did y'all learn about—" I stopped when I realized he'd hung up. My gaze closed in on Eve's face.

"It's fantastic that you discovered all that information," she said.

"Mm." I grimaced.

"Sunny, that is really fantastic." She gave me the biggest hug, and I leaned into it, not ready to tell her I had made up most of what I'd said— although I hoped the officer determined it was all true. "Did you learn anything else?" she asked, pulling out of the hug.

Dave asked about me slid across my tongue. I tightened my mouth and kept the words inside. Running my thoughts to another area, I said, "We need to get to Cherry's place and see what we can do with the damage."

Eve frowned again. "You still can't remember what granite you picked?"

I shook my head. "I'm certain I didn't really choose anything. I just pointed back in the building and ran out."

"Uh-uhn, I hope the manager didn't just send something ugly that they couldn't move."

That was my hope, too, but I kept it inside while I went with her to her car, pleased that I had gotten one stumble out of the way. If we were extremely fortunate, we would find the situation at Cherry's house easy to fix.

Something told me we wouldn't be.

Chapter 26

"Oh no," Eve said, but at least kept the words soft. Maybe Cherry, standing across her kitchen from us, didn't hear.

"What?" Cherry's eyes widened with fear. "You don't like it either?"

We were all in her kitchen, Eve, her, and me. And that horrible, uglier than sin or anything resembling it might be granite top that now lay newly installed on the island we had planned to make the showpiece of her remodeling.

"Oh, no," Eve said louder than before, "I just realized my nose started to run." Give one to my sister. She recovered from that goof-up nicely. She reached into her purse and dug inside it while our customer gave her worried eyes.

"I can get you some tissue," Cherry told her.

"No, that's fine. I'm good. Yes, here it is." Eve's attempt at making the time pass while we could think up some explanation for that eyesore in the room was admirable, but made me sad for her. I needed to help out.

While she took a small pack of tissue from her purse, pulled one from the pack, and wiped her already dry nose with it, I gave Cherry the most open-eyed incredible stare I could muster and forced out words, using the best acting I could muster. "You mean there's someone who doesn't like this?" I moved to the granite and set my hand on it. The gross blend that made me think of avocado and lemons squashed together with baby poop made me want to pull my hand away.

Cherry's eyes moved closer together, her face sincere. "So you really like it."

"Who couldn't love this?" I tapped the granite and hoped nothing came off on my fingers. With only a little struggle, I kept my face straight.

A long exhale blew out of her nostrils. Her shoulders sank lower, and her whole body relaxed. "See? That's what I told Charles. He didn't think it was so pretty." Her lips twisted to the side in a half smile, yet also a half frown. "But what does he know? He operates in people's stomachs after all."

"Ah, and what he finds in there isn't the same as what's here." Again, I rubbed the granite top, trying to feign appreciation.

"Are you okay?" Cherry spoke to Eve, concern in her eye. "You're still blowing your nose. Maybe you need something else. A cough drop. Cough syrup." She scurried across her kitchen and yanked a cabinet door open. Inside sat lots of meds. She grabbed a handful. "Look, we have something for sinus problems if that's what you have, or if you think you're getting a cold, here's a pill for that. Or, let me see."

While she flipped back around, tip-toed and perused her medicines, Eve rolled her eyes at me.

"Oh, look, this." Cherry thrust everything back in that cabinet, shut the door, and came toward Eve with water she'd retrieved from the front of her fridge and an orange pill. She held them both out to Eve. "Take this with a little water. It's a kind of heal-all pill that will stop noses from running and clear up sinuses and stop coughs."

Eve's eyes at me over the rim of the glass while she sipped after swallowing the pill showed concern. Neither of us usually took meds that weren't prescribed for us or over-the-counter medicines unless we read the labels well first. This time seemed like an emergency of sorts with a client we needed to satisfy. Besides, her husband was a doctor. He shouldn't have anything in that cabinet that would hurt her. I was certainly glad he wasn't here, and we didn't know him. I hoped I never had to face the man. He probably wasn't nearly as easy to appease as his wife.

She watched Eve with hopeful eyes, leaning forward, watching so closely it was as though she expected my sister to sing, "Alleluia, I'm healed," the moment the pill slid down her throat.

"Thank you. I almost feel better already," Eve said, and Cherry's eyes lit with pride. She reached out for Eve's used tissue.

Eve drew it back. "I see your garbage can. I'll just drop it in there."

The white garbage can stood out, an unattractive stained thing standing in the room. When Eve stepped on the foot press, the top opened to reveal take-out containers and two liter-and-a-half bottles that recently held wine.

"Do y'all have parties?" Eve asked, trying to discreetly look away from their trashcan's contents. "Lots of company comes over?"

Cherry, the constant mover, kept shaking her head. "No. That's the reason we want the kitchen finished so fast. Well actually, I do. Charles doesn't really seem to care about much except his surgeries—oh, and this granite top. But I'm sure he'll love it once you're finished with the room."

I had to blurt to get in my question. "So you were saying the reason you want the kitchen finished so fast—"

"Is so we can have our first real visitors over. Our families and whoever else might come."

She had told us about the big family get-together, not that the people who attended would be the first real visitors to their house. Now I really understood why the work we would accomplish in here would become so important to her. From her trashcan's contents, I also perceived why she might be so happy all the time. Or maybe her husband imbibed quite a bit? I hoped not while he was on call.

"We'll need to hide the receptacle where you keep trash," Eve said, giving a nod toward where she'd discarded her tissue.

"Oh, yes, good idea." Cherry spoke with big nods as though it had never occurred to her to do that. She leaned in closer to Eve. "What else?"

"Umgg," or something like that came from my sister's mouth and then her lips went slack. She swayed back and grabbed the top of the island.

I grabbed her around the waist. "What's wrong?"

"Uk." A smaller sound.

"Let's sit her down." Cherry caught hold of a chair and pushed it behind Eve. "I'll call my husband."

I stood beside Eve and supported her upper body, which leaned hard against me. "You're going to be all right," I promised her. Promised myself. One sister died beside me. This one that I equally adored couldn't also vanish.

Cherry yelled into her phone, barking out orders, seeming quite a different and stronger person than the one we'd met. "I don't care if he's in surgery. Tell him it's an emergency. I need to know what to do."

She waited and paced and came close to Eve to check her out. "You doing okay?" she asked.

Eve gave her head a slight nod, which also pleased me. She pulled away from me and sat straighter, but then leaned back against me. I gripped her tight, not about to let her fall.

"Okay, okay," Cherry said annoyed, again in her phone. "Then tell him this. We have a guest in the house, and she had the sniffles, so I gave her an OTC tablet to help clear it up." She gave the name of the product, which she must have been asked. A minute later, she came and stooped beside Eve. "No, her lips aren't blue. I don't see a rash around her face or neck. And her nose isn't swollen." Cherry flicked her gaze toward me. "Is it?"

I shook my head. Eve watched and looked relieved at my headshake.

An extended minute later, Cherry started nodding again at her phone. She told the person okay and hung up. Darting to their kitchen's medicine cabinet, she took out a box I recognized. It was a product I'd sometimes used when my sinuses required help.

"Have you ever used this before?" Cherry held the box up to Eve.

"Yes, once or twice." At least her voice was stronger.

"This is what I gave you, but you've become allergic to it. Don't ever use it again." She set the box down. "Do you feel like you'd need an ambulance?"

"Absolutely not."

"Do you want us to get you to an emergency room to get checked out?"

"No, I'm fine." Still seated, Eve swayed a little. "Or I'm getting there."

"Okay then. Charles couldn't leave his patient but heard everything I relayed about you. He said you need to take this." She replaced her OTC sinus meds and grabbed another box. Eve was shaking her head as Cherry came toward her, taking out two pink tablets and refilling water in Eve's glass. "Don't worry, these can't hurt you. They're to stop an allergic reaction." When she pressed the tablets to my sister's lips, Eve opened her mouth and allowed them in. Then she sipped water.

"But that never happened to me when I took those other things before," Eve said.

Cherry stopped moving. "Anyone can become allergic to anything at any time." She spoke slower than I had ever heard her. "You could have taken some type medicine or used some other product all your life and then one day, you become allergic to it. Just leave those other pills alone, and you should be fine."

Eve had straightened her spine and sat straighter to drink the water, but began to slant toward the side. I pressed against her.

"You just had a mild reaction to that product," Cherry told her in a slow, gentle tone. "You should be fine." Our hostess looked up at me. "You need to take her home, or I can help drive her there if you'd like." She saw me shaking my head and continued. "That reaction could probably make her feel a little woozy, and the pill she took for sinuses sometimes causes drowsiness. Oh, and meds I gave her to counter that reaction normally make people quite sleepy."

"I'll take her to my house."

Cherry was shaking her head, tapping the granite top on her island. "I never would have imagined putting a color like this in here," she said, and I awaited an outburst. We would need to foot the bill? Her lips moved into a smile. "You two are so talented. I love this."

I faked a smile, the same as I figured she was doing with her words. "Come on, Eve." I slid my shoulder under hers and placed my arm around her, gripping her tight. Cherry got the other side and supported Eve by holding one arm and watching her. We all three walked out of that ugly kitchen and helped Eve stumble through the living room. At the door, Cherry held onto her while I got Eve's keys out of her purse and went to get her car, driving it up to Cherry's door. Both of us helped her get inside. I strapped her in and ran around to the driver's seat.

"Please let me know if she needs anything, anything at all," Cherry called out once I lowered a window. "If she needs any emergency care, Charles will be there." I was certain she meant if he wasn't involved in an operation like right now. "I'm sure she'll be fine, but I'll call later and check on her."

Cherry nodded and gave us big waves while I drove away, down their long driveway past all the big oaks. By the time I got on the highway, I said, "I guess doctors get sued so often, they're really afraid something might happen if a person gets hurt at their house. Especially from taking medicine either of them gave a person."

Getting no reply, I glanced at Eve, worried.

Her head was slumped to the side toward me. The big snorts that came out of her brought out my laugh. My sister was sound asleep.

Cherry called later that evening and again fairly early at night. She wanted to assure me that if Eve needed anything—anything at all—I should just let them know. If we wanted Charles to check her out, he would be glad to come out and do that.

"She's fine. She's just really sleepy," I assured her as I had the first time she'd called. I managed to wake Eve enough to help me walk her inside my house and then down the hall to the first bedroom, where she slumped onto the bed, clothes and all. I slid off her shoes, pulled the covers from the other side of the bed and placed them over her. She kept snoring so loud I thought she might wake Mrs. Hawthorne down the street.

When I finally went to sleep myself after replaying all of the events of the day, snorts and snores occasionally woke me. At least I knew I still had a sister.

Chapter 27

"I can't believe I slept so much." Eve drank coffee while she sat at my small kitchen table wearing an unusual look. She was all rumpled. From the top of her hair down to the hem of her dress, she had parts out of place. A wide swath of her red wavy hair stood up in back, mascara made a wide black rim a quarter of an inch beneath her eyes, and her dress bunched up with creases.

"But you feel better now?" I sat beside her, had cooked her breakfast, and we'd eaten. "Are you doing okay?"

She waved a hand to brush off any idea of ill effects. "Don't worry. I'm great. Did I miss anything?"

Surely she missed seeing herself in a mirror yet. It was difficult to hold a serious conversation with her now. Bright crimson lipstick remained on one side of her lips, but not the other. Watching those lips move and looking into her eyes that appeared raccoon-like this morning made me only want to grin. Instead, I took a swallow of my dark roast hot coffee and told her about Cherry's offer to have her husband help. "But the big plus was that right before we got you out of her house, she praised the granite."

Eve chuckled. "She did not."

"I'm pretty sure she was only trying to appease us since you seemed to have a reaction to something she gave you. Oh, you remember that you can't take that medicine anymore, don't you?"

"Yes. I won't, but the other one helped me, right?"

"It sure did. Okay, so what happened at their house probably scared the couple so much that we might sue them that it should give us a little breathing room to try to decide what in the world we might do in that hideous kitchen."

Eve was nodding. "It is bad." She widened her eyes. Made me think of
an owl. Would she turn her head around on her neck? "Or maybe I was
having a nightmare about what I saw in there."

"No, it was real. That's a color we never would have chosen. Anyway,
we'll need to come up with really good ideas on how to fix that kitchen and
make it look much better." Impossible was the thought that came to mind.
I didn't voice it. "We need the income, and the granite store will send us a
bill for those materials and their installation. Just their time driving here
and back from New Orleans will add a bit. But even worse, after we or
I am cleared of murder, word will spread that we're horrible at selecting
materials to remodel anything."

Eve took a swallow of coffee and set the cup down. "Right. Even if
they let us out of completing the job, some doctors and other people with
large budgets will be going in their kitchen. They certainly won't consider
us now." She carried her cup to the sink. "I need to get home to shower.
We'll get together afterward."

I watched her walk outside and get into her car, assuring myself that
she was no longer woozy or unsteady. She seemed fine.

Returning my attention inside, I got out the lists I had made of suspects
and such, considering what we might do next. Looking through the pages,
I knew we'd have to try to bandage or somehow otherwise fix up the huge
mistake I had made with the granite. The days were counting down until
the big party at Cherry's house, but we wouldn't deal with it today. I put
the sheet mentioning remodeling behind the others.

Thoughts focused on anyone else beside me who could have killed
Eve's neighbors, I considered phoning Detective Wilet and asking what he
found out about the tip I'd given him yesterday. If it was a tip. Or possibly
the whole story of Royce impregnating that woman at the manor was
fabricated. Hoping that wasn't the case, I put aside the idea of calling him.

What Eve and I needed to do was return to the manor and try to discover
more, like had any of our mother's other friends heard about that possible
affair. Darn, considering an affair and Mom at the same time made scenes
flash into mind that I didn't want to imagine. Mom. That new guy. Both
coming down that hall about the same time. "Uhn-uh." I fixed another cup
of strong coffee to send my thoughts other places, and sat again, placing
the tip of my pen on one possibility after another and making notes while
I came up with ideas.

An image came of that alligator swimming in the bayou beyond Dave's
camp in the direction of the camp beyond, where a man had been using
fine tools to work on his wharf. I had no idea whether he would be around

his camp since he lived out of state, but was fairly certain Detective Wilet
had investigated him. Eve and I could run out there to see if we'd find
him although I had no idea what good that would do. The man certainly
wouldn't admit to us that he'd killed Mrs. Wilburn and brought her dead
body out to Dave's. Considering that idea made the concept of him being
a suspect in the murders of her and her son seem ridiculous. I crossed him
out as a suspect. Something worked the edges of my mind. I tried to focus
on it but could not grab onto that thought and pull it into view.

The young fellow behind the Wilburns' fence was another one I wondered
about. In my mind, he was a distinct possibility for Royce's death. But
his mother's? If that guy were the killer, I would only find out when the
detective was ready to tell me or if he announced it to the public. I made
a large question mark.

A similar mark went next to what I'd written about the killer being
someone Eve and I didn't know at all. Somebody else could have a motive,
means, and opportunity to kill both of them.

Moving along to those we knew about left only a couple of possibilities.
Rayne, the woman in navy at the manor. Mrs. Wilburn's nephew Andrew
Primeaux whose niece Jessica lived with him. I had seen him first at the
manor, and he'd told me none of Mrs. Wilburn's relatives liked her. They
both had the older relative residing at the manor that I'd seen but hadn't
been able to speak to at first because another resident told me mealtime or
right afterward was a bad time to do that. The person who said that was
Cherry's grandmother, whose table in the cafeteria was two before hers.
Cherry's grandmother would soon see her horrible kitchen and then the
entire manor would know about it. Twin Sisters Remodeling and Repair
would quickly be junked out the window.

I drove to Eve's house with my lists of names and notes. It didn't take
long for me to fill her in on what I'd thought of. We agreed that the manor
was the place we needed to start.

"You look nice," I had to say on our way outside. Her slender dress
showed off her trim figure from all of her workouts and healthy meals.
Her makeup and hair all looked perfect.

"I can't believe you didn't tell me how awful I looked this morning."

I grinned at her.

Midmorning at the retirement home was the liveliest time in the place.
Everyone had gotten up early and eaten a substantial breakfast. There
was still a little time before lunch—that brief time between meals when
kitchen staffers would clean used items and start preparing the next dishes.

We'd passed a handful of residents going out while we came in. Some of them may have wanted to sit awhile in the sunshine on one of the many benches. Others could go off in their cars to shop, visit friends or family, or eat out. Maybe see a dentist, a doctor, or who knows where else? We hadn't seen anyone we wanted to speak to in that group, so we'd only exchanged greetings with individuals and moved on.

An administrator standing behind the check-in desk eyed me and then the book we should write in and the long-tailed white pen standing in its holder. I sped my gaze away from hers and kept going.

"There's Mom's group." Eve pointed toward where they normally sat. "But Mom's not there."

I didn't want to think of where she could be.

"Hello, you two. Your mother should be out here soon." The speaker played with her pearls.

One woman on the sofa and another on a loveseat that helped create this cozy seating area tapped places beside them. "Come join us. Tell us what you've been doing," the one on the sofa said, and Eve and I took the seats offered.

"And don't leave out the juicy parts." This came from the person we'd looked for who kept her phone in her bra, and again I was grateful I'd discovered and called in Rayne Adams's name on my own.

"There are no juicy parts in our lives right now," Eve said, prompting an uninterrupted discussion from the senior women.

"We know that man you're all hot for is still in jail, but what if he never gets out?" asked the negative Ida.

"My son is a widow and a nice man," a wheelchair-bound woman said.

"No, he's too old. How about my grandson? He likes girls...I think," another one offered.

"We have lots of visitors who come to this place. You should come and sit out here." This suggestion was directed at me. "Then you could introduce yourself, start up a conversation."

"Just don't get too pushy at first." That love advice was aimed at my sister. These women knew her.

A familiar female staff member wearing navy walked into view. She stopped to speak to a man whose lap was covered with a blanket in a wheelchair.

"That's a nice woman," I said, pointing to her and interrupting some other advice aimed at Eve. "She has such an unusual name." Yes, I was pulling for anything.

"She does." Ms. Grace shoved her hand down into the top of her dress. "I think I have her picture." Her hand resembled a third boob dancing around behind those buttons. I was no longer interested in that photo.

"But it's a shame she has to miss so often," another one said, this statement truly drawing my attention. "All that morning sickness she has."

Eve and I whipped our faces toward each other and then the last speaker. "She still has morning sickness?" Eve asked.

"Yes, I wouldn't say she's a floozy or anything," the person still digging said, "but she's pregnant, and she's not even married."

"I'll be right back." I rushed to the exit and got outside, my fingers locating the contact info for Detective Wilet. When he answered, I said, "She's still pregnant."

"Who?"

"Rayne Adams. This is Sunny, and I'm at the manor and just found out Rayne didn't abort Royce's baby. She's still carrying it."

"Okay." His hesitancy to say anything else gave me pause. What could this mean? Would this info help me? Hurt me?

My stomach tightened at that thought. "I knew you'd want to know," I said, hoping for something positive. Hearing silence, I moved on. "So can you tell me anything about what you've discovered?"

"In those murders? No." Maybe he wanted to soften the blow. "But you'll know in time."

Whatever that meant, at least he wasn't saying he wanted to lock me up. "Okay, thanks. I'll let you go now."

He let out a small laugh that I figured meant he was aware of what I was doing and then he hung up.

A full breath released from my nostrils. I trotted back inside, not wanting to think of whether what I'd just done was good or not. At least it was truthful. Second thoughts made me pause. No one had told me the child Rayne carried was Royce's. I hurried to Mom's group. Maybe they knew.

Eve was standing when I rushed near. It looked like she was being introduced to someone. Our mother was doing the introduction. It was to that new man.

Chapter 28

I hesitated before going forward but knew I had to. I tried to plaster a smile on my face but could only fake a tight one while I stepped to her as she stood in the center of her buddies. "Hey, Mom." I gave her a kiss.

"Hello, sweetheart. I want you to meet my friend Alexander McCormick. He's new here. Alexander, my daughter Sunny."

My glaze flitted to Eve's face that appeared apprehensive and then to him. His hair was salty gray and his white eyebrows shot through with a few traces of black. His eyes flitted toward my mother and came to rest on me. I accepted his handshake, which was firm. "Miriam told me she had two gorgeous daughters. I can see that she wasn't exaggerating."

Okay, maybe he wasn't so bad. "From your accent and last name, I know you're not from here."

"You are very clever, too." He gave me more flattery but not information. Didn't the man realize I was checking him out? Where are you from? Were you married? Are you now? Do you have children, grandchildren, dogs, guppies, hangnails?

"Ladies, it's time to eat." The woman searching her bra must have given up on finding her phone. Her attention was aimed at the dining room.

"Yes, indeed." One woman got her cane in position to use.

"What's for lunch?" Eve asked.

Pearl lady glanced at a sheet of paper she pulled out of her large pocket. "Mm, we're having chicken, okra, and sausage gumbo with potato salad and French bread. And milk and lettuce and tomato salad with a slice of avocado."

"That does sound delicious. My sweet daughters, I hope to see you again soon." Mom dismissed Eve and me with quick kisses. The man we just met gave us nods. Then he walked off beside our mother. His gait was as strong as hers.

One woman from the group who normally held quality discussions rose from the sofa. I touched her arm and leaned close, nudging my head toward Mom and that fellow. "They aren't... you know, are they?"

She gave me a wide grin and pat on the back. "Don't worry. They only sometimes hold hands." As I was breathing a sigh of relief, she added with a wink, "That I know of." And then she was off.

"Eve," I said, stepping close to my twin but not knowing what to add. Her halfhearted smile and shrug told me she felt the same—uncertain of this new situation with our mother. Dad had been gone quite a while, but still—this was our mother.

Movement from others going to the dining area made us both watch them. One person I noticed too late was Adrienne Viatar eating with two silent others at her table.

Eve pointed a couple of tables over. "And there's Cherry's grandmother. Maybe Andrew Primeaux and Jessica are around."

We took a quick spin of the area, watching for those coming near and those eating. Mom and her new friend stood with their trays, selecting food items. We didn't see Andrew or Jessica.

"Come on, let's go eat," Eve said, and I agreed that their meal also made me hungry. I drove to Swamp Rat's Diner where we ordered the exact same thing the people at the manor ate. The only thing missing was the avocado slice on our salads.

"Eve, I have an idea." As thoughts rushed to mind, I considered even more of them, and she added other suggestions until everything blended together about what we could do with Cherry's kitchen. Our meal arrived, and we ate.

Afterward, Eve got Cherry on speakerphone. Once she assured Cherry she was still feeling fine, she asked whether Cherry and her husband enjoyed Mexican food. "It's our favorite," Cherry enthused, and Eve and I gave each other high fives and huge smiles. "Here's what we'd like to do," Eve said. "That granite color, of course, will make you two and other people think of guacamole."

"You're right!"

"So what we planned to do was give your kitchen a Mexican theme but not totally since you'll want it to blend in with the rest of your house and your beautiful sprawling lawn. We'll use a bright lemon yellow on your stove's long hood and the slim wall on both sides of it, but only on one wall to make it pop. We'll use much lighter matching shades on the other walls."

"Excellent," Cherry said.

Eve mentioned a couple of other things and then told her, "Wait, here's Sunny. She can fill you in with our other ideas." She handed the phone to me.

"Hey, Cherry. To tie it all in, we suggest framed prints of Mexican dishes on the wall. A thick colorful ceramic bowl filled with fresh lemons and limes would go well on the island, and for the sides of the island, we've ordered faux leather padded tiles in pale ecru that will blend in well. They're fire resistant and waterproof and look exquisite."

"You two are brilliant!" the woman who was about to become our most pleased customer said. "I knew it."

"My sister and I will get our tools and other gear, and we'll come over this afternoon so we can get started if that's all right."

Our suggestions were perfect with Cherry, so she and her hubby should be satisfied. We could get our remodeling completed fast, and I would be able to do some of the things without aggravating my left shoulder too much.

Eve was changing into work clothes and going to grab a few things we might need from her place, while at home I did the same. I kept more tools than she did so I gathered them from the storage room behind my carport, lifting Dad's tool belt with loving care and placing it with the other items I would bring. From there I drove to the lumberyard. In it, I stepped to the back of the building to learn whether the faux leather squares I'd ordered for the sides of Cherry's island arrived. Thank goodness, they had. While a salesman gathered those boxes for me and also the glue I would need, a man who looked familiar walked past. I could only see the back of his head. "Hi, Jake."

He glanced back. "Oh, hello. Good to see you again," he said and continued out a wide rear door. He hadn't mentioned my name since he probably couldn't tell which twin I was. Few people could, even if we stood next to each other.

While a salesclerk rang up our charges, I pointed to the rear. "I thought only people who work here use that back entrance where they bring out lumber and other large items to their trucks."

He nodded, moving the last boxes of nails closer to add them. "They do."

"I just saw Jake Angelette going out there. He's a financial advisor. He certainly doesn't work here. Or maybe he works on your books?"

"He does some of our bookwork and once in a while does a couple of deliveries for us. You know times get slow for people like him who want to tell people what to do with all their extra income. I never have any extra cash. You?"

"Not me."

"Yeah, times are tough. A little extra money comes in handy for anybody." He pointed to a line. "Sign right there."

He helped me load the boxes in my truck, and I drove to Eve's. As usual ever since the people died on the opposite side of her place, I drove up in front of Jake's house, not theirs. He was walking across his yard toward Eve's, carrying his toolbox.

I parked in her drive and stepped across the grass toward him. Apprehension made the center of my back suddenly pull tight, the picture of the man on his wharf beyond Dave's camp working with good tools running along the outskirts of my mind. He had no ties to both murdered victims.

Jake began pounding a post into the ground. He paused and watched me walk over.

"I was surprised to see you at the lumberyard," I said, my gaze falling to his tools now scattered on the ground.

"Oh, that was you? I couldn't tell if it was you or your sister." He lifted his hammer and again beat the post.

"Your permit must have come through so you can get that fence built now," I said, and he nodded. I skimmed his tools, didn't see a certain one, and thought of the neighbors two doors over. Both dead. Hard object hit them. My mouth dried. Still I had to say it. "You know I loved to use my father's ball peen hammer, but my mother never found it after he died. Do you think I could use yours? Just for old time's sake."

Redness flushed up his neck to the outer rim of his face. His eyes narrowed. He bent to his tools, touched handles of a couple of hammers, and lifted a large one. "Sorry, I seem to have misplaced the ball peen for now. I'll probably find it in my garage. Why don't you try this one instead? Just give the post a few hits."

The tight set of his jaw make me pull my head back. A Christmas carol rode up my throat and spewed out. I turned to get away and felt a striking blow against my back. I fell on my stomach. He hadn't struck solidly since I had been turning, but the next hit with his hammer would surely be on the head and do me in. I clawed at grass and scrambled to my knees, felt it strike my shoulder, knocking me over on my side. He bent over me, eyes furious, hammer raised high.

"You won't get her!" Eve slammed something against his head that made him yowl and drop, his face close to mine. His eyes shut.

Excruciating pain ran through every place on my body he had hit. My eyes shut, too.

As I drifted off, I could hear Eve yelling, giving information about me being hurt by a man and her possibly killing him with her pneumatic nail gun.

Chapter 29

Awake later in the hospital, I ached everywhere, especially from my head to left shoulder and upper back. Drifting in and out of consciousness, I sometimes found a nurse or doctor or Detective Wilet and always discovered Eve at my side. Bits and pieces filled in empty spots floating around my mind.

Eve had been right inside her back door, gathering power tools from a closet when she'd heard me blast out a carol outside. She grabbed the nailer and rushed out there.

Jake might survive her attack since it wasn't right into his skull, but he wouldn't do well for a long time. I'd managed to tell Eve he worked part time at the lumberyard, and learning that made me recall the lumber stacked under the carport at Dave's camp. Thoughts of the man owning the camp beyond Dave's and using tools there brought my mind to consider who else I had seen using some that might possibly have ties to Eve's neighbors. The answer was Jake—her neighbor on the opposite side.

"And I thought you two might get together, like he might be your soulmate," I told Eve once when my mind sort of cleared.

"Oh, no. Jake might be good looking, but I'm only waiting for the one man who's meant for me. Dave should be released from jail soon."

Maybe it was good that the meds kicked in again and sent me back to dreamland before a response crossed my tongue.

Once, hearing my mother's voice, I opened my eyes. Hers went from pulled together with concern to widening. "Ooo, you're doing okay, sweetheart. The doctor says you'll do fine. You'll probably be out of here anytime now."

"Good to hear. I'm okay, Mom." To ease her mind, I smiled although felt it crooked.

She kissed my cheek. "You asked around at the manor about Rayne being pregnant. Yes, she is, and she'll have Royce's baby. He was looking forward to it."

How sad that he would never get to see or hold his child.

Why Jake killed him and his mother I learned gradually, some from Eve but mainly from my now-friendly detective. Actually, neither of the victims knew Jake, but he had had an affair with a woman and in a fit of rage in his house, murdered her. He carried her out in a large garbage bag at night and dumped her in a swamp. The police were currently trying to locate what was left of her.

After that murder, he became more watchful and paranoid and noticed Mrs. Wilburn always peeking out the window that faced Eve's house and his. Mrs. Wilburn sent him a signed note: *I know what you did. If you don't want others to know, I want $100,000.*

How hard it was to discover she had done something like that, even though we hadn't really known her well. Maybe she was greedy. Possibly, she wanted to pay off large debts for her son to protect him from his debtors.

Becoming more vigilant, Jake saw Eve leave her house one evening and then Royce left his. He called Mrs. Wilburn and told her he knew they had both left. She should come to his back door, where he would have her money. He didn't respond when she got there and knocked on his door, but he'd left the door unlocked.

When she walked in, Jake was ready with a vinyl sheet on the floor and the ball peen hammer ready to beat in her head. He set her dead body in another garbage bag. He was making a delivery to the carport of a camp and knew the address but not who owned it and brought her there. Instead of tossing her into the bayou, he spied the tip of a small key on the floor, climbed on the lumber he had unloaded, and used that key to open the attic door. He pulled himself up and went down inside the camp, where he unlocked the back door. From there he brought in the black bag holding Mrs. Wilburn. Locking the door from inside, he returned through the attic and threw that key away. It must have fallen off Dave's key ring with the other key we had seen in there from the day Dave tried to give me one.

Maybe Dave was distracted being around me then like I had been with him.

At his house, Jake tried to hurry and build a fence to keep what he did at home private. Then he needed to stop and wait for that permit. In the meantime, he'd noticed Royce was outside more often. He had seen Royce standing at that window behind his mother a couple of times, and after she died, he was out front, placing a sign, sporting a new car and revving a motorcycle in front of Eve's. More afraid of being discovered, Jake determined Royce could have figured out what happened. He snuck into Royce's backyard while Royce was peeking through a hole in the back fence. One hard smash with a hammer did the young man in right there on the ground where I found him. The hammers Jake used had been tossed into different bayous.

Soon after doctors released me from the hospital, I went to Eve's house so she could keep me under her watchful eye. My neighbor Mrs. Hawthorne came to visit. With the rich chocolates she carried, she also brought the news that even if I never asked her cousin about doing repairs, he said he would fix my truck's rear end and the squad car I'd backed into for nothing.

"Just a good meal after you're feeling better," she said, and I gratefully promised I'd fix him more than one.

"Cherry's house needs to be fixed! It's a mess," I told Eve when we were alone and my thoughts shifted there.

She lifted a hand to stop my concerns. "A pipe burst behind their washer and did a bit of damage. They needed to postpone their big family hoo-ha."

"Okay, then let's go see what we can do there."

She barely touched my bandaged left shoulder. Fiery pain shot through every muscle to my fingers. "Sit back down."

I did, and she explained that because of all our troubles and with our terrific ideas on how to remodel their kitchen, they would be paying us triple what we would normally charge.

Eve having a reaction to a pill Cherry gave her probably added to their desire to do that.

"So you're going to allow your body to heal a little longer, and I will do some of the remodeling there myself and be able to hire help for a day or two."

"All right, but I'm going to study online sites to get more ideas for tasteful redecorating for them. I'll want to go there as soon as I can." I thought about more and said, "And I'll make them a big bowl of homemade guacamole."

"Good ideas. Oh, and Cherry said she's going to take lots of pictures after everything's done and post them all over social media and tell all of their friends about our great ideas and terrific work."

I smiled. Then went back to sleep.

Nicole, her husband, and baby Noah came to visit. "We needed to make sure Nanny Sunny was all right," Nicole said. That's what they planned to have the little one call me. I was Noah's godmother. I got to hold him and take in his sweet face and comforting body that I gripped with my good arm. I loved that he sucked on my chin. A special glow took over my sister's face while she was around her daughter and that child.

After their family left, Eve spent time in her art room. I sat and watched her. On a new canvas, she painted hearts, some tiny ones that I imagined belonged to the baby. The hearts she created grew larger and rose across the space. I wondered if she was considering Dave while she drew those.

* * * *

Once my body healed except for the continued pinch in my shoulder and ache in my shoulder blade, Eve and I went to help Dave fix up his camp. Calls and e-mails kept coming with people wanting Twin Sisters to do some clever remodeling like we had done in Cherry's kitchen.

Dave looked wonderful, Eve and I both told him, and he'd laughed, saying he hadn't spent years in prison. It had only been a few days, and the food was surprisingly good. At least it was okay. The jumpsuit also wasn't too bad.

We were helping him float an attractive vinyl floor over the worn one in his camp and change locks on his attic and doors. Eve went outside to get a Phillips screwdriver from my truck.

"I thought a lot about you while I was in jail," Dave told me, and I smiled. And then he added, "I am so glad to have you as a special friend."

Special friend? I didn't voice the words while Eve stepped back inside.

Possibly that's all he and I were meant to be. That thought hurt. But then I thought more about it. What a terrific friendship that would be. While my sister and I worked with him on his camp, he and I smiled at each other often. Eve also smiled at him and he at her, but it wasn't the same. No, not quite the same.

She was a much happier person now. Soon she would be going to stay with Nicole's family in Houston for a while. I felt a wider smile cross my face. Maybe then Dave and I could become one-step closer to each other.

Also by June Shaw

A Fatal Romance

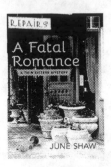

Twin sister divorcees Sunny Taylor and Eve Vaughn have had their fill of both heartaches and headaches. So when they settle down in the small Louisiana town of Sugar Ledge and open a remodeling and repair company, they think they've finally found some peace—even though Eve is still open for romance while Sunny considers her own heart out-of-business.

Then their newest customer ends up face-down in a pond, and his widow is found dead soon after. Unfortunately, Sunny was witnessed having an unpleasant moment with the distraught woman, and suspicion falls on the twins. And when an attempt is made on Eve's life, they find themselves pulled into a murder mystery neither knows how to navigate.

With a town of prying eyes on them, and an unknown culprit out to stop them, Sunny and Eve will have to depend on each other like never before if they're going to clip a killer in the bud.

Chapter 1

I stood in a rear pew as a petite woman in red stepped into the church carrying an urn and stumbled. She fell forward. Her urn bounced. Its top popped open, and ashes flew. A man's remains were escaping.

"Oh, no!" people cried.

"Jingle bells," I hummed and tried to control my disorder but could not. Words from the song spewed out of my mouth.

"Not now," my twin Eve said at my ear while ashes sprinkled around us like falling gray snow. She pointed to my jacket's sleeve and open pocket. "Uh-oh. Parts of him fell in there."

I saw a few drops like dust on the sleeve and jerked my pocket wider open. Powdery bits lay across the tissue I'd blotted my beige lipstick with right before coming inside St. Gertrude's. "I think that's tissue residue," I said, wanting to convince myself. I grabbed the pocket to turn it inside out.

"Don't dump that." Eve shoved on my pocket. "It might be his leg. Or bits of his private parts."

"Here comes Santa Claus," I sang.

She slapped a hand over my mouth. "Hush, Sunny."

The dead man's wife shoved up from her stomach to her knees, head spinning toward me so fast I feared she'd get whiplash.

"Sorry," Eve told her. "My sister can't help it."

Beyond the wife a sixtyish priest, younger one, and other people appeared squeamish scooping coarse ashes off seats of the rough-hewn pews. An older version of the wife used a broom and dustpan to sweep ash from the floor. People dumped their findings back into the urn. Other mourners scooted from the church through side doors. A boiled crayfish scent teased my nostrils. Someone must have peeled a few crustaceans for a breakfast omelet and didn't soap her hands well enough.

Ashes scattered along the worn green carpet like a seed trail to entice birds.

"Look, there's more of him. I'll go find a vacuum," I said.

The widow faced me. "No! Get out."

"But she's my sister," Eve said.

"As if I can't tell. You leave with her. Go away." The petite woman wobbled on shiny stilettos, aiming a finger toward the front door.

I sympathized with her before this minute. Now she was ticking me off. I'd been kicked out of places before, but never a funeral. "I didn't really know your husband, but Eve did. I stopped to see if she wanted to go out for lunch, and she asked me to come here first. She said y'all were nice people."

"We are!" The roots of the wife's pecan-brown hair were black, I saw, standing toe-to-toe with her, although my toes were much bigger inside my size ten pumps. I was five eight and a half. She was barely five feet. Five feisty feet. "But you're not going to suck up parts of my husband's body in a vacuum bag." She whipped her pointed finger toward me like a weapon. "And you need to stop singing."

I wanted to stop but imagined parts of the man that might be sucked into a vacuum cleaner and ripped out a loud chorus, my face burning. Nearby mourners appeared shocked. Mouths dropped open.

"You don't know my sister," Eve told the little woman who'd just lost a spouse. Actually, lost him twice. "Sunny can't help singing when she's afraid. And that includes anything dealing with sex, courtesy of her ex-husband."

"What does sex have to do with Zane?" The wife's cheeks flamed.

Should I tell her about his privates possibly being in my pocket? Second thoughts said not to. "Who knows? But you don't need to worry. I certainly wasn't having an affair with your husband," I said, quieting my song to a hum.

"Just the thought of sex makes her sing," my sister explained. "Maybe it's a good thing she doesn't think of it often."

The widow shook her finger. "Zane was always faithful to me."

"I'm sure he was," I said, working to get my singing instincts under control. Nodding toward the carpet, I spoke without a hint of a tune. "I'd really like to help you get those pieces of him out of the rug. If we can just find an empty vacuum bag, I'll—"

"Go! Get away!"

I stomped out of the church into muggy spring air. Eve clopped behind me toward her Lexus in the parking lot.

"You told me they were fine people," I said.

"They are. At least he is. Or was." Eve shook her head, making sunshine spread golden highlights over her flame-red waves. Her clear blue eyes sparkled. I was glad few people could tell us apart. "I only met his wife that day I laid their pavers, and Zane stayed and helped a little. When she got home, he introduced us. She seemed pleasant."

"I guess you never know."

"Good grief, Sunny. You kept singing after she spilled her husband."

I lowered my face toward the chipped sidewalk.

Eve touched my arm. "I know, but maybe you can try harder."

I nodded. She knew how long I'd fought to stop the songs that began when a major tragedy threw my life into an unending tailspin. Junior high had been especially painful.

At the next corner, we waited for a truck to pass. I checked my sleeve in the sunshine, relieved that if any ashes had been there, the breeze had blown them off to a better place. "There weren't many people in church."

Eve frowned. She started across the street. "They've lived here less than three years and don't have much family. Zane's job kept him out of town a lot. When he joined our line-dance class, he said his wife was shy and didn't like to dance anyway."

"I don't think she's shy. I think she was involved in his death."

"What?" Eve stopped. "The man drowned. It was an accident."

I spread my hands. "In his own yard? Why didn't he fall in that pond before now?"

"Because this week he tripped on a cypress knee near the job we did in their yard and knocked his head on the tree and fell in. He couldn't swim. And you don't even know his wife."

No, neither she nor her husband had been home when we created that seating area in their yard. I tugged on Eve's arm to get her across the street so oncoming cars waiting for us could turn.

She kept talking. "Darn it, Daria Snelling might not be the sweetest person right after her husband's ashes flew to the heavens, but that doesn't make her a killer."

"Eve, you know I have good instincts about people. And covers on burial urns are sealed. They aren't supposed to come off." I created a mental picture of what happened. "Besides, she was walking along carpet. There weren't any bumps for her to trip over."

My twin's face pinched up. Not a pretty picture. "How do you know that?"

"Her shoes. When the organ music started and everyone turned to look back, I noticed her shoes."

"I can't believe this, Sunny. You aren't usually that shallow." She stomped off ahead of me.

I strolled faster behind. "You know I can't even pronounce the brands of expensive shoes. I saw she was tiny but looked extra tall, so I glanced at her shoes. Her heels must be four inches. That's really showy for a grieving widow."

"Wearing stilettos make her a murderer?"

"And a bright red dress. Red?" I caught up with Eve. "I think she wanted to dump her husband so his remains couldn't all be buried together."

She threw up her palms. "You are so sick. The man was my friend."

"Geez, you worked for him briefly and saw him a couple of times in dance class."

"That doesn't give you the right to cut down his family."

"And if you hadn't made that dig about my unhappiness with sex, his wife wouldn't have gotten so upset."

Eve knew my limited experience with sex had come with Kev soon after our marriage. If I'd known how unpleasant one man could make the quick chore, I would have started chuckling in bed much sooner. Eve and I were both divorced—she, three times, her choice—and her admiring exes still showered her with gifts. Kevin left me with little and did so after my spontaneous laughter about frightening things escalated to include sex. But he made the intimacy so unpleasant I had begun to dread it.

Watching my sister, I saw myself a little slimmer, wearing dressier clothes and an unpleasant grimace. At thirty-eight, she was fairly attractive in a black knit top and skirt, emerald green jacket, and spike heels. I wore low heels and tan slacks with a white shirt and my favorite jacket, a rust-colored silk. With a pocket that now held parts of Zane Snelling.

"Sis," I said, "do you see any ashes in my hair? Or on my sleeve or other places on my clothes?"

She did a quick inspection of my hair and looked longer at my clothes, while I did the same to her. "I don't see anything anymore." She checked inside my pocket. "Except in there."

"You're clean," I said, voice dull from knowing I still wore parts of a man. I slid my jacket off and carefully folded it, not letting anything escape.

Eve wrenched her car door open and flung herself inside. I slid onto the passenger seat. "Buckle up." She waited until I did before pulling onto the street.

"Do you want to go out for lunch?" I asked.

"My stomach's too upset. I'm going to change clothes and hit the gym."

Positive news came to mind. "Anna Tabor wants us to give her a price to replace the picture window in her den with a glass block one." It wasn't much of a job, but we were still pleased with every one that came in.

"Why does she want that?"

"She said it would be unusual and attractive. I'll do the estimate this evening."

"Okay. I'll check your work tomorrow, and we'll schedule her in."

I nodded. Our deceased father had been an excellent carpenter who made us enjoy working with our hands. We'd done quite a bit of work with him and liked changing the design of some of his jobs. Ever since I convinced Eve to join me to start Twin Sisters Remodeling & Repairs months ago, we were gradually building up our name and earning people's trust. We were both strong and knew how to use subcontractors and power tools. So far my estimates all turned out correct. Still, being dyslexic made me want all written work and numbers double-checked. Early struggles and some teachers' hurtful comments made me still doubt myself.

Most of the sugar cane stalks in fields Eve drove past stood three feet tall. On the opposite side of the highway, the brown bayou lazed along, shielding gators, turtles, catfish, and other water creatures. We sped by shotgun houses dotted between brick homes in our small town of Sugar Ledge and entered our subdivision. Houses were brick and stucco and most of the lawns well-tended, especially on Eve's street. She reached her house, remoted the garage door, and pulled in.

"I shouldn't have snapped at you. I'm sorry," she said.

I leaned over and kissed her forehead like Mom used to do to let us know anytime we were forgiven. "To make amends, can I see what you're working on?"

She considered a minute, then led the way through her picture-book house. The lingering fragrance from vanilla triple-scented candles made me want yellow cake. The spacious den held large windows and pale neutral shades, its main color from Mexican floor tile and Eve's muted-tone abstracts, which I determined she painted when she was between dating or marriage.

She kept most of her home with a colorless feel like a blank canvas, letting her imagination soar. Pulling a key from the second drawer of an end table beside the white marshmallow-leather sofa, she unlocked a door off the den.

Shell-shocked. Her studio made me feel that way even more so than usual. While the rest of her house gave off a bland feel, this room was infused with color, especially on a huge canvas on an easel in the center of the room. Splashes of color and bright dots of varying sizes filled almost every inch of the canvas.

"Intriguing," I said. "Who does it represent?"

"Dave Price. That man is terrific."

"I can tell. Y'all must have an explosive relationship."

"I only know him casually. Of course I'm planning to change that." Her grin widened. "This is how I'm expecting our relationship to become."

"Impressive."

The other dozen or so paintings on easels and standing on the floor represented men she'd dated or married. Some wore drab shades. A couple of canvases showed small vases. Others held crudely-drawn flowers or apples. She wasn't a proficient artist, but while our business grew, this gave her something to do with extra time besides line dancing once a week and working out at the gym. She didn't get to see her daughter in Houston often enough. A sex therapist would enjoy analyzing what she did in here.

"Thanks for letting me see your latest work. Sorry about the funeral ruckus."

"You didn't cause it." The fair skin between her eyes creased. "I'd like to know what happened after we left the church."

I'd prefer to know what really happened to the dead man before we went there. "Maybe you'll find out. See you later." I locked the stained-glass front door on my way out.

Ambling alongside her taupe stucco house, I paused in back to admire the fountain burbling on her patio. Inside it, a stone angel poured bleach-scented water. Again, I wished the fountain held live fish instead of the almost real-looking plastic gold ones. Angling through the little grass path between the yards behind her house, I passed a dog-eared cedar fence on the right and white solid vinyl fence panels on the left. Then I stepped across the next street, which was mine. Yards and cars here were less fancy than on hers. A couple of clunkers sat in circular drives. Even the air smelled less pure.

"Your petunias still look good," I told Miss Hawthorne, kneeling beside the purple blossoms lining the concrete path to her front stoop.

"Thank you. Oh, Sunny, look. The girdle you sold me still works great. Two years old and still holding me in." She struggled up to her feet. Miss Hawthorne was probably older than my mother and didn't like help. She'd insisted on a girdle, not that newer stuff she said was smaller than her gloves, and bought it from me while I still worked at Fancy Ladies, our town's only upscale dress shop. I'd needed to quit that job since I had developed excruciating heel spurs that wouldn't get better until I stopped standing all day every day, and surgery wouldn't correct them.

The top of Miss Hawthorne's plump face hid beneath the wide floppy brim of her straw hat, which didn't hide her pleasant smile. Dirt tumbled off the knees of her slacks. The girdle pushed her stomach up and made the thick roll above her waist more pronounced through her knit shirt. I'd learned to notice details while I fitted ladies with undergarments and determined she had gained fifteen pounds since I sold her that girdle.

"You look good, Miss Hawthorne. But next time you're at Fancy Ladies, you might check out the newer styles. You could find a control panty or shaper that's more comfortable."

"Oh no, hon, this works just fine."

"Good. I'll see you later." I strolled off, pleased to know her smile finally returned after her misery because a relative's pet she had been keeping escaped from her fenced backyard.

A couple of houses to the left, I reached mine, a gray brick with a darker gray stucco entrance. I entered, experiencing the same stir of unpleasant emotions as every other time I returned from Eve's. My place was pleasant, yet now felt like it held too much clutter, even if there wasn't much extra. The house even smelled dull. I plugged in a vanilla-scented air freshener.

Standing beneath the foyer light, I yanked my jacket pocket wide open. Course grayish bits of a man lay inside. I strode to my kitchen trashcan and stepped on the pedal to pop it open, ready to turn my pocket inside out.

No, that wouldn't be right. I let the can's top close. Where else might I put these powdery flakes? I couldn't dump them in my yard or even think of flushing them.

This was part of a person that needed to be treated with respect. I hung the jacket in the foyer, grabbed a phonebook, and looked up a number, relieved to find the person listed. I punched in numerals and listened to the phone ring. A click sounded.

"Snelling residence," a woman said. "We can't get to the phone now, but we will return your call as soon as we're home if you leave your number." Daria Snelling sounded much more pleasant on the machine than she had in church.

I hitched up my chin and tried to sound cheerful. "Hello, Mrs. Snelling. This is the tall redhead who blurted a song this morning at St. Gertrude's. I'm sorry I sang and really sorry about your husband." I cleared my throat. "I called to tell you I have something of his. I'm sure it's something you'll want." I gave my number in case she didn't have caller I.D. and hung up.

My stomach rumbled, reminding me of why I'd stopped at Eve's in the first place. I considered eating leftover red beans and sausage, but instead yanked rice from the fridge, heated a pile of it in a bowl, and squirted my initials over it with ketchup. I munched on this entrée with a chunk of lettuce topped with a few raisins, fat-free ranch dressing, and crunchy chow mein noodles.

In my bedroom, I peeled off church clothes and struggled to snap my jeans, then yanked on a purple T-shirt with gold letters in front that said TWIN SISTERS. Small letters on its back said Remodeling & Repairs.

I slipped into my backyard, where flats of flowers waited. Sunshine and temperatures in the mid-sixties made the spring afternoon appealing. A cool breeze pushed off earlier mugginess that reminded us soon south Louisiana would treat us all to steam baths.

Digging up scraggly plants, I tossed them aside, noting sirens in the distance. A harsh memory trying to erupt froze me in place. I fought the remembrance from my youth and forced it away.

I stabbed soil with my shovel, knowing something was definitely not right with Daria Snelling. Years of working in close contact with women at Fancy Ladies let me learn much more than I wanted to about their private lives so that now my initial instincts were normally correct. Dragging topsoil to the flowerbeds, I mentally weighed the probability of what police decided happened to Zane Snelling and shook my head. Why had he tripped and slid into the deep water in their backyard near the seating area Eve and I recently completed?

Uneasy about his drowning, I added weed preventer to my beds and topped the mounds with cypress mulch. Next came tall coneflowers as a nice backdrop. I set daylilies in front and filled in the closest section with coreopsis.

When the sun was dipping behind rooftops, my riot of color pleased me. I watered everything and kicked off my dirty shoes near the backdoor. Walking into the kitchen, I was ready to develop a bid for Anna Tabor's window that would add to our other pending jobs. A flashing red light on the answering machine caught my attention. I pressed the button, expecting Mrs. Snelling.

"Sunny! Where are you?" Eve yelled.

My heart slammed against my ribs. Something happened to Mom?

I played the next message. "Sunny, it's Eve. I need you!"

My quivering finger pressed her number in Memory on my phone.

"Where have you been?" she asked with a sob. "I've been calling."

"Planting flowers. Is it Mom?"

"Somebody broke into my house!"

"What? Are you okay?"

"No. Come over."

"I'm there!" I raced toward my sister.

Meet the Author

From the bayou country of South Louisiana, **June Shaw** previously sold a series of humorous mysteries to Five Star, Harlequin, and Untreed Reads. *Publishers Weekly* praised her debut, *Relative Danger*, which became a finalist for the David Award for Best Mystery of the Year. A hybrid author who has published other works, she has represented her state on the board of Mystery Writers of America's Southwest Chapter for many years and continued to serve as the Published Author Liaison for Romance Writers of America's Southern Louisiana chapter. She gains inspiration for her work from her faith, family, and friends, including the many readers who urge her on. For more info please visit juneshaw.com.

Printed in the United States
by Baker & Taylor Publisher Services